I0604278

SONG OF THE SEA

CHRIS LONGMUIR

BARKER & JANSEN

Published by Barker & Jansen

Copyright © Chris Longmuir, 2025

The moral right of the author has been asserted.

Cover design by Cathy Helms, www.avalongraphics.org

All rights reserved.

No portion of this book may be reproduced,stored, or transmitted in any form, or by any means electronic, mechanical or photocopying, recording or otherwise, without the prior permission of the publisher or author.

Song of the Sea is a work of fiction. Names, characters, places and incidents are the product of the author's imagination or are used fictitiously. Any resemblance to actual events, locales or persons, living or dead, is purely coincidental.

ISBN: 978-1-0684185-0-1

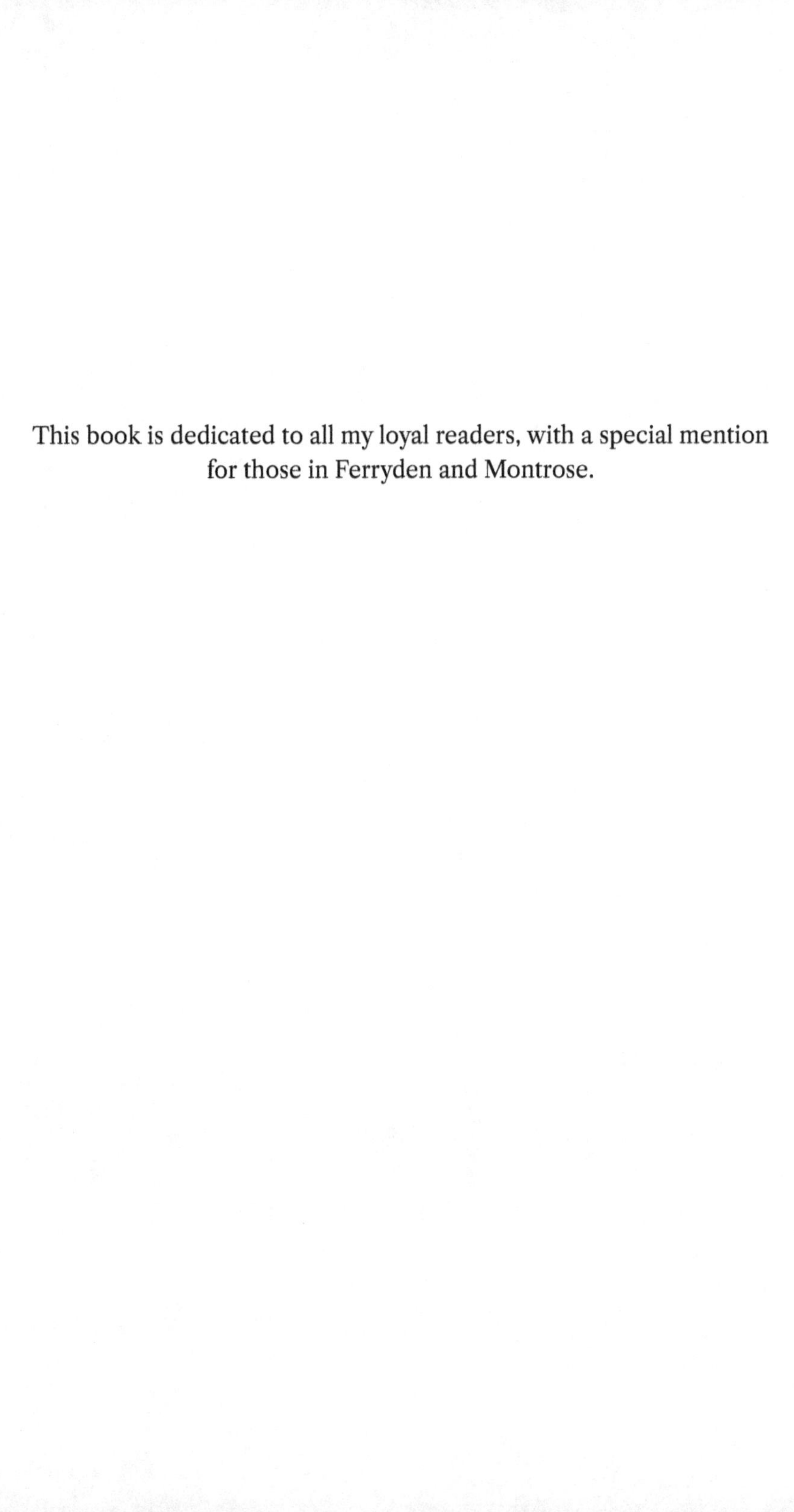

This book is dedicated to all my loyal readers, with a special mention for those in Ferryden and Montrose.

1

February 1840 - After the Fire - Monday

A flicker of torches advancing along the riverside path drew Annie Watt to the door. What she had feared was happening and, despite her efforts, the women were not to be swayed.

Sunday's sermon, where the minister preached about Jezebels in their midst, had inflamed the congregation. Ellen was the worst. She'd incited them to take action, and this was the result. Even Ian said his wife was immovable, but he'd agreed to warn Belle and ensure her safety.

'What's up?' Davie's tousled head looked down from the opening to the net loft.

'Trouble, that's what,' his father growled before leaping out of the box bed. He pulled Annie inside and slammed the door shut.

'If ye know what's good for ye, stay inside. There's trouble brewing. And the rest of you, get back to your beds and cover your ears. This is not something we aspire to be part of.'

The torches were nearer now, casting a glow into the dark room.

Unable to stop herself, Annie peered out of the window in time to see her daughter-in-law, Ian's wife Ellen, brandishing a flaming torch. As she watched, Ellen waved it above her head, sending sparks flying skywards.

Ellen's voice soared over the chanting of the women who followed her. 'We'll rid ourselves of the Jezebel tonight and she'll burn in Satan's Hell.'

Annie shivered and bit her lip as the horde moved on.

'Come to bed, Annie. Don't attract their attention.'

'I'll not rest until I know it's over.'

'Please yourself.' James pulled the blanket over his head. Nothing sounded from the loft above and Jeannie, tucked up in her truckle bed, appeared to be asleep.

It didn't take long before the horde reached the inn, and now, the first flames were licking at the wooden structure. How much time before it became a pile of ash?

Annie creaked the door open again and stood in the shadows, watching. She pulled the edge of her shawl over her nose and mouth as choking acrid smoke filled her nostrils.

Flames leapt upwards, turning the sky red, and the burning timbers crackled as the fire took a greater hold. Banshee shrieks pierced the night, and the women brandished their fiery torches, for all the world like witches dancing around their cauldron.

'What have ye done, Ellen,' she muttered, 'what have ye done?'

For it was her daughter-in-law's vituperative words, combined with the hellfire sermon the minister had delivered yesterday, that set them on their murderous errand.

'What's going on, Ma?'

Annie hadn't heard Jeannie come up behind her.

The girl's eyes widened as she surveyed the carnage close to their home.

She made to run out of the house, but Annie grabbed her arm. 'Stay here, lass,' she said. 'There's nothing you can do.'

'But Belle,' Jeannie gasped, 'and the bairns. They're in the inn. They'll burn.'

'I sent Ian to get them out,' Annie said. 'Pray God they're safe.'

Jeannie shook her mother's hand off her arm and ran off. The sky, reddened by the flames and sparks soaring upwards, bathed everything in a red glow. Was this Satan's inferno, which the minister was so fond of preaching about?

'Ye shouldn't be here, wee Jeannie.' Lizzie McNab waved her torch in the square's direction. 'It's no place for a lass.'

'Neither should you,' Jeannie retorted. 'It's murder ye've done the night.'

Lizzie shrugged and continued walking. 'What's done is done,' she said.

Anger bubbled inside Jeannie as the woman walked away. She'd known these women all her life and thought she knew them. How could they do something like this?

She reached the village square and found it deserted, with flames flickering around the inn's remains.

A sudden flare-up illuminated someone crouching in an alley opposite. Jeannie narrowed her eyes. The figure wore a dark-flowing garment, but it wasn't a woman. He turned away when the flames took a firmer hold, but not before she recognised the minister. His expression chilled her and sent her scurrying home. She didn't feel safe until she felt her ma's arms encircle her.

'Ye shouldn't have run off,' Annie said. 'There's madness in the air and I feared ye'd come to harm.'

'But everyone's gone now, and they've left the inn to burn.' Jeannie tilted her head back to look into Annie's face. 'D'ye think Uncle Ian got Belle and the bairns out?'

'Have faith, lass. He'll have got them away.'

But she saw her mother's worried look, and it didn't reassure her.

'I saw the minister hiding up a closie. He was watching the fire, and he was smiling.'

Annie snorted. 'Calls himself a man of God. My James is more of a man of God than he is. If it wasn't for his spouting hellfire and damnation, that lot would never have done what they did.'

In that moment, Jeannie lost her faith in the church and vowed she'd never let it rule her life.

The acrid smell of smoke in the air reminded Ellen of a job well done. Not a soul moved on the river path as she made her way home. The others had slunk away into the night, fearing they would be caught, but Ellen had no such fears. Tonight, she had done the Lord's work, and the two harlots were burning in hell.

She paused a moment on the doorstep to look up at the red glow in the sky. Without Belle and Madge to tempt the men, the village would be free.

Exhilaration pulsed through her. She had never felt so alive. Her lips curved into a smile, and she was laughing as she entered the house.

'What mischief is this ye've been up to?'

Her father's harsh voice deflated her, and she scowled.

'I don't call doing the Lord's work mischief,' she retorted.

'What else could it be? Setting fire to the inn without warning those inside. That's not the Lord's work. And don't deny it. I saw you with the burning brand in your hand. It's the Devil's work ye've done tonight.'

'What do you know about it? You haven't set foot inside a church for years. If you had, you would have heard the minister preaching against the harlots in our midst. He said, "The flames of hell shall devour them," and it came to pass tonight.'

'If that's what the church preaches, I want no part in it.'

'I say it's good riddance to the two of them. We want no Jezebels in our village tempting the men.'

'So, ye would have blood on your hands to rid the village of them?'

'Aye, and proud of it.' She stared him out and watched as his body deflated.

'To think a daughter of mine could do such a thing. Ye're as mad as your mother was before ye.'

'Because my mother ran away from you when I was wee doesn't mean she was mad.'

Ellen's voice shook with rage, but her father was no longer there. She was shouting at the closed door of the boxroom he called his bedroom.

2

The flames from the inn had settled into a red glow that lit up the darkness and reflected across the water like the molten stream of a lava flow. Two women and three children huddled together at the end of the bridge they had crossed to reach the unknown safety of Invercraig.

Belle knew many of the women who had been part of the mob. A group of fishwives who, encouraged by her sister-in-law, Ellen, started the fire and thought their victims had burned inside the inn. She thought some of them might now have guilt pangs about the children. However, she doubted this would apply to Ellen, who was so consumed with hatred, and the bitterness caused by her own inability to have children, that she had little sympathy for anything connected with Belle.

The night was quiet except for the shushing of the waves and Jamie sobbing into Madge's skirt. Davy, his twin, gripped Belle's hand. He said nothing, although his lips were compressed, and his face was white. Belle knew Davy, at six years old, considered it a weakness to cry and she hoped he wouldn't tease Jamie later on.

Sarah stood slightly apart from the rest of the group. At ten, she was already independent and behaved like an adult. Belle supposed it was her fault. She'd never allowed Sarah to be a child and depended on her to mind the twins while she worked at the inn. If she could only love her a little, it might be different. She still remembered Jimmie's wonderment after Sarah's birth and her resentment at having to share his love. But she'd been consumed by an irrational possessiveness, a jealousy that warped her love for her child. It was too late now, for only the sea had Jimmie. He'd never returned from his last whaling trip.

Belle reached out and placed an arm around Sarah's shoulder. Maybe it wasn't too late to make it up to her. Sarah stiffened under her grasp, but Belle pulled her closer, determined to show she cared for her and things would be different from now on.

The faintest smell of burning wood drifted over the water, reminding them of the danger they'd been in. If it hadn't been for Ian, her husband's brother, they would never have escaped. She watched him now, striding across the bridge, back to Ellen, and knew if she'd wanted him to stay with her, he would have stayed.

She turned to Madge. 'There's nothing left of the Craigden Inn, except some ashes, so what now?'

'That inn was my life; my future; my security. I worked hard to build it up from a broken-down ale house into a going business. And what do I have to show for my work? Nothing.' Madge's voice was thick with bitterness. 'All because some jealous-minded fishwives couldn't bear to see us make a success of it.'

Belle was convinced the jealousy ran deeper than Madge thought.

'Maybe they were afraid their men would leave them,' she said.

'Aye, perhaps they were, and it would have served them right if we had taken their men.'

Madge moved off. 'Come on, Belle,' she said. 'The further away we get from Craigden, the better it'll be for all of us.'

'Where will we go?' Sarah asked her.

'That's a good question, lass. But I have the inn's takings here, so we have some money, and I'm sure my brother will be glad of an extra two barmaids.'

Belle joined her, turning her back on the ashes of her old life.

Ian strode towards Craigden, but once he was sure Belle and Madge were no longer watching him, he stopped to look back. He didn't continue on his way until they passed out of his sight.

What would become of them? Their worldly goods and possessions were gone, up in flames. But at least they were safe. They had their lives.

And what did he have? A loveless marriage to a murderous bitch.

The echo of his mother's voice ran through his mind. 'You make your bed; you lie on it.' It was a common saying, meant as a warning for them to behave themselves.

Well, he'd made his bed when he took Ellen for his wife, so he'd have to endure it. But he knew each time he looked at her, he would see that crazy look in her eyes and the murder in her heart.

Shivers engulfed Belle as she urged Sarah and the twins to follow her and Madge.

The wind had risen since their hasty departure from Craigden. It tore at her shawl and whipped her skirts around her ankles, chilling her to the bone.

Boats creaked and groaned against the harbour wall on their right and the smell of fish permeated the air. No lights shone from the dilapidated cottages on the other side of the road where the fisherfolk of Invercraig lived.

She tucked her chin into her shawl and kept her head down; she was finished with the fishing life and everything it entailed. The time had come to start anew.

They continued onwards, walking past a row of tall tenements with dark and lifeless windows. Further along, moonlight silhouetted the ships berthed in the docks, silvering the masts which pointed starkly to the heavens, looking like a forest of trees with no leaves.

'We're here,' Madge said.

Belle raised her chin from the folds of the shawl to stare at the Ship Inn. It looked shabby and uncared for, but Belle had worked long enough as a barmaid to realise its position, central to both the docks and the Fishtown, ensured it would be a gold mine.

Her eyes roamed over the two-storey building. It looked as if everything could do with a coat of paint, from the whitewashed exterior to the doors and windows.

'Is this your brother's inn?' Belle stared at the uninviting frontage and the black, empty windows. It didn't look welcoming.

Madge nodded and thumped on the door.

Belle wrapped her arms around Jamie and Davy. 'I need you to behave,' she whispered to them. She feared Madge's brother might not take kindly to two rowdy boys and use it as an excuse to turn his back on them.

Sarah stood apart from them on the pavement's edge. Belle ignored her as she often did. It was easier to do that than try to understand why the child lacked enjoyment. The only time she had ever seen her smile or heard her laugh was when she was with Jeannie, her mother-in-law's youngest child. How she had birthed such a serious child was beyond her.

The twins, however, were always laughing, always up to mischief, and if truth be told, they were wild.

'Are you sure your brother will give us shelter?'

'I'll make certain he does.' Madge thumped the heavy double doors. The sound echoed into the building. After waiting for a moment, she hammered on the doors again.

A window above them slid open. 'Bugger off, we're closed.'

Belle's fears increased. There was no welcome for them here.

'Damn you, Gregor. It's me, Madge. Open up. It's perishing out here.'

After a brief silence, the window slammed shut and the sound of feet shuffling inside filtered out to the waiting group. The rasp of bolts followed, and the door creaked open.

A man stood in the doorway holding a lantern. He was swarthy and no taller than Belle. His uncombed hair reached in a shaggy mess to his shoulders, while his face and hands looked as if they only had a passing acquaintance with water.

'What d'you want?' He scowled at them.

Madge pushed past him. 'That's no way to greet your sister.'

'Sister?' He snorted. 'How many years is it since I've seen you?'

Madge shrugged. 'I've been busy running my inn at Craigden. You know how it is, business before pleasure.' She beckoned Belle to follow her inside.

Belle, grasping the boys' hands, edged past Gregor. She felt him watching her and sensed his interest. Maybe she could turn it to her advantage.

'If you're so busy with your inn, what are you doing here?'

'Cast your eyes across the river. You see that red glow? That's my inn burning, which means I no longer have a business or a home. But you wouldn't like me sleeping on the street, would you? You are my brother, after all.'

Gregor grunted but didn't raise any objection.

'I knew you wouldn't let me down.' She patted his arm.

Gregor scowled and held his lantern up to look at Belle. 'This one.' He jerked his head towards her. 'Who's she?'

Madge smiled and patted his arm again. 'This is Belle. The best barmaid I ever had. Men came from miles around to be served a drink by her. It wouldn't do you any harm to hire her. She'd improve your business enormously.'

'Oh, she would, would she?'

His eyes raked over her, and Belle shivered. She didn't like the gleam they held. But they needed shelter and a place to stay, so she smiled at him and lowered her eyelids, feigning shyness.

The scowl left his face for the briefest of moments, and although they were already inside, he said, 'I suppose you'd better come in then. But don't think I'm going to give you a room and a bed, and don't get too comfortable because you'll be out in the morning.'

Madge bristled. 'You can't turn your sister out into the street. Da will spin in his grave.'

'Da's not here. I'm in charge now.'

'You could at least let us have an attic room.'

Gregor scowled at them. 'You can bed down here, like it, or lump it. Come morning, I'll decide what to do.'

He stamped out of the room, slamming the door shut behind him, leaving them in the dark except for the flickering flame from the dying fire.

Belle flinched when another door upstairs slammed. Whatever was in front of them, she'd have to make the best of it.

3

Jeannie gripped her ma's hand. The screeching women with their flaming torches had terrified her, and she couldn't get the minister's manic smile out of her mind as he watched the inn burn. Her worries about Belle and the bairns increased. Had Ian got them to safety? Or were their bodies lying in the building's shell?

Little remained now. The roof had caved in a short time earlier and the flames were nearer to the ground.

Annie drew back, pulling Jeannie with her when two women scurried past. One of them stopped on the river's edge and threw her spent torch into the water.

'Aye, Lizzie McNab, that'll not change what ye've done the night,' she muttered under her breath.

Annie and Jeannie sidled out of the shadows once the baying mob was further away.

'It's a sad day when something like this happens among the folk ye thought ye knew.'

'Why did they do it?' Jeannie tightened her grip on Annie's hand.

'Ye widnae understand, lass. Ye're just a bairn yet.'

'I'm not a bairn. I'm sixteen and I'll be seventeen come this June. Belle was wed and had Sarah when she was seventeen.'

'Aye, well, don't think you're going to follow her example. I'll not have any daughter of mine cheapening herself the way Belle did.'

Jeannie stayed silent. She knew full well her ma disapproved of Belle. She'd made that plain ever since she'd come to Craigden as Jimmie's wife. But Jeannie liked Belle. She was different. More delicate and with bonnier clothes than any of the other women.

10

Ma didn't know, but she'd often visited Belle. She'd fingered the silk dresses and wished she could put them on even though she knew they wouldn't look as good on her as they did Belle. For Belle was a lot bonnier and shapelier.

She would miss Belle with her quick wit and laugh, but she would miss Sarah even more.

Sarah was seven years younger than Jeannie, but the two had been inseparable since Sarah's birth in the summer of 1830.

'D'ye think Belle and the bairns escaped the fire?' Tears pricked her eyes when she thought of their bodies burned to ash.

'Ian will have done his best, lass. No one can do more than that.'

Footsteps on the gravel path sounded over the dying crackles. Jeannie held tight to her ma's hand as they both shrank into the dimness of the cottage. They waited in breathless silence until the figure of a man appeared. His stride was purposeful, and he was heading for them.

'Is that you, Ma?' Ian peered at the shadowy figure standing in the doorway.

'Aye, lad. Are Belle and her bairns safe?' Annie emerged from the gloom, followed by his sister Jeannie.

'I walked with them to Invercraig. They'll be safe there.'

'What will they do there? Where will they go?' Jeannie's voice trembled.

'They'll not land up in the workhouse if that's what ye think.' His confident tone masked Ian's fear that this might be a possibility.

'Madge mentioned a brother who keeps an inn. Perhaps he'll shelter them.'

Ian made a silent vow to himself to check up on them. It ran in his mind that families over in the town didn't share the same closeness and loyalty that was a part of village life. Here in Craigden, no villager would turn their backs on family, but in the town, it was different.

Ian's mood darkened as he walked home. Ellen had a lot to answer for, but he couldn't confront her. Not as long as the old bugger, her father lived, for he was reliant on them for the fishing boat, which would eventually be his own.

Ellen had different ideas, though. As soon as Ian walked through the door, her shrill voice echoed through the house. 'You have the cheek to come back here after being with her?'

Ian took a step backwards. 'And what was I supposed to do? Leave them to burn and be complicit in a murder. Do you think I want my wife to dangle from the hangman's noose?'

He grabbed her arm and twisted it. 'Be thankful they're not dead.'

'Thankful, is it?' Ellen's face contorted. 'The village is well rid of those two whores.'

'What about the children, Jimmie's bairns, your kin? Do they deserve to die because you're jealous of Belle?'

'Belle's brats are no kin of mine. Jimmie was your brother, not mine.'

'Aye, and you married me, which makes them your kin. Have ye no shame about what you've done?'

'Why should I feel shame? I have nothing to be ashamed of. I live a god-fearing blameless life, not like those harlots who'd lift their skirts for any man who gave them a second look. Even the minister called the wrath of God down on them.'

Ian drew a breath. Was Ellen's mind so twisted she thought she was carrying out the will of God?

'I am sure God would not approve of burning people alive.'

'It's no more than they deserve, and I would do it again if I had the chance.'

Spittle sprayed his face, and he drew back, unable to hide his disgust.

Ignoring his response, she advanced and pushed her face closer to his. Hatred transformed her features, and her eyes gleamed with malice. He shuddered. This was a stranger in Ellen's skin. There was no saving her.

He turned on his heel and left the house, his marriage, and the boat that ensured his future. The price was too high.

Annie and Jeannie remained watching until the last of the flames flickered into smouldering ash. The smell of smoke lingered, but the night sky no longer glowed red and the darkness crept back, wrapping them in its chill embrace.

Annie shivered and pulled her shawl tighter around her body. 'It's over. No point standing here any longer. Best we get some sleep before morning dawns.'

She watched Jeannie return to her truckle bed and knew in her heart the lass would have trouble sleeping. It showed in the slump of her shoulders and the look of despair on her face.

With a sigh, she climbed into the box bed beside her James. Despite the clamour of the evening, he hadn't stirred. But she had her doubts whether he'd slept through it. He was like all men, wary of interfering with the womenfolk.

Come morning, she'd have it out with him.

4

February 1840 - The day after the fire - Tuesday

Daylight had not yet penetrated the room when Belle woke with a start to the sound of wind and rain lashing the windows. Her recollection of how she came to be here after the horrific events of the night before was vague. Sitting up, she swung her feet off the bench and rubbed her aching back. She peered through the gloom to get her bearings, but the place was unfamiliar. The bar must be at one end of the room. But which end? Madge had bedded down on another of the benches, while the bairns had tucked themselves under a table, huddling together for warmth and safety.

'Madge?' Her voice echoed in the large room. 'Are you awake?'

A movement over to her right caught her eye. 'I am now.' Madge sounded peeved.

Outside, the inn's sign creaked and swung as a gust of wind caught it and, further away, she heard the clatter of bins and other debris being tossed around.

Belle shivered and wrapped her arms around her middle. Everything had been going so well. Her work in Madge's inn was enjoyable. She had money to spend and no worries about how to survive. Life had been good until last night when everything had gone up in flames. Now she had nothing. No job, no income, and only the clothes she wore.

The rustle of Madge's skirts and the pad of her feet on the floor suggested she was on the move.

'What are you doing?' she whispered into the dark room.

'Looking for a candle or a lantern.' Madge's voice echoed back to her. 'Ah, here we are, found one.'

Madge's feet padded across the floor again, followed by a scrabbling noise and the clink of something metallic. The cloying smell of ash made Belle cough, and she covered her mouth with her sleeve.

'What are you doing now?'

'Stirring some life into yesterday's fire so I can light this taper. The bugger's just about dead, but there are some cinders at the bottom.'

A flicker of flame glowed briefly, giving Madge enough time to light the candle.

'That's better,' she said, holding it aloft.

The smell of the tallow was worse than the ash and Belle held her nose.

'This will be enough for me to light the lanterns behind the bar.'

'How do you know where to find the lanterns?'

'This was where I was brought up. It was my da's pub before he died and left it to Gregor, even though he's younger than me.' Madge returned with a lantern. 'God, this place is a mess,' she said. 'It's no better than a pigsty. Come on. Let's get it cleaned up.'

'Why should we? It's nothing to do with us if your brother wants to live like this.' Belle looked around with disgust on her face.

'Because I'm going to convince Gregor he needs us, and it will be in his interests to allow us to stay.'

5

It was dark when Annie slid out of bed, and outside a gale was howling. The heavens had opened, sending lashing rain and wind screeching up the river from the sea. An omen, Annie thought, God expressing his disapproval of the previous night's activities.

She stirred the ashes in the grate and laid sticks to kindle a new fire. The men would be up and about soon, looking for their breakfast.

Jeannie stirred in her truckle bed. At least the lass had got some sleep. Whether or not it was restful was a different matter. She'd seen the look on Jeannie's face when she returned last night.

A spurt of flame from the newly kindled fire in the grate resurrected her memories of last night's hellish scenes. With a shudder, she suppressed them and poured water into the pot sitting on the trivet. She had a family to feed.

Before setting down the wooden pail, she gave it a shake. The water inside slurped from side to side, but from the weight and sound, she knew there wasn't enough to last the day.

'Run for some more water while I make the porridge,' she said to Jeannie, who was scrubbing her face with a wet cloth. 'By the look of the women last night, I don't think there will be much of a queue at the pump.'

Jeannie's expression darkened, and she grabbed the bucket and ran out the door.

It had been the wrong thing to say. Reminding Jeannie of the madness of the women during the night.

With a sigh, she swung the trivet over the fire, threw in a handful of salt, and waited for the water to boil before adding the oatmeal.

By the time Jeannie returned with the pail of water, the porridge was simmering, and James was pulling on his trousers.

Noises from the loft showed the boys were awake and before many minutes had passed, Davie clattered down the ladder, followed by Angus.

Davie stretched, yawned and combed his hair with his fingers. At twenty-two he still looked like a boy, probably because of his thin, lanky frame and smooth skin, which never became weatherbeaten like his father or brothers. Annie never understood why she and James had managed to produce this lad, a dreamer ill-fitted to a fisher's life.

Angus, at twenty-five, was stockier and looked like a fisherman. It was clear to see he was following in his father's footsteps.

She narrowed her eyes and compressed her lips as she looked at them. They'd refused to get involved with the previous night's activities. How was it possible for them to ignore the ruckus and the acrid smell of smoke? It was baffling. But not one of them had poked their heads out from under the blankets while she and Jeannie stood at the door. What good were menfolk when they weren't willing to protect their kin?

Jeannie placed the pail of water in the larder before setting the porridge bowls on the table.

'What's the matter, Jeannie, lass? You're not smiling this morning.' James pulled a stool over to the table.

'Fine you know what's the matter. Jeannie watched what was going on last night while you cowardly lot covered your heads with blankets.' Annie slapped a dollop of porridge on each plate. 'Best eat your breakfast. It's all you're good for.'

'You know it was impossible to stop those screaming banshees. There's not a man in the village could have stopped them.'

Annie threw the pot in the sink and scowled at them. She placed her hands on the table and leaned towards James until her face was so near their noses touched. 'You'd rather see Belle, and her bairns burned to death,' she hissed. 'Your own kin.'

James leaned back. 'Belle's not of my blood,' he said.

'No. But the bairns are.' She stopped for breath. 'Our Jimmie's bairns. All that's left of him.' She straightened and turned away. She'd never allowed her family to see her cry before, and she didn't intend to let them see it now.

James stood and put a hand on her shoulder. 'Ian said he'd get them out.'

Annie pulled away from him. 'I never thought I'd see the day I'd say this. But Ian's a better man than the lot of you.'

'Ach, Annie, don't be like that. You must know there was nothing we could do to stop what happened.'

'Maybe so, but once the laird finds out what the women have done, he'll throw everyone out. We'll be homeless. You'll lose your boat unless you have enough money saved to pay for his share. Have you forgotten he owns the village, every stone of it, and he has a share in most of the boats?'

'And who do you think is going to tell him who was responsible for last night's mischief? I can't see anyone in the village telling him that.'

'The minister was there. I saw him watching.' Jeannie's voice was low, but what she said struck fear into their hearts.

'We're done for,' Annie said. 'The minister won't hold his tongue.'

'We'll see about that.' James grabbed his jacket.

Wind whistled into the room, bringing with it a splatter of rain when he threw the door open and strode outside.

Murdo McAllan washed his breakfast plate and cup in a basin of cold water. He was in between housekeepers. They never stayed long. Not that it worried him. His needs were few, and he ate sparingly, so the lack of cooked meals did not worry him. After all, greed was a sin, and Murdo had been preaching about sin for most of his life.

He blew on his fingers to get warmth into them before adjusting his clerical collar and pulling on the long black robe he thought gave him an air of authority. It was time to visit his cousin, Sir Roderick Craigallan.

His mission, to tell Roderick about how the women of Craigden set fire to the inn, filled him with pleasure. In his eyes, Eve offering the apple to Adam meant women were evil and required saving. Certain

Roderick would agree Murdo was the one to save them and ensure they were penitent, made him rub his hands in anticipation.

He was turning the key in the lock of his front door when he sensed someone looming over him.

A man stood there with rain streaming from his sou'wester hat onto his waterproof jacket.

'James,' he said, 'I didn't recognise you for a minute. Was there something you wanted?'

'It's a wild day, Reverend. We'd be better inside.' James motioned towards the door.

Murdo sighed and unlocked it.

James didn't wait for an invitation. He marched inside, took off his jacket and hat, shook the water off, and hung them on a coat hook on the lobby wall.

'Don't want to drip on your furniture,' he said as he walked into the minister's sitting room and planted himself on a wooden chair.

Confusion swept over Murdo. The village men were not prone to be so forward. They usually showed him respect. He pulled over another chair and placed it in front of James.

'Is something on your mind, James? Is something worrying you?'

'It's like this, Reverend. There was a riot in Craigden last night which led to the inn being burned to the ground.'

'Ah, yes. I had heard about that. When you arrived, I was on my way to inform Sir Roderick of the horrific events of last night.' He rubbed his hands together and tightened his lips to suppress the smile of anticipation hovering on his lips. 'Such a sad business.'

'Sad indeed.' James nodded his head. 'I heard some muttering among the women after Sunday's church service. They thought your sermon was inspiring. Such a pity it inspired them to violence.'

It took a moment for Murdo to understand what James was insinuating. But the man was of no importance. A fisherman. What right had he to make such comments? He stiffened.

'I preach the word of our Lord, and I never condone violence. But that inn was a den of iniquity inhabited by women of ill repute who put temptation in the way of the men in this village.'

'Jezebels I think you were referring to.' The man's voice was steady, containing no element of incrimination.

Murdo relaxed. 'Yes, we had Jezebels in our midst. I am not sorry they are gone.'

James leaned forward. 'Gone, yes. But it's lucky for you they aren't dead.'

'What happened last night had nothing to do with me.'

James leaned forward and stared into Murdo's eyes. 'And the flames of Hell shall devour them.'

'What?' Murdo stared at James in confusion.

'That was the part the women liked the most. And don't forget, Sir Roderick was present and heard your sermon.'

'You presume to lecture me when the men of the village cannot control their women. If there is anyone to blame, it is yourselves. I think you've said enough, and it's time for you to leave.'

'Aye, perhaps you're right. But I reckon by nightfall the village will be empty after the laird throws us out because of what the women did. You will have lost your congregation.' James turned before he left the room. 'I am sorry for you. What good is a minister with no one to preach to?' With that parting remark, he left.

Murdo remained seated, his thoughts in turmoil. His planned visit to his cousin no longer afforded him pleasure, but it had to be done. Sir Roderick needed to be informed. But Sir Roderick was not known for compassion, and James had been right when he surmised that when the laird found out the women were responsible, he would evict the villagers.

Not that Murdo concerned himself about the fate of the villagers, but he was concerned about his own fate. How could his church survive with no congregation? This was his home, and he didn't relish being called to another parish.

He pulled his robe about him, preparing to face the storm outside and his cousin, although he didn't know which was the worst.

6

The howl of the wind and the patter of rain lashing the window woke Lachlan. He resisted the temptation to roll over and go back to sleep and, throwing back the blankets, he rubbed his eyes and stretched to bring vigour to his limbs. No doubt his father was already up and about, for both father and son had little liking for staying abed most of the day.

Once he completed his ablutions and dressed, he sauntered out of his room in search of breakfast. He stopped outside Clarinda's door but heard no sound from within. Not surprising because Clarinda was not likely to rise before midday. Unlike him, she had a fondness for her bed. He sighed. His marriage had been a disappointment. He would have preferred to wed Belle, but his family would never have countenanced it. Besides, Belle resented him for deserting her and marrying Clarinda, and she refused to speak to him.

His father grunted at him when he entered the breakfast room. He supposed it was too much to expect him to say good morning, for Sir Roderick was not one who embraced the niceties of life.

Lachlan gave the porridge bowl a miss and helped himself to bacon, sausage, cold meats, and some kidneys. He preferred fish, but the lack of it didn't surprise him. The February storms had been worse this year, keeping the boats beached for longer than usual. Maybe when today's storm blew itself out, there would be enough calm for the boats to sail to the fishing grounds.

He barely had time to sit at the table and lift his fork before the door burst open and a bedraggled Murdo appeared with the butler bringing up the rear.

'I'm sorry, sir,' Bates said, his voice heavy with disapproval, 'but the minister insisted on coming straight in without being announced.'

Murdo removed his cape and shook it before handing it to the butler, who received it with an expression of disdain, which the minister ignored. With a flick of his fingers, he dismissed the man.

Bates raised his eyebrows and looked at his master for confirmation before leaving the room.

Sir Roderick laid down his knife and fork and looked at the minister. 'What is so urgent you need to interrupt me at the breakfast table?' His voice expressed his annoyance mixed with a modicum of curiosity.

Lachlan had little time for the minister. He thought him pompous and overfull of his own importance. Why did his father tolerate the man? Was it because Murdo was his father's cousin, a recognition the man was of their blood? His father set a lot of store on blood, but Lachlan was less sure.

Murdo approached the table, looking pious. 'I come with bad news.' He kneaded his hands together. 'Bad news,' he repeated.

'Spit it out, man. We don't have all day.'

Lachlan pierced a lump of sausage and thrust it into his mouth. While he chewed, he watched his father's patience erode as Murdo hesitated. No doubt the man aimed to gain an advantage from the situation.

As Lachlan continued to watch, Murdo cast a glance at the food on the sideboard and then the table. The damned man was angling to be asked to eat with them. But that was a step too far, even for his father.

Sir Roderick drummed his fingers on the table and scowled.

Murdo cast him an anxious glance before speaking. 'The hand of God has driven out the Jezebels in our midst.' He placed his hand on his chest in a dramatic gesture.

'Stop talking in riddles, Murdo, and tell me what has happened.'

Murdo gulped. 'The inn, Sir Roderick, has burned to the ground and God has cleansed the village of the evil within.'

Lachlan choked on the sausage. Surely the man didn't mean Belle and Madge had burned with the inn. And what about the children? The twin boys who might have been sired by him, although he wasn't sure about that.

'The occupants of the inn. Have they perished?' A sense of doom enveloped him.

'You mean the Jezebels. If they have met their end, it is only what they deserve. The Bible tells us, "The flames of Hell shall devour them." If you recall, it was part of my sermon on Sunday.'

Lachlan wasn't sure that was what the Bible said. It sounded more like a Murdo quote rather than a biblical one.

'And the children. Did they deserve such a fate?'

'The spawn of Satan deserves no less.'

Lachlan turned from him in disgust. 'We need to find out if there was anyone in the inn when it burned,' he said to his father.

'I agree,' Sir Roderick said. He looked over at the window. 'Best wait until the storm has abated somewhat.' He seemed to have forgotten Murdo until the minister cleared his throat. 'You may leave now.' He dismissed him with a wave of his hand.

Lachlan pushed his plate aside. He was no longer hungry.

Had the flames consumed Belle? Bile rose in his throat, and he stumbled from the room without a backward glance at his father.

Lachlan paced up and down the courtyard while Hamish got the coach ready for the drive to Craigden. The rain had abated and was only a drizzle, although the wind still tossed the trees and thunder rumbled in the distance. For once, Lachlan was thankful his father was accompanying him as he didn't fancy riding Raven today. The horse was too high-spirited and more difficult to control in this weather.

After what felt like an eternity, Hamish nodded to Lachlan. 'You may tell the laird the carriage is ready,' he said.

A retort hovered on Lachlan's lips at the effrontery of the man telling him what to do, but he was eager to get on the road and simply scowled before turning to the house to collect his father.

The road to Craigden was waterlogged. Several times, the carriage slithered on the mud. But Hamish was an expert coachman, and he soon drew the coach to a halt at the village square.

Without waiting for his father to alight, Lachlan jumped out. His feet slipped, and he grabbed the coach's door to regain his balance before turning to inspect the pile of ash and rubble which had once been the inn.

His father joined him and poked at some remnants of charred wood. 'At least the rest of the buildings in the square have survived. It's a blessing they're stone built.' The laird picked up a stick. He fingered the burned rags at its tip. 'Last night's fire was no accident.' His voice was rough with anger. 'If I find out who started it, I'll make sure they pay for it.'

The words made no impact on Lachlan. He was too busy concentrating on the rubble and wondering if it contained any bodies. He shook his head to clear his thoughts. What had happened to Belle and the children?

'Are you listening to me, Lachlan? Someone must know who started this fire, and I want you to find them. The innkeeper and barmaid are nowhere to be found. That's damned suspicious? It suggests they either started the fire themselves or they know who did. Find out where they've gone and what the villagers know. And find the culprits, even if it requires threatening the entire village with their removal if they don't talk.'

Lachlan stared in dismay at his father. He had no illusions about the fisherfolk. They were a close-knit community, and they were unlikely to tell him anything. But although he had no liking for Murdo, his chances would be better if the minister accompanied him.

'I have my doubts whether the villagers will talk to me, but if I ask Murdo to help, I might have more success. They have respect for the church and if Murdo threatens them with hell and damnation, I'm sure they'll tell us what we want to know.'

'Whatever, the man's a buffoon, but if you think it will get a result, then do it because I want to find the person responsible for setting fire to my property. I'll make sure they hang for it.'

'Not good for business all this mess. Who's going to clear it up? That's what I'd like to know.'

The voice startled Lachlan, and he turned to the speaker. A small man wearing an oversized apron.

'And you are?'

'Fraser Watson, although most folks call me Wattie. I run the general store over there.' He nodded to the opposite side of the square facing the rubble of the inn. 'Lucky for me the shop is stone built.'

'Well, Wattie, what can you tell me? How did the fire start?'

7

Annie hurried to the window when she heard the clatter of hooves and the sound of coach wheels. It could only be the laird come to inspect the damage to the inn.

She shivered. What did he know? What had the minister told him? James had talked with the man, but that meant nothing. Murdo McAllan was known for keeping his own counsel. He liked to think the villagers looked to him for guidance in their lives in the same way the farm workers did. Truth to tell, the fisherfolk were more dismissive and worshipped God rather than the minister.

Mud splashed onto the window when the coach passed, and despair coursed through Annie. Her home was this house and this village and the thought of having to leave because of the reckless behaviour of the women struck fear into her heart.

James hadn't stirred from the fireside since his return. Annie could hardly bear to look at him sitting in the ingle nook smoking his pipe.

'Did ye not hear the coach?' Annie demanded. 'That's the laird. He'll be here to find out what's happened.'

'Dinnae fash yourself, wife.' James leaned over to stir the fire with a poker. 'The minister will not tell him it was the women.'

'Aye, that's all right for you to say. But what if he finds out?'

She stepped outside into the wind and rain. Pulling her shawl closer she peered towards the square. The laird stood there, glowering, and poking the debris with his stick while his son stared at the rubble with a wild expression.

A door facing the burned-out inn creaked open and Wattie the shopkeeper emerged. He hovered on the doorstep for a moment before stepping outside.

Annie gasped. Wattie must have seen what happened.

She scuttled back inside the house. 'Quick Jeannie, get hold of Wattie. Stop him telling the laird what happened, or this will be the last day we spend in this house.'

'But what can I do?' Jeannie grabbed her shawl.

'He likes you lass, anyone with half an eye can see that.' She groaned. 'Do what you can.'

She watched Jeannie run to where the men stood, but feared there was nothing the lass could do.

Jeannie reached the village square in time to hear Lachlan, the laird's son, ask Wattie what he knew about the fire.

She grasped Wattie's hand, and he turned to her with a startled look.

Jeannie forced tears to her eyes and looked up into Lachlan's face. 'It was scary, the fire. I feared we were all going to burn. It was such a quiet night, not like today, and the flames were everywhere. I came to the square to see if my guid-sister, Belle and her bairns were safe, but no one was here except for the minister. I saw him watching from that pend over there.' She pointed to an opening between the remaining buildings. 'I thought if he was there, he would help, so I went back home.'

'What about you, Wattie?' Lachlan turned to the shopkeeper. 'You were about to say what you saw when this lass interrupted you.'

Wattie hesitated. Jeannie held her breath, willing him to confirm what she'd said.

Sir Roderick, still grasping the makeshift torch, stopped poking the ashes and rubble and joined them.

'Speak up, man. What did you see?'

'It must have been as Jeannie said, sir.' Wattie paused, as if thinking. 'I'd had a busy day sorting out stock and went to bed early, so I don't know how it started. The last thing I remember before falling asleep was some lads heading home. They were merry and making a bit of noise. Madge was locking up the inn, and I heard her shout to the lads to be quiet and not wake the bairns. But later, I woke in the night, choking and spluttering on the smoke. Nothing I could do though, it were too far gone by then.'

'What about this?' Sir Roderick waved the stick at him, thrusting the charred rags at the tip under the man's nose. 'If I'm not mistaken, this is a torch.'

'I know nothing about that, sir. Like I said, the inn were burning something fierce when I woke.'

The laird snorted his disbelief.

'What about the inn's occupants? Did they escape?' There were no signs of charred bodies, so Lachlan presumed they'd fled.

Wattie shrugged. 'I didn't hear no screams so I reckon everyone must have got out.' He sighed. 'Nice folk they were, Madge and Belle. I hope they've come to no harm.'

Jeannie squeezed his hand. 'I'm sure you would have helped them if you'd heard anything.'

'Aye, that I would.' Wattie's voice was husky as if he was on the point of tears.

Jeannie wasn't sure how much he knew, but it was enough the laird and his fancy son seemed satisfied with the explanation.

'I think we've seen enough, Lachlan.' Sir Roderick walked over to the carriage and, without another glance at Wattie and Jeannie, he clambered aboard.

'Thank you for your help,' Lachlan said. 'I will speak to you again later.'

Jeannie shivered. His eyes had been on her when he spoke.

The coachman touched the flanks of the horses with his whip and with a clatter of hooves and rumble of wheels, the carriage moved off, trundling along the river path.

Wattie still held Jeannie's hand and seemed in no hurry to let it go. No boy or man had ever held her hand before, not even her father, and it was comforting but also embarrassing. She wriggled her fingers free from his grasp.

'I need to get home,' she said.

He grabbed her hand again. 'Not before you tell me why you stopped me from telling the laird about last night.'

'You saw what happened? How the fire started.'

'Yes, Jeannie, I saw, but it was clear to me you didn't want him to know. Why was that? Were you one of them?'

'Me? One of them? I wouldn't be so daft.'

'Then why protect them?'

'Because if the laird finds out, we'll all be evicted. That's why.'

Wattie stared at her. 'That means the village will be dead.'

'Yes. What will happen to your store then, with no customers?'

She wrenched her hand free and ran down the road. 'Think on it. Do you really want the laird to know what happened?'

Wattie watched Jeannie until she vanished inside the house. The warmth of her hand in his had felt so right, and he'd been reluctant to let go. It was strange. He'd paid little attention to her before and now there was this feeling coursing through his body. A feeling he'd never experienced before. He hesitated on the threshold of the shop before entering. This was not the time to run after a girl he barely knew.

The bell above the door jangled when he pushed it open and a puff of ash floated in the air, no doubt part of the aftermath of last night's fire. It would take him all day to clean up, and he wasn't looking forward to it.

The overcast morning allowed less light than usual to enter through the small shop window and he blinked in the gloom. Ash covered everything. The floor, the oatmeal bin, the rack of turnips and vegetables in front of the wooden counter. The weighing scales with the weights piled up at the side. The bowl of eggs. And the other bits and bobs cluttering the countertop. Thankfully, the lids on the various boxes of fresh food, protection against marauding mice, meant the ash couldn't infiltrate there. It was only yesterday he'd scraped a layer of mould from the surface of the cheese, scraping it again would reduce the size even more.

With a sigh, he grabbed the broom from behind the counter and swept the floor. It wasn't a task he liked. The shop needed a woman's touch. But what woman would want him? The village girls only had eyes for the fisher lads who were younger, bigger and stronger than him. Next month he'd be thirty and the women nearer his age were all wed.

He sighed again and concentrated on sweeping the floor.

8

Ian woke up stiff and sore. Where was he? Memories of last night flooded back. The fire, Belle, Madge, and the bairns, and his argument with Ellen. In his anger, he'd left the house, throwing away his life and his future as a boat owner. What was a fisherman without a boat? He'd stomped along the road, his anger growing with every step. But no light shone from his ma's house and the door was closed.

The rain, which had come too late to save the inn, battered his body. He needed to find somewhere to sleep and anywhere outside wasn't an option. He'd turned towards the river and the boat that was no longer his and crawled aboard.

Now it was morning and the tarpaulin covering him felt heavy. He threw it aside, dodging the water which had pooled on the top before it soaked him.

The storm and the rain had abated while he slept, but his mood remained dark. There would be no return to Ellen and the home they had built. He'd seek refuge with his ma and help man his da's boat. Or follow Jimmie's lead and go whaling or seek a berth on a ship that traded with foreign countries. Ellen and her father could keep their boat. After what had happened, the price was too high. He'd make money, somehow or other, and get a boat of his own. That way, he'd keep his self-respect and independence.

He had almost reached his ma's house when he saw the carriage on the road beside the village square.

The laird's voice was unmistakable, loud, gruff, and more refined than the dialect of the villagers. His intention to evict everyone was clear unless he found the culprits who set the fire.

He drew back into the shadow of a house as the carriage bowled past him, taking the laird and his son back to Craigallan Castle.

He must warn his parents, and make sure the villagers knew what the laird had threatened.

Jeannie ran home from the square. It wasn't far, but her heart was thumping by the time she burst through the door of the cottage. She'd never been so close to the laird as she had been that day, and it had taken all her willpower to face his anger about the fire. Then there had been his son who quizzed her about Belle. He had been polite, but said he'd talk to her later. She didn't want to talk to him later or at any other time. But what choice did she have? He was the laird's son.

Her father looked up from his seat at the fire and, removing his pipe from his mouth, he said, 'Did Wattie tell the laird what happened, or were you able to stop him?'

'It's all right. I got my word in first and Wattie went along with it. But after the laird left, I had to explain to him why we have to keep quiet. I think he understands.'

'Good work, lass. I feared we were done for.'

Annie laid down the knife she'd been using to pare the skins of some potatoes. 'I was watching from the window. I couldn't hear anything, but the laird had a look on his face that sent shivers through me.'

'Aye, fear of him near made me turn back.' Jeannie shuddered as she remembered her fear. 'He'd found a burnt-out torch, and he was so angry I nearly ran off. But I gripped Wattie's hand and stayed the course.'

Before Jeannie could continue, the door slammed open and Ian loomed in the doorway, blocking the light.

Annie's eyes narrowed. 'What are you doing here? Shouldn't you be with Ellen?'

'I've left her.' The bitterness in Ian's voice was unmistakable. 'How can I stay with her after what she's done?'

'She's your wife, that's why.'

'Wife no more. I'll be having nothing more to do with her.'

'You'd bring disgrace to our family and the village.'

'Disgrace!' Ian laughed. 'I think Ellen has already done that. That's the least of our worries. There might not be a village once the laird finds out what went on last night.'

James got up from his fireside seat. 'And how is he going to find out, lad? I've already talked to the minister, and he'll not be telling him.'

'He thinks someone deliberately set the inn on fire and is swearing vengeance. I heard him instruct Lachlan to search for Belle and Madge to find out what they know, and question the villagers about the fire. He is threatening to remove everyone from the village and won't rest until he finds the culprit. He wants someone to hang for it.'

'Surely it won't come to that,' Annie said.

'If you'd heard the anger in his voice, you'd know he meant it. And I'm sure setting fires is a hanging offence.'

'We must warn the women to hold their tongues, and we need to find Belle and Madge, before the young Craigallan returns.' Annie untied her apron and slung it onto the back of a chair. 'Ian can take Jeannie with him to Invercraig to look for them. They might not pay any heed to him, but I think they'll listen to Jeannie. While they do that you can warn the men, James, and I'll see to the women.'

'Aye, but what about Ellen? She's so full of bile I can't see her holding her tongue.' Ian's voice was bitter. 'She won't care whether the village suffers.'

Lachlan stared out the coach window, his mind in turmoil wondering what had happened to Belle, so it took him a moment to register his father's voice.

'Damnable thing to have happened.' Sir Roderick scowled at him. 'But we can't leave it like that. After you've found out who was re-sponsible, the place will have to be rebuilt, and a new innkeeper put in charge.'

'Madge ran a good inn. I'll try to track her down.' If he found Madge, he knew Belle wouldn't be far away.

His father snorted. 'And let her burn it down all over again?'

'I hardly think she allowed it to burn down. After all, it was her home.'

'But she didn't stop it burning. Any responsible innkeeper would have taken precautions.'

Lachlan sighed. There was no arguing with his father when he was in this mood.

'If the inn had been built with stone instead of wood, it wouldn't have burned.'

'That inn was there before any of the other buildings. It was there in my father's time and probably before it. There was no need to take it down and rebuild with stone when the structure was adequate.'

The growl in his father's voice was louder now, and Lachlan decided to say no more.

They travelled in silence until the carriage stopped in the courtyard and they entered the house.

The boot room led off from the back corridor. Waterproofs and outdoor coats hung from pegs protruding from the wall, while underneath the benches lining the room was a motley collection of wellingtons and boots. Lachlan shed his wet garments and hung them on a spare peg.

His father, struggling to remove his boots, looked up. 'Blasted boots,' he said. 'Damn things won't come off.'

Lachlan suppressed a smile. His father's paunch had increased over the past year, which was why he was struggling.

'Here, let me.' He stooped and pulled each boot off.

'The rebuild of the inn,' his father said. 'I'll put it in your hands. You'll need to hire labourers to clear the site and then stonemasons to rebuild it. After that, we'll see about installing an innkeeper.'

'What about the fishermen? They could start clearing the site.'

'Don't be daft. They'll be out on their boats as soon as the weather clears. There are plenty of dock labourers going idle at this time of year. They will be glad of the work.'

Lachlan shrugged. When had his father ever taken his advice?

'If that's what you want,' he said. 'I'll go to Invercraig later today.'

At least it would allow him to check if anyone knew where Belle had gone.

9

It was mid-morning before Gregor stumbled down the stairs from his room in the inn's attic. Outside, the rain had stopped and the wind abated, while a watery sun shone through the windows which were now sparkling.

Belle was exhausted after the spate of cleaning she and Madge had done while Gregor slept the morning away, and the last thing she wanted to do was be civil to this unkempt boor of a man. But she forced a smile to her lips when she looked over at him. Their future depended on his decision for them to stay or find shelter elsewhere.

At least the bairns were outside, where they wouldn't remind Gregor of their presence. She'd told Sarah to sweep the pavement and get rid of any rubbish. The twins were probably getting in her way although they were supposed to be helping. Sarah doted on them so she wouldn't mind.

'You still here?' The growl in Gregor's voice didn't bode well.

Madge stepped out from behind the bar where she'd been polishing glasses. 'Yes, and you should be thankful we are. This inn is a disgrace. Da would turn over in his grave if he knew the disgusting state it's in. I thought you had a wife. Where is she?'

'Dead this past year.' Gregor glowered at his sister. 'If you'd kept in touch, you would have known.'

'Me keep in touch with you? When did you ever look out for me?'

She glared back at him. 'Maybe if you'd had our backs, the fishwives over the water wouldn't have burned us out of my inn.'

Gregor shuffled his feet and looked away. 'Not much I could have done there,' he mumbled.

35

'No, but it would have been nice to have your support.' Madge leaned over and waved her washcloth under his nose. 'The least you can do now is give us somewhere to stay.'

'I don't have to do any such thing.' Gregor backed away from her. 'But I suppose I can't have my sister sleeping in the gutter.'

'What about Belle?'

'I don't owe her anything.'

'Maybe not, but she's the finest barmaid you'll ever get. She draws men in like moths to a flame. You wouldn't regret employing her. Besides, you need a woman's touch to keep this place clean.'

Belle thought he was weakening until the sound of the door opening, as Sarah and the two boys came in, made him stiffen.

Sarah set her brush against the wall. 'It's tidy outside now. Is there anything else you want me to do?'

Belle stifled a groan. Why didn't they stay outside until after Gregor agreed they could stay? Looking at his face, she reckoned there was little hope of that now.

Sarah flinched when Belle glared at her. Her shoulders sagged. Why was it nothing she did ever pleased her mother? And why was she now smiling at the horrible man? He was dirty, his hair flopped in tangles around his face, and she didn't like the look in his eyes.

The man was looking at her now.

'I suppose I could find a use for the lass, but I refuse to have the boys running wild in the inn.'

His eyes glittered, and Sarah's stomach churned. She didn't like this place and wanted to return home, but that was impossible. She no longer had a home and was dependent on her mother.

Belle sidled over to stand at Gregor's side. 'The boys won't be a problem. Sarah will look after them. She's good with them. They do what she says.' She glanced over at Sarah. 'Isn't that right?'

Sarah nodded even though she didn't want to be here. She willed her mother to take them away. Anywhere else would be better.

'Why don't you take the boys outside while I sort things out? I'm sure they'll want to explore.'

Sarah felt behind her for the door handle, opened the door, and beckoned to her brothers. The man's eyes followed her every move and it made her uneasy.

She only breathed freely again when the door closed behind her.

Belle sidled nearer to Gregor. 'I'm a good barmaid and you wouldn't regret taking me on. Madge said her trade went up after I started working for her.'

'Aye, that's right.' Madge glared at her brother. 'With the two of us working for you, the inn would attract more customers. Seems to me this place is suffering from neglect. It needs the services of two barmaids.'

'Barmaids are two a penny.' Gregor returned her glare. 'I'd only have to snap my fingers to get anyone I wanted.'

Madge bristled. 'I'm sure any number of doxies would like to serve up your ale, but we are more experienced.'

'Aye, well, you can stay. Ma wouldn't have wanted me to turn my back on my sister, but she's no kin to me.' He nodded his head toward Belle. 'And I'll not have bairns running about my inn getting under the feet of customers. They'll need to be out of here before the day is done.'

Belle's stomach churned. She'd hoped Gregor would have let them stay longer, but his voice was firm and surly.

She smoothed her hand down his arm until her fingers rested on his wrist. He turned to look at her with furrowed brows and narrow eyes.

'I'd be a real asset to your inn.' She introduced a seductive note into her voice. 'You wouldn't regret it.'

His eyes glittered and Belle suppressed a shiver at what she sensed in them, but she felt him waver and for a moment thought he was going to agree.

He eyed her up and down. 'Aye, you could be good for business right enough, but this is no place for bairns.'

'I'd make sure they stayed out of your way,' Belle said.

'And how could ye do that when the inn is open from morning until night? Would ye be prepared to turf them out to fend for themselves all day?'

Despair engulfed Belle. It had been easier in Invercraig. The stairs to the house above the inn had been at the back of the building. Here the stairs were inside. Could she let her children roam the streets from early morning until late at night?

'I'll find a way,' she said.

Gregor snorted. 'The only way I'll let you stay is if you get rid of the kids.'

He stomped to the door and opened it. 'That's us ready for business and the bairns can't be here while we're open.'

'What am I going to do, Madge?' Belle turned to her friend. 'I need somewhere to stay until I get sorted out and a place of my own.'

'You could send the bairns back to Jimmie's family in Craigden.'

'But you saw what the women did. They fired the inn. The bairns wouldn't be safe.'

'It was us the women wanted out. They'd never hurt bairns.'

Belle turned the idea over in her mind. Maybe Madge had a point. It would only be for a few days. She had the money to start a new life, although she hadn't told Madge that. Twenty sovereigns nestled in the leather pouch tied around her waist. Lachlan gave them to her when he left for London to woo a new bride, something that still rankled. Jimmie's whale money was also in the pouch. Four pounds and ten shillings from his last whaling journey before the one when he was lost to her forever. It was enough to get her settled in a house with her own things. The problem was, she didn't know where to start and who to trust. And she needed a few days to sort things out.

'If I had some money to pay Gregor for a room, do you think he might change his mind?'

'Do you have money?' Madge sounded surprised.

'I've got Jimmie's whale money from his last trip. He was saving it to buy his own boat, but he won't be needing it now.'

Belle bit her lip. It hurt when she thought of Jimmie. She had been so careless of his love when they were together. It was only when his ship failed to return from the Arctic, she realised how much she loved him. But by that time, it was far too late.

'How much do you have?'

'Four pounds, ten shillings.' Belle didn't tell her about the twenty sovereigns.

'That's a fair bit. You could rent rooms with that kind of money. Give me a minute to check out with Gregor whether old Granny Mutch is still renting rooms, and we'll go along the road to talk to her.'

'What about Gregor? Would he rent me a room in the inn?'

'Best not be too dependent on Gregor,' Madge said. 'If you rent elsewhere, he won't have a hold over you.'

Belle shivered in the draught which whispered around the room when Madge opened the back door to shout to Gregor. What did Madge mean when she advised her not to become dependent on him? She shrugged. It wouldn't do to be choosy if he offered her a way out.

The door remained open while Madge conferred with Gregor. His demeanour was still sullen, and he glanced over at her from time to time, but Belle wasn't close enough to hear what they were saying.

After a few minutes, Madge returned to her, and Gregor stomped back out to the yard.

'He didn't look pleased. What did he say?' Belle's heart raced as she waited for the answer.

It was irrational. She had no reason to feel worried as she had the money to secure her independence. If only she knew how to go about it. Having the money was the easy part, gaining her independence was harder.

Madge laughed. 'I've never known him to look pleased about anything. Even as a bairn, he was surly. I suppose it didn't help that I interrupted him when he was shifting ale barrels in the yard. But he's gone back to that, so he won't interfere with us for a while.'

'Does he want me to leave?'

'You can stay, but he won't budge about the bairns. He refuses to have them in the place. But the good news is Granny Mutch still rents out rooms. Some of them she rents by the day or the week, and some of them by the hour.'

'Why would she rent them out by the hour?' Belle had never heard of such an arrangement before.

Madge ushered Belle outside. 'Why do you think?' She waved a hand towards the busy dockside teeming with men. Workers, sailors and all sorts. 'Where you find this number of men, you'll find women who are prepared to pleasure them for a price.'

Belle stopped and stared at Madge. 'You mean Granny Mutch runs a bawdy house? I can't take the bairns there.'

'It's not a bawdy house. It's a rooming house. Granny Mutch takes the view it doesn't matter what her tenants get up to as long as they pay the rent and don't make trouble. The bairns will be all right there. Granny Mutch won't let any harm come to them.'

'If you say so.' There was a flicker of doubt in Belle's voice. Heaven knows she was no angel, but she drew the line at providing the services these dockside girls did.

The house was only two doors away from the inn and was an impressive building, three storeys high, plus attics. Granny Mutch lived in the rooms at ground level, facing the street. The smiling, grey-haired woman who answered the door to their knock was not what Belle had expected. She'd envisioned an old crone with grasping, talon-like hands.

'I expect you're looking for a room,' she said. 'Is it for the two of you?'

'You don't remember me?' Madge smiled at her.

The woman frowned. 'Should I?'

'I'm Madge, Gregor's sister. My mum and dad had the Ship Inn. When I was a bairn, you used to give me a sweetie to run your messages.'

Granny Mutch beamed. 'I remember you now. You were a wee rascal. But you can't be needing a room. Surely your brother will put you up.'

'It's for my friend Belle. Gregor is giving her a job to work in the bar, but she's got three bairns, and he won't let them into the inn.'

'He's a hard man, your brother, that's for sure. Shame about his wife. He didn't treat her well, you know. She used to come here, and we'd have a sit down and a wee blether. I miss her.'

'I didn't know she'd passed. What happened to her?'

The older woman's face darkened. 'They found her in the lobby at the bottom of the stairs. Gregor says she got out of bed in the middle of the night when it was dark, and she tripped over the cat at the top. Broke her neck, she did. Mind you, I have my suspicions.'

'I didn't see a cat at the inn.'

'Nor will you. Gregor killed it and threw it in the river. Said he'd rather have the mice than a cat any day.'

Belle shivered. After listening to Granny Mutch's exchange with Madge, her opinion of Gregor worsened. The sooner she built a life of her own the better. But in the meantime, she'd have to make do with what was available.

'You'll be Belle then.' Granny Mutch's eyes swivelled away from Madge. 'I haven't seen you around here before. What brings you to Invercraig?'

Belle sensed what was in the woman's mind and she stiffened. Why did everyone think she was a harlot because she liked to dress in silks and bright colours? But the drab clothes worn by other women didn't appeal to her, and she was damned if she would wear them.

'I was working for Madge at her inn in Craigden, but the villagers took against us and burned us out. So we came to Invercraig.'

'Ah, yes. I smelled burning last night, and when I looked across the water, I saw the flames. I wondered what it was, but didn't reckon it to be the inn. So, you're both homeless.'

'Aye,' Madge said, 'but Gregor has agreed to give me a room, but he won't do that for Belle because of the bairns.'

'I see.' The woman's eyes turned back to Belle. 'And the bairn's father? Where might he be?'

'He was away at the whaling, but his ship never came home last year.' Tears seeped from Belle's eyes and dribbled down her cheeks. She dashed them away with the back of her hands.

'Ah, that would be the *Eclipse*. Such a tragedy. A lot of good men lost.' Granny's voice softened, and she grasped Belle's hands within her own. 'Come back and see me this afternoon. One of my tenants hasn't been paying her rent. You can have her house, two rooms it is, so it should suit you and the bairns just fine. But I need to see the bairns first, so when you come, bring the bairns with you.'

'The rent,' Belle said as the woman turned away from them. 'How much will it be?'

Granny Mutch paused with her hand on the door, which was now half-closed. 'Two shillings a week and that's a bargain. I'll need it in advance mind.' She closed the door without further ado.

Gregor stood in the doorway and watched the two women walk along the street. His life had been ticking along until his sister and Belle appeared and upended it. He was fond of his sister, up to a point, and he couldn't refuse to give her sanctuary. But Belle wasn't family.

His eyes followed Belle and something stirred in him. Heat spread through his body as he watched the provocative swing of her hips.

He forced himself to look away. The sooner she was gone, the better. There was no point in getting involved with a woman who had bairns.

But Madge had been adamant Belle would draw the customers in. That might be a benefit because, if there was one thing he liked before anything else, it was emptying the pockets of his customers.

But she had bairns. He shook his head and scowled. He couldn't be doing with bairns.

Thoughts swirled around his brain. He wasn't a deep thinker, and they confused him. He grabbed a cloth and polished the top of the bar. If he kept busy, maybe the image of Belle with her swinging hips and low-cut dress would go away and leave him in peace.

10

Jeannie's breath wheezed out of her chest as she kept up with Ian. Her brother was taller than her, with longer legs, making it difficult for her to match his strides as they hurried along the village path to the bridges leading to Invercraig.

Curtains twitched at the windows of a line of cottages, alerting Jeannie to the multitude of eyes watching them pass. How many of them had been part of the horde waving burning torches? Jeannie shuddered.

The last cottage in the row was the one Ian shared with Ellen, but he glanced neither to the left nor the right when they approached it. And he tried to keep walking when Ellen jumped out in front of them with a screech.

'I knew you'd be going to that whore. You can't keep away from her.' Spittle flew from Ellen's mouth and her crazed eyes flared with fury.

Ian pushed her aside. 'You don't know what you're saying. You're a crazy bitch and, but for the grace of God, not a murderer.'

Alarmed, Jeannie sidled past them.

When she reached the first bridge that crossed the river to the island in the middle, she stopped and leaned her arms on the parapet while she got her breath back. This bridge was a smaller version of the next one, with only one arch spanning the river at this side, which wasn't much more than a stream.

After what seemed to be an eternity Ian pushed Ellen aside, but she still tried to prevent him leaving Craigden by clawing and tearing at his jacket.

Ian was out of breath when he joined Jeannie on the bridge and a nasty scratch on his face leaked blood down his cheek.

'I'm at my wit's end with Ellen. It's as if she's been taken over by a devil.' He dabbed at the scratch with a grubby handkerchief. 'I don't know what to do.' His eyes were black holes of misery.

Jeannie patted his arm. 'There's nothing you can do until after we find Belle and Madge. We'll think about Ellen when we return. Ma will know how to handle her.'

Ian laughed, but there was no joy in it. 'I think it's gone beyond that. She's gone mad.'

Jeannie agreed, remembering how scared she'd been when Ellen leapt out in front of them.

'Come on,' she said. 'We'd best get to Invercraig before the laird finds Belle.'

After crossing the island and bridge to Invercraig, the weather cleared enough for a weak sun to glimmer through the clouds.

'Where now?' Jeannie asked.

The bridge lay behind them and the road in front led into the town while the road on their right meandered along the waterfront.

'I think Madge said sailors and dockworkers frequented her brother's inn, so it's likely to be somewhere along here.' He pointed to the road on their right.

The river's noise as it rushed from the inland basin filled Jeannie's ears as they trudged along the road. She loved the sound, and she'd often sat on the pebbles of the foreshore at Craigden watching it, as the turbulent stream met the sea. But on this side, the river was deeper and more dangerous.

They passed a small pier where several small boats tied to it bobbed on the ebbing river. Further along, a ship with furled sails lay at anchor. It reminded Jeannie of the whaler her brother Jimmie had sailed on last year. The voyage from which he never returned. She blinked back a tear. Jimmie had been older than Ian, who strode at her side, and he'd been her favourite. Jimmie had been a bit of a rogue, but he'd been kind and didn't have a nasty bone in his body, whereas Ian's rough side often made her wary of him and she thought it best never to rile him.

Ian stopped in front of a building that had seen better days.

'I think this must be it.'

A creaking sign above the door of the age-blackened building said Ship Inn.

Jeannie wasn't sure why, but she had a bad feeling about this place.

11

At the other side of the river in Craigden, Annie threw her shawl around her shoulders. 'It's time,' she said to James. 'You need to talk to the men while I tackle the women. Between us, maybe we can prevent the laird from finding out how the inn caught fire.'

James grunted in reply and followed her outside.

'Mind now,' she said, 'you need to make the men understand our homes and living depend on the women holding their tongues.'

It didn't take long for Annie to go from house to house with muttered instructions about a meeting. Her hand was sore from rapping on so many doors, and the women's resistance was getting her down.

'If you want to keep your home, you'd best come,' she said, although she felt like berating them for their foolish behaviour. But, when she saw the women congregating on the foreshore, she smiled with satisfaction.

Further along, James addressed a group of men, and the low rumble of their voices drifted towards her. Their hunched shoulders and nodding heads suggested James was convincing them of the seriousness of their situation. But the men had taken no part in last night's activities. It was different with the women. Most of them had been involved and their guilt might lead them to confess their sins, particularly if the minister was involved in questioning them. Annie shuddered. She'd have to convince them otherwise.

The women's muttering silenced when Annie joined them. Although most of the women looked cowed, anger simmered among some of them. They were the ones Annie would have to watch.

'We have a problem,' Annie said

'Aye, but it's gone now.' The voice was strident. 'We made sure of that last night.'

'You're proud of what you did last night, Jessie Cargill?'

'Aye, and I'd do it again.' A snigger floated around the group.

'You'll not be so proud when the laird throws you out of your home and bans you from the village. What will you do then? Will your pride feed and house you? And what will your man do when the laird takes back his share of the boat? Ye cannae fish with half a boat.'

'The laird will not do that. He likes his share of the catch and the fish we bring him.'

'That's not what my Ian heard him saying when he was here this morning. Ian told me he was in a rare paddy, swearing to hunt for those responsible, even if it meant throwing everyone out of the village. He threatened to see the culprits hang for it. How d'ye feel about swinging from the end of a rope, Jessie? Will ye be so bold then?'

Jessie scowled at Annie. 'He widnae dare.'

'Aye, but he would. He's the laird. He can do anything he likes, and fine you know it.'

There was a shuffling of feet and the murmur of voices as several of the women turned away from Jessie and put their heads together.

Lizzie McNab stepped forward. 'But what can we do? What's done is done and cannae be undone.'

'We hold our tongues,' Annie said. 'If everyone stays silent, he'll not be able to prove anything.'

'But what if he sends the minister? We cannae tell a lie to him.'

'The minister won't be a problem. My James spoke to him this morning and convinced him that with no villagers there will be no church and he'll lose his living. So, think on it as a wee white lie to protect everyone here, including the minister.'

Mutters rippled around the group, and Jessie Cargill stepped forward. 'That's all very well, but what about your guid-daughter, Ellen? I saw her this morning spitting fire at your Ian. She's not here and if I'm any judge, she'll never hold her tongue.'

'Leave Ellen to me. I'll see she holds her tongue.'

'Good luck with that.' Jessie glared at Annie, and then the other women. 'I'll not be telling the laird anything,' she said, 'and it's best we do what Annie says.'

Annie breathed a sigh of relief. Jessie was not well liked, but the women would follow her lead.

'I can't be standing here all day,' Jessie said. 'There's work to be done.'

She strode off toward her house and, after a few moments, the rest of the women drifted away.

Annie watched them go. That was one problem solved, but there was still Ellen to convince, and that would be far more difficult.

Ellen waited until everyone had gone before she stepped out from behind the boat where she had hidden when the village women gathered on the foreshore. She scowled at Annie's retreating figure. If her mother-in-law turned and saw her, she would give her a mouthful. She'd tell her about her good-for-nothing son who neglected her, his wife, to chase after that trollop, Belle. But Annie didn't look back.

Her face twisted, and she breathed heavily as her anger increased. It was Ian's fault those two harlots didn't burn to a cinder. She glared across the river at Invercraig. That was where he'd gone, panting after her petticoats like a dog chasing a bitch in heat. And now, Annie had turned the village women against her. She hoped they rotted in hell.

She spat on the stones at her feet, and her fingers curled into claws. If she'd been a witch, she would have cursed both Belle and Ian.

But the plan coming together in her head was better than a curse. Even better than the trollop burning to death.

Fragments of Annie's words echoed in her mind, and she planned what to tell the laird's son when he came to question her. If the laird was looking for the culprit who started the fire, then Ellen knew where to place the blame.

She'd see Belle hanged and laugh as the harlot dangled at the end of a rope.

12

Lachlan found his mother ensconced in an armchair in front of a blazing fire in her cosy sitting room, working on her needlepoint. She preferred this room to the larger lounges and public rooms, which to her mind were too formal and cold.

She looked over at him with a smile and laid her sampler on the small table next to her chair.

'I heard about the fire in the village,' she said. 'Was it as dreadful as they say?'

'Yes, Mama, there is nothing left of the inn but ash.'

'Oh dear, that is unfortunate. I expect it has put your father into one of his black moods.'

'I'm afraid that's putting it mildly. He found evidence the fire was deliberate and is now vowing to evict the villagers unless they disclose who started the fire.'

'I expect he'll calm down.'

'I'm not so sure about that. He wants someone to hang.'

Catherine Craigallan stared into the flames of the fire. Lachlan wondered if she was imagining the scene of the disaster and the outcome of his father's ire. After a moment, she sighed.

'Your father has always been a stubborn man, but it will vex me if he makes the villagers suffer for the sins of one person.'

Lachlan shivered. If the villagers remained silent and his father kept his word, that did not bode well for Belle and Madge. He knew his father's thoughts had turned to the two women and if he blamed them for the fire, he would see them hanged.

He turned his thoughts away from that distressing scenario and squatted on the carpet at his mother's knee. This was always where he'd sought comfort, first as a child and even now he was an adult. Her hand settled on his head. 'You've been a good son, Lachlan. I'm sorry things have not worked out well for you.'

Lachlan knew she was referring to his relationship with the cousin he'd taken as his wife. Clarinda had never forgiven him for insisting she leave London to live in the ancestral home. And she blamed him for making her go through the throes of childbirth.

After the baby's birth, Clarinda declared herself an invalid and took to her bed. She took little interest in her daughter, and Lachlan wondered if she would have behaved differently if she had fulfilled her duty by birthing a son.

Wee Catherine, named after his mother, was now nine months old and still Clarinda hid from him behind her bedroom door. She also ignored Sir Roderick's demands for the boy child they all desired. Lachlan thought there was little hope of that as long as Clarinda barred her door to him.

He wondered if she would ever open it to him again, although the prospect of union with her was a joyless task, unlike the passion he'd experienced with Belle. But his father was adamant he should sire a son to carry on the family name. As things were, that seemed unlikely as long as he remained married to Clarinda. But he was saddled with her. 'As long as ye both shall live.' The minister's words echoed through his mind. Marriage was for life, and the only way out was death. And despite her professed invalidity, Clarinda appeared healthy.

For a moment he indulged in the fantasy of a life with Belle but, even if Clarinda were no longer here, his father would never countenance marriage with a commoner.

'Father is losing patience with me. He thinks it's time Clarinda got over what he describes as her vapours and provides him with the grandson he wants. He has instructed me to be a man and force Clarinda to do her duty as my wife.' Lachlan, unable to mask the misery in his voice, continued, 'I don't know how I can do that.'

The thought of facing up to Clarinda and demanding his conjugal rights chilled him. Clarinda had a talent for making him feel small, like a child. She robbed him of his manhood. It was a pity she wasn't more like Belle, who encouraged his virility and made him feel like a man.

Sadness crept over him, and he wished he could be with Belle again. But, since his return, she had rejected him. Belle's anger, because he had deserted her six years ago to go to London had never left her. His subsequent marriage to Clarinda had only intensified that anger.

'I don't know how to handle Clarinda,' he said, more to himself than his mother.

'I'll talk to her. Perhaps I should have done it earlier and not let her lapse into such a sad state.'

Lachlan relaxed as his mother ruffled his hair. It made him feel like a child again. A child with no wife and no responsibilities.

'Do you think that will work?'

'I can but try.'

Lachlan wasn't convinced. He knew Clarinda wasn't sad. She was sulking because Lachlan refused to allow her to return to London. And then, there had been the unpleasantness about the baby's name. She objected to Lachlan naming the child Catherine after his mother.

'A mother should have the right to name her child,' she'd said. But Lachlan and Sir Roderick overruled her.

'It's a family tradition to give the firstborn child a family name,' his father had said, and that was an end to it.

Clarinda hadn't taken kindly to losing the battle and had retired to her rooms, declaring she was too unwell to care for the child or take part in family life. She demanded no one but Aunt Beattie attend to her. Since then, she'd been like a ghost in the house.

'Perhaps she is suffering from some kind of mental aberration,' Lachlan said. 'It might be best to pave the way by having a chat with Aunt Beattie. She is the only person Clarinda trusts.'

His mother drew in a sharp breath and removed her hand from his head, startled at the suggestion.

'I'll talk with Beattie when she brings the child to see me later today and I am sure, between us, we can resolve the problem, whatever it is.' She paused for thought before continuing. 'It might be helpful if you were present. It would provide you with an opportunity to spend some time with your daughter.'

Lachlan wasn't sure he wanted to spend time with the child. She was at an uninteresting stage. What on earth did you do with a baby who could not walk or talk?

'I'm afraid my father wants me to go to Invercraig to hire labourers to rebuild the inn and after that, I have to find the culprits who started the fire.'

'Surely that can wait.'

'No! Father lacks patience and expects everything to be done the minute he issues the order. I don't want to disappoint him again, although I'm not sure how successful I'll be in finding the fireraiser.'

His mother sighed. 'You are right, of course. You must do what you have to do.' She patted his hand. 'You are not a disappointment to me, Lachlan.'

'If only Father thought the same,' he said. But he knew, in his heart, he would never measure up to his father's unrealistic expectations.

'I'd best get Raven saddled up and be on my way to Invercraig. If he finds me here, it will give him another chance to berate me.'

The longer Jeannie looked at the inn, the more she shivered. The bad feeling she had about the place intensified. She glanced at Ian and knew the Ship Inn had affected him in the same way.

She gripped Ian's arm, feeling the need for his support. He patted her hand to reassure her, and she took some comfort from it.

'Come on,' he said. 'We'd best go inside to see if Belle and Madge are here.'

She nodded but clung to him as he pushed the door open. The hinges squealed and the swinging sign above them creaked. It sounded like an omen.

The unkempt man rolling a barrel across the floor didn't look at them until it was deposited behind the bar.

He straightened. 'What'll it be? I've just set up a new barrel of ale, or maybe a whisky straight from Glen Clova.' He leered at them and winked. 'I have a good supplier.' He leaned toward them and whispered, 'Or what about a drop of French Brandy? Fresh off the boat.'

Jeannie sensed Ian was tempted, so she tugged at his arm. 'That's not what we're here for,' she whispered.

She felt Ian brace himself. 'No thanks,' he said. 'Drink isn't what I've come for.'

A look of alarm crossed the man's face. 'What then? You don't look like an exciseman, not with the lass in tow.'

'We're looking for two women who might have sought shelter here.'

'Women, is it? Men don't usually bring a lass along when they're looking for company.' He leered at Jeannie.

'We're wasting our time here.' Jeannie glared at the man. 'He won't help us.' She dragged Ian toward the door.

'Wait a minute,' the man said. 'Can ye not take a joke? I never said I didn't know them. But ye can't be expecting me to be giving out information after what happened to them.'

'Have they been here or not?'

Ian's temper was rising, and Jeannie laid a restraining hand on his arm.

'Why d'ye want to know? And what's in it for me?'

The door behind them opened, and a gust of air swirled around the room.

Jeannie turned and her heart lifted when she saw Belle and Madge framed in the doorway. She ran to Belle and hugged her.

'I'm so glad you're safe,' she said. 'I feared for you when the inn burned.'

'Safe I may be,' Belle replied, 'but I've lost everything and daren't set foot in Craigden again. The women over there have a lot to answer for.'

'That's what we've come to talk to you about.' Ian glanced at Gregor, who had gone back behind the bar to wrestle with the barrel. 'Shall we go outside where we won't be overheard?'

Jeannie followed them outside, but when she glanced back at the man, he was scowling. She shivered. The bad feeling was back again, and it convinced her Belle wasn't safe here.

Belle's mind buzzed with questions. What did Ian want from her? Had he decided to leave Ellen and follow her here? But if that was so, why did he bring Jeannie with him? She stepped outside and turned to face the river while she waited for the rest of them to follow.

They made an odd group, standing outside the Ship Inn. Madge and Belle in their colourful smoke-stained silks. Jeannie in her drab woollen skirt and shawl, and Ian in his roughly woven fisherman's jacket and breeches.

Once the door closed behind Ian, cutting them off from Gregor whom they'd left inside the inn, Belle turned to face him.

'I thought we'd said goodbye last night. Why have you come?'

Ian reached a tentative hand toward her but drew it back before it made contact. 'I promised Ma I would speak to you.'

'Annie? She can't want me to return to Craigden, not after what the women did last night.' Belle shook her head. Why would Annie want her to return? Neither woman liked the other. But Annie had never rejected Sarah and the twin boys. Like most of the villagers, her mother-in-law never let her emotions show, but Belle could swear she was fond of the bairns.

'No, it's not that.'

'What then? Does she want the bairns to go back?' For a fleeting moment, Belle thought that would solve her problems and enable her to carve out a new life here at the inn without the encumbrance of bairns. But she dismissed the thought with no hesitation. The bairns were part of her and part of Jimmie. How could she think of giving them up?

'Where are the bairns?'

Jeannie had been silent up to now, but her question made Belle suspicious.

'They've gone exploring. They'll be back soon.' Her voice was sharper than she meant it to be. 'I'm not sending the bairns back to Craigden. So, if that's what Annie wants, she's going to be disappointed.'

'It's nothing to do with the bairns,' Ian said. 'It's about what happened last night.'

'We all know what happened, and we all know who was responsible.' Belle glared at Ian, even though it wasn't his fault. He couldn't help it if his wife was a vicious bitch who'd encouraged the village women to attack them.

'Aye, we do.' Ian's voice faltered. 'That's the problem. The laird is vowing vengeance on those who torched the inn. He's threatening to evict the entire village.'

'Why should I care? It serves them right.'

'Aye, but that would include those who weren't involved, like my ma and da.'

'Do you think I care? What have Annie and James ever done for me?'

'They were Jimmie's ma and da too, and they're grandparents to your bairns. What do you think Jimmie would have wanted?'

Belle lapsed into silence. She thought of all the times Annie had belittled her. She had never been good enough for Jimmie in his mother's eyes. But she was Jimmie's mother, and Belle didn't wish her harm.

'What do you want me to do?'

'Stay silent when the laird's son comes to question you. Say you don't know who started the fire. You too, Madge,' he said, looking at the other woman.

Belle and Madge exchanged glances and then nodded.

'Thanks,' Ian said. 'We'd best get back.'

Belle's heart raced as she watched them go. Lachlan was coming to question her about the fire, and she hadn't decided whether she wanted to see him again.

'I'm worried,' Jeannie said as she and Ian retraced their steps across the bridge and left Invercraig behind.

'I don't think that's a good place for Belle to be, and I didn't get a chance to check on the bairns. What if that man causes them harm?'

Ian concentrated on the road ahead and didn't break stride. 'Belle may have her faults,' he said. 'But she widnae see harm come to the bairns.'

Not convinced, Jeannie shrugged and pulled the shawl more tightly around her shoulders while the wind whipped it back. Choppy water churned underneath the bridge as the inland basin emptied and the tide roared seawards.

'I don't like leaving her there.'

They were now at the windiest spot on the bridge, and she wasn't sure Ian heard. But his pace quickened, his head was down, and the scowl on his face deepened

Her breath whistled through her lips as she strove to keep up with him. If she had been with any of her other brothers, she would have grasped his arm so he could pull her along. But not Ian. There had always been a dark side to him, although he mellowed when Jimmie didn't return from the Arctic. His resentment toward his older brother dissipated after he was no longer overshadowed by him. A thought niggled at her that Ian might have been glad Jimmie didn't return, but she banished it from her head. It was unworthy of her.

An eerie silence hung over the village, although Jeannie sensed eyes peering at them as they walked along the road. There were no women hanging their washing on the foreshore. No one shelling mussels at the doors. And no shouts of greeting as they passed. She had never known it to be so quiet. It felt like the villagers were experiencing a sense of doom after last night's activities.

Annie standing in her doorway was a welcome sight, and Jeannie ran to her mother. She wanted Annie to wrap her arms around her to drive away the feelings of despair that engulfed her. But she knew that was too much to expect from her mother.

Suddenly, Jeannie yearned for Belle, who wouldn't have thought twice about it.

'Did ye find Belle and Madge?' Annie demanded as soon as they were inside.

'Aye. We found them. They were at the Ship Inn, which is run by Madge's brother. That's the one just before ye come to the dock where the ships lay at anchor.'

'Did ye talk to her? Tell her to hold her tongue about the fire.'

'Aye. She was a wee bit unwilling, but when I explained why, she saw the sense of it.'

'That's good. Your da has talked to the men and I've talked to the women. It took a bit of doing to convince them, but they see the sense of it. The only thing is, your Ellen wasn't there. You'll need to speak to her.'

Ian's expression darkened. 'Whatever you say. But she wasn't in the best of tempers the last time I saw her.'

'It needs to be done, lad. It needs to be done.'

Jeannie watched him go as he shuffled out the door. The slump of his shoulders and the glower on his face made him look like a man going to his doom.

'I think Ian and Ellen had a fight,' Jeannie said. 'I don't think she'll listen to him.'

'Maybe not, lass. But he has to try.'

Belle clutched Madge's arm and waited until Ian and Jeannie were no longer in sight before she turned to enter the inn.

Gregor stood a few steps inside and Belle wondered if he'd had his ear at the door listening. She decided she didn't care and met his glower with a toss of her head and a flip of her skirts. Earlier in the day, she'd seen the hunger in his eyes when he leered at her. Men were easy to handle when their minds were controlled by their instincts.

'This barmaid job you wanted me for,' she said, peering at him through lowered eyelashes.

It had the effect she wanted, and he struggled for breath before he said, 'I don't recall making that offer.'

'But you know you want me.' She leaned towards him.

He gulped. His eyes fixed on her low neckline.

This was too easy. Belle wondered when he'd last had a woman. Probably not since the demise of his wife. Women weren't interested in the likes of him with his slovenly ways and boorish attitude. He'd be easy pickings. Her problem would be how to keep him at bay once she'd reeled him in.

'I'm a good barmaid, one of the best,' she said. 'Ask Madge.'

'That's right.' Madge stifled a smile. 'The best barmaid I ever had, and the men came from miles to be served by her.'

'Well, I suppose.' Gregor's voice sounded hoarser than normal.

'I can only work evenings.' Belle drew back slightly. 'But evenings are always the best time to convince men to drown their sorrows in ale.'

'I won't have bairns in the inn. The drinkers wouldn't like it.'

'That's taken care of. I've rented rooms and Sarah will see the twins are bedded while I'm working. Is it a deal?'

'Aye,' he said. 'It's a deal.'

'What about my wages?'

'What about it?'

'I'll need four shillings a week. I'll not take less.'

Gregor choked. 'Four shillings? That's ridiculous.'

Belle moved nearer to him and leaned forward. Her eyes shone with the hint of a promise, although she had no intention of keeping that promise.

'I'll not take less,' she said.

He removed a dirty cloth from his pocket and wiped his brow.

'She's worth it.' Madge didn't try to hide her smile.

'Ye strike a hard bargain,' he growled and leaned toward her.

'Aye, and you won't be sorry.' Belle moved away from him with a smile and a teasing look. 'I'll see you later. I need to find my bairns and keep my appointment with Granny Mutch.'

She flounced out of the door, leaving Gregor standing with his mouth open.

Once outside, she leaned against the stone wall of the inn and gulped air into her lungs. Nausea churned in her stomach, and she tasted bile in her throat. Gregor disgusted her, but she'd have to keep stringing him along until she worked out something better. She fingered the leather pouch hidden under her dress. Lachlan's twenty sovereigns were the key to her new life. It wouldn't be enough to start her own inn, but it might be enough to start a shop if she found premises to rent. In the meantime, she'd take Granny Mutch's rooms and work for Gregor until she found what she was looking for.

14

Ian had no appetite for facing up to Ellen again, but his mother's last words rang in his ears.

'It has to be done, lad. It has to be done.'

But the more he thought about the confrontation to come, the less he relished it. The black mood which engulfed him after he left Belle at Invercraig increased. He was a strong man, but the energy seeped from his body and his shoulders slumped, while it felt as if a steel band tightened around his head. His breath wheezed from his chest in quick gasps and his legs no longer propelled him forward.

It was a strange feeling he'd never experienced before, and he wondered if this was what people felt when they were dying. He shrugged the thought away. He was a Watt, a fisherman, and they were a healthy bunch. Everyone in his family before him had lived to a grand old age. Except for Jimmie, of course. But that was his own fault for sailing off to the Arctic on a whaling boat.

Ian sat on the stones next to the river and contemplated it. The tide was running seawards. Like the rhythm of life, it ebbed, and it flowed. His life was bound up with the river and the sea. It was in his blood. There had been Watts in Craigden since time immemorial, and they had always made their living from the sea. But if the laird carried out his threat, where would they go?

He wasn't sure how long he sat there, although it was long after his breathing calmed and his head stopped pounding. But the reluctance to confront Ellen remained.

Eventually, he decided he could not put it off any longer. He stood and turned to walk toward the house he shared with Ellen and her father.

He paused for a moment with his hand on the door before pushing it open, bracing himself to meet Ellen's anger. But Ellen wasn't there. The figure sitting before the ash-filled fireplace was her father, old Hector Bruce. He was an unexpected sight because he rarely ventured out of his room, preferring his own company to that of his daughter and her husband.

'It's you then,' Hector said without looking up. 'Ye'll be looking for my Ellen, no doubt.'

'Aye, that I am. There are things we need to talk about.'

'I don't think Ellen is much in the mood for talking. The madness has taken her.' He sighed and tapped his pipe out on the fender to loosen the tobacco inside. 'Like her mother before her.' His voice was bleak.

Ian slumped onto a stool. It had been six years since his marriage to Ellen, and all that time the old man had kept his distance. He still went out with Ian on the boat but rarely passed more than a couple of words with him. Ian accepted that and held his counsel. Everyone knew Hector was dour and had no time for others. Ian was no different from the villagers who let him go his own way.

Ian puzzled over Hector's words, the most he'd heard him utter at one time during his stay in this house.

'What d'ye mean?'

Hector clamped his lips on his cold pipe. 'It's just the blethers of an old man.'

But Ian thought it was more than blethers.

'I've never heard you mention Ellen's mother before.'

'Aye lad, and ye're not likely to hear me mention her again.'

After waiting in silence for Hector to continue, it was obvious the old man didn't intend to explain what he meant.

Ian got up from the stool. 'I'd best go look for Ellen.'

Hector grunted and continued to gaze with unseeing eyes at the ashes in the fireplace.

Ellen's mood darkened as she tramped along the road to Craigallan Castle.

'No time to lose,' she muttered to herself. Her head was full of voices and the name Belle resounded over and over again. 'Bloody Belle,' she said. 'Harlot, whore, deserves to hang.' She continued muttering as she strode along. The voices were so real she jerked her head from side to side to see where they were coming from. But nothing was there except for the wind swaying the bushes. The trees with their branches whipping in the air. And the water rushing from the wide expanse of the inland basin in a frenzy to reach the sea.

Last night had been a triumph, and she would never forget the feelings of exhilaration and power as she led the women to the inn. The flames fanned those feelings, and she laughed as she thought of Belle burning to a cinder inside. But Belle hadn't burned with the inn. She'd escaped and run off to Invercraig. And her bloody Ian had helped her. She scowled at the thought. Not only that, but Annie, his bloody mother, had turned the village women against her. She'd make them pay. After she talked to the laird, he'd throw them all out and Belle would hang.

She continued to march along the road, looking neither to left nor right. As her muttering grew louder, it blocked out the sound of the voice shouting her name.

She had a mission to complete, and nothing was going to stop her.

Intuition led Ian to the rough track leading to the big house. Remembering Ellen's anger and spite when they argued earlier, he wondered whether she was capable of sabotaging the entire village. He wasn't sure. What he did know was that she would gladly see Belle in the grave. He needed to find her before she talked to the laird or his son.

Seeing Ellen in the distance he quickened his pace and shouted, but she didn't turn her head. He broke into a run. He needed to catch up with her. Stop her. Make her see sense.

But on she strode like a valkyrie with her hair whipping in the wind and her shawl and skirts billowing behind her.

She was talking to herself, her words getting louder and louder, and he heard references to Belle, himself, and Annie. Swear words predominated. Words he had never before heard her use. What had come over her?

When he reached her, he grasped her arm and pulled her around to face him.

Her eyes narrowed and her mouth twisted as she shook his hand off.

'Stop, Ellen. You need to come home with me.'

'Home,' she said. 'With you? What about your precious Belle?'

'You've become obsessed with Belle. She's nothing to me. You're the one I wed.'

'Aye, that may be so. But it's Belle you go panting after, with your tongue hanging out. D'you think I can't see that?'

'That's not true.'

She laughed, but it wasn't a pleasant sound.

'Isn't that why you helped her last night? Why you took her over the water to Invercraig?' She glared at him with something that looked like madness in her eyes. 'She should have burned last night like the witch she is.'

'I helped her because I didn't want my wife to be hanged as a murderer.' Ian pulled her into his arms. 'I was protecting you.'

Ellen struggled to free herself from his embrace. 'Aye, we'll see who is to be hanged after I've seen the laird. Your precious Belle will get what she deserves.'

'You can't do that.'

'I'll not be stopped, so don't try.' She struggled some more.

'You're not thinking straight. Think about the village and your neighbours. The folk you've known all your life. What will become of them if the laird evicts everyone?'

'What do I care? They should have stood up for me instead of listening to your ma. I hope they all rot in hell.'

She glared at Ian, and her body went limp in his arms. He relaxed, thinking she had given up her struggle, but her eyes still flashed with anger or madness.

'Come home with me,' he pleaded.

A smile flickered around her lips. She bent her head forward and clamped her teeth into his arm.

With a yelp, he released his hold on her and she scampered off into the woods that bordered the track. He thought about chasing after her, but that would be pointless. She'd made her mind up and there was no stopping her. He turned and walked back the way he had come. He'd better alert his ma. She would let the villagers know what to expect.

Despair flooded through him. His feet stumbled on the ruts in the track and his arm ached. He suspected she'd drawn blood. A dog bite would have had less effect, although there was no danger of contracting rabies from his wife's bite.

His heart sank even further when the village came into sight. How was he going to explain to his ma and the village folks he couldn't control his own wife and, as a result, disaster loomed?

15

Anger swelled in Ellen as she stood in the shadow of the trees and watched Ian turn back along the track. It would take a better man than him to prevent her from doing what she had to do. She couldn't allow the harlot to live. If Belle wasn't stopped, she'd tempt every man in Craigden and Invercraig to stray from the straight and narrow. The wives would thank her when she accomplished her task. And God would smile on her for doing his work and removing temptation from the men.

Once Ian was out of sight she returned to the road and plodded on, muttering as she walked. Her mind buzzed with thoughts until she felt it might burst. Mud from the rutted track clung to her shoes and spattered her stockings, but she paid no heed.

Her muttering increased when she reached the path that branched off from the track and led to the castle. This was the path the fishwives used to take their fish to the laird's kitchen. Jeannie trod this path every time the boats landed their catch of fish. But before Jeannie it had been Belle, and she was walking in the harlot's footsteps.

'Jezebel, harlot, whore.' The words reverberated around her brain and spilled from her lips in a frenzy of vitriol. With each utterance, her anger increased.

She was out of breath when she rounded the last bend in the path. The arched entry to the stables and the servant area faced her, but she turned her back on it and trudged around the building to the front.

She stared in amazement at what she saw. She'd been prepared for it to be a lot larger than the village houses, but it was beyond her imagination to visualise what now stood before her. The mansion house was only two stories high, but the turrets at each side of the imposing front and the battlements flanking the roof increased its height. Pale sunlight dappled the windows. Windows that were larger than the front doors of the village houses.

Two sets of stairs, one at each side of the entrance, curved upward, meeting in front of a massive door at the top. Her feet dragged as she approached one of them. She stopped at the bottom, drew a deep breath, braced herself, grasped the balustrade, and mounted the stone steps. Double doors recessed behind two matching pillars greeted her at the top. The burnished wood and brass fixtures gleamed, and she rubbed her hands on her skirt before she dared to knock.

Her heart thumped as she waited for the door to open, but it wasn't forceful or loud enough to drown out the cacophony of thoughts invading her mind.

The gnawing ache in the pit of Ian's stomach grew as he strode along the village road. He found the change in Ellen incomprehensible. She'd never been the most biddable of wives, that was for sure. But over the past few months, she'd stopped laughing and become moody.

He puzzled over when the change had begun. It was true she'd never been the same after she lost the bairn she'd been carrying five years ago. Then her failure to conceive again hadn't helped. But when his brother failed to return from the Arctic, it fuelled her fears he would stray and her obsession with Belle increased. Jealousy? Was that the reason?

But this change. This madness.

It had begun on the day of the fire. Or had it been before and he hadn't noticed? The minister's sermon on Sunday had been about Jezebel, and Ellen had been sure he was talking about Belle. She'd talked about the sermon for the rest of the day. Was that why she'd whipped the women into such a frenzy? Would they have followed her with flaming torches if Ellen hadn't stirred them up?

His stomach churned, and the ache increased. What was he going to say to his ma?

Annie crouched over the pot on the sway hook and the smell of turnip filled the room. No doubt his younger brother, Davie, had been raiding the fields bordering the village.

Ian slumped onto a stool opposite her. 'Where is everyone?' He looked around the room, empty except for him and his ma.

'Jeannie's gone to the shop to see if Wattie will give her a wee bit of something to go with the soup, although we owe him a fair bit already. But he's got a soft spot for our Jeannie.' She replaced the lid on the pot. 'The menfolk have gone to get things ready for the boat. Now the weather's cleared up, they might get off to the fishing this afternoon. Times have been hard and we could do with the fish.'

'Aye.' Ian stared into the remnants of the fire heating the soup. The way things were going, there might not be a village or boats to sail to the fishing before long.

Annie pulled another stool over and sat.

'I take it Ellen wasn't to be persuaded.'

'There's no reasoning with her. She's determined to talk with the laird.' Ian couldn't keep the despair out of his voice.

'That means she'll tell him the village women set the fire, and she was part of it. Will she tell him she was the one that got them worked up? Surely she wouldn't put her own neck in a noose.'

'No, she won't risk her own neck. She plans to tell the laird Belle fired the inn. It's Belle who will hang if she gets her way.'

Ian bent his head and covered his face with his hands. 'What can I do? I think Ellen has lost her wits.'

Annie patted him on the shoulder. 'You stay here and keep an eye on the soup pot. Don't let it boil over. And I'll go see Ellen's father. Hector doesn't mix much with other folks, but we go back a long way. Between us, we'll figure out how to handle Ellen.'

'Aye.' Ian removed his hands from his face and stared into the burning coals in the grate. The flames reminded him of the burning inn, and he shuddered. It was all too much for him, and knowing Hector Bruce, he reckoned Annie was wasting her time.

16

Annie strode along the path bordering the river. The fresh air revived her after being cooped up in the house all morning, but she couldn't shake off her worries.

Forefront in her mind was her worry about Ian. She'd never seen him so dejected before. Although he was dourer than his brothers, he was usually full of energy and she couldn't shake off the image of him hunched on the stool, steeped in misery.

Belle filled her thoughts as well. She had no love for her daughter-in-law, but Jimmie had wed her, and she was the mother of his children. Besides, no one deserved to hang for the sins of another.

The door to the house opened before she reached it.

'I saw ye coming.' Hector Bruce stood framed in the doorway. 'Ye'd best come inside.'

Annie followed him in and he gestured for her to take a seat.

'It's been a while,' he said.

'Aye. I think Ian and Ellen's wedding was the last time we spoke.'

Hector sighed. 'I thought that would be the making of my Ellen.'

Annie thought back to when Ian had courted Ellen. She'd thought them well matched. But she realised she knew nothing about their daily lives. Had they been happy? Ian was so dour it was difficult to tell.

'What do you mean? Ellen seemed to be such a capable person.'

'In a way she was, but she'd always been moody and never having a ma to advise her made life a wee bit difficult. Despite that, I thought she'd settled. She'd turned into the woman her ma never was.'

'What does she know about her ma?'

'I told her she'd run off when she was a wee bit bairn, and I didn't know where she went.' Hector looked away from Annie. 'What else could I say?'

'Ian thinks Ellen has lost her mind. D'you think she's taking after her ma?'

'She's just a bitty upset.'

'Ian thinks it's more than that.'

'Mayhap she'll snap out of it.'

Annie leaned forward and grasped Hector's hand. 'She set fire to the inn. That wasn't a sensible thing to do. And now, she's threatening to tell the laird it was Belle who did it. She says she wants Belle to hang but, despite our differences, I widnae see her hang for something Ellen did. Nor do I want to see Ellen hang. So, we have to think about how we handle this.'

A tear slipped down Hector's face. 'I dinnae want her to hang, but I couldn't bear to see her shut up in the lunatic asylum, either.'

Annie squeezed his hand. 'It's not as if she'd be alone in there. She'd be able to meet her ma.'

Hector stiffened. 'She doesn't know about her ma, and I want it to stay that way. I'll not see my lassie locked up. She'll come round.'

'I hope you're right. Think on it and ye know where I am if ye want help.'

Annie hesitated in the doorway before she left. It tore her heart to see Hector sitting there in much the same position she'd left Ian. His misery at the thought his daughter was following in the footsteps of his mad wife was destroying him.

The man who opened the door took one look at Ellen before snapping, 'No tramps here,' and slamming it in her face.

Heat rushed from her neck to her face. 'I'm not a bloody tramp. It's the laird I need to see. I have something to tell him.'

She lifted her fist and thumped on the shiny oak of the closed door. Her voice rose to a scream. 'He'll want to hear what I have to tell him.'

The sound of footsteps crunching on gravel barely impacted on her consciousness and she continued to hammer on the door. It was only when rough hands grabbed her arms and pulled her away, she registered the two burly stablemen at her side.

She struggled, but their grip was too strong for her to shake off. They manhandled her down the steps and along the drive.

'Take your bloody hands off me,' she hissed, before launching into a string of expletives.

'You shouldn't be here,' the older man said. 'Mr Bates said we have to remove you.' His hand tightened on her arm.

The younger stable hand's grip was less firm, and she tried to wrench free from him. 'You need to stop struggling,' he said. 'You'll only get hurt.'

Ellen glared at him. 'I came here to speak to the laird,' she said. 'I have information for him.'

'The laird doesn't speak to the likes of you,' the older man growled.

They continued to drag Ellen down the drive and when they reached the iron gates, they threw her onto the road outside, clanging the gates shut behind her.

'And don't come back,' the older man shouted. He turned to the younger one. 'Come on, Alfie, we've work to do.'

Ellen scrabbled to her feet and spat at the gate. 'I'll see you in hell,' she shouted after their retreating backs.

The sound of screeching outside had drawn Lachlan to the window overlooking the front of the house. He'd watched while Fred and the stable boy manhandled an unkempt woman down the stairs and dragged her across the forecourt to the drive.

He hadn't envied their task as the woman struggled and screamed at them. He reckoned some of her kicks must have hurt, but Fred hadn't flinched.

After the screeching faded into the distance Lachlan wandered through the house on his way to the stables. He took his time because he reckoned it would be a good half hour before the stable lads returned.

The smell of baking filtered into the back lobby from the kitchen, and he poked his head around the door. 'Something smells good,' he said, eyeing up the array of scones and sweetmeats on display.

'Keep your hands off, Master Lachlan.' Cook waved her rolling pin at him.

'You know how much I like your baking. Surely you can spare a wee taste.' He reached out a hand and snaffled one of the biscuits cooling on a tray.

'You'll be the death of me, so you will.' Cook scowled at him, but her eyes crinkled at the corners.

'Thanks.' He grabbed another biscuit and backed out of the kitchen before she had a chance to stop him.

He was still chewing when he reached the stable yard. Old Hamish looked out from the coach house as Lachlan crunched his way across the cobbled courtyard.

'I heard ye coming,' he said. 'Ye'll be wanting your horse saddled. I'd do it for ye but I'm a wee bit busy the now. The lads will soon be back, though. Ah, speak of the devil,' he said as the stable hands turned the corner into the courtyard. 'They'll soon see ye right, Master Lachlan.'

'Ye'll be wanting Raven, I reckon,' Fred said when he reached Lachlan. 'I'll have him saddled in two ticks.'

Lachlan leaned on the stable door. 'What was the fuss about?'

'Ach, just a tinker demanding to see the laird. Cannae have that though, so we saw her off the premises.'

Fred finished tightening the saddle. 'That's him ready,' he said, giving the horse an affectionate tap on his rump. 'He was skittish because of the stormy weather this morning, but he's calmed down now.'

Lachlan nodded his thanks before mounting and galloping out of the courtyard.

He guided his horse to the track at the rear of the house, which was a shortcut to the village and the town. A run-in with the tinker woman wasn't something he relished, and it was a longer walk from the main gate.

Once he left the track behind and reached the road, he turned the horse's head towards Invercraig. He hadn't yet thought about the intricacies of hiring men to rebuild the inn, but he refused to let it worry him until he got there. What was more important was finding Belle.

A watery sun broke through the clouds as Annie walked home and the river was no longer choppy, so it didn't surprise her to find James outside sorting out his lines.

He looked up at her approach. 'How did your chat with Hector go?'

'He's worried about Ellen. I think he fears she's going the same way her mother did before her. But he won't admit it.'

James let go of the nets and stood, placing a hand on his back as he did so.

Annie frowned. He wasn't as young as he used to be, and she was conscious he'd developed more aches and pains over the past year. There was a stiffness in his posture that hadn't been there before. The sea did that to a man. Constant exposure to the elements took its toll.

'I mind Mary-Ellen,' James said. 'A bonnie lass, she was. It was a shame when they took her away after she lost her wits when Ellen was born.' He gazed across the river and Annie wondered if he was visualising the grim building that housed those who lost their senses.

'Hector had little choice after she tried to harm the bairn. What else could he do?'

'I suppose.' There was a hint of doubt in his voice. 'I cannae help thinking what I might have done in his place.'

'You would have done what you had to do, the same as he did. Mind you, I think he's been grieving ever since.'

'So, what happens now? What happens when the laird comes with his questions? What do we tell him?'

Unaccustomed to feeling helpless, Annie stared out over the river as she searched for an answer. But no answer came. Despair gripped her, but she knew she had to stay strong. Her family relied on her. She was the glue keeping them together.

'I don't rightly know,' she said, 'but I'm sure we'll think of something.'
It felt like an admission of failure, and she turned away.

'While you're getting ready, I'll talk to Ian. Maybe he can reason with Ellen and make her see sense. Give me a shout when you want me to carry ye to the boat.'

With a heavy heart, she entered the house. The soup bubbled softly over the dying embers of the fire while Ian sat hunched on the stool, staring into space.

'Ach, you've near let the fire go out. Could ye not have added a lump or two of coal to keep it going?'

Ian looked up and shrugged. 'It's still got a bit of life in it and there's not much coal left in the scuttle. I didn't want to waste it.'

'That's real thoughtful. But there's a wee drop more in the coal shed out back, enough for about two days. And now the weather's cleared enough for the boats to go out, and if the fish are biting, we'll be able to get another sack when the coal cart comes round.'

'Did Hector have anything to say?'

Annie knew by his tone he expected her to have failed.

'He says he'll talk to Ellen.'

'I've tried that, and it was no use. She's too fired up.'

'Aye, but he's her da. He knows how to handle her.'

Ian stiffened. 'I'm her husband. If she'll not listen to me, he has little chance of making her see sense.'

'Give it time.' Annie put a modicum of hope in her voice, but she was inclined to think Ian was right. 'In the meantime, the boats need to get ready to sail. You'd best go along the road and give Hector a hand.'

'I hadn't intended to return there. Not after what Ellen did and how she treated me. Maybe my da will let me go out on his boat.'

'It makes no difference whether you and Ellen are seeing eye to eye. You'll get yourself along that road. Hector won't be able to put to sea without your help and fine ye know it. Besides, if ye won't talk to Ellen, how do you expect her to come round to our way of thinking?'

Ian got up from the stool and stalked to the door.

When Annie saw his expression, she anticipated him storming out of the house without a backward glance. But he hesitated in the doorway and turned to face her, his brows drawn together in an angry frown.

'Whatever you say. But if you think Ellen will come round, then I fear you're sadly mistaken.'

With that parting shot, he left.

17

Ellen screamed a last curse after the retreating backs of the men who had thrown her on the road before she set off on her long walk home. The storm had gone, taking the clouds with it, and a pale sun glimmered in its place. Too wrapped up in her thoughts, Ellen didn't notice.

When the road forked, she ignored the lower road along the river's edge and turned to the right. This road led to the church, winding its way along the clifftop overlooking the houses below. Halfway along, she flopped onto the damp grass. Lying on her stomach, she peered down at the village below, where the fisherfolk were gathering on the foreshore.

The weather had cleared since the early morning storm and no doubt they were getting ready to take the boats out.

She ought to be down there with them, helping to get the boat ready. Carrying her da and Ian out to it so their clothes remained dry before they sailed. But she wasn't sure of her welcome.

Dampness from the grass she lay on seeped through her skirt and blouse. She squirmed, thinking of the comfort of her house in the village, and knew she had to return home. But her thoughts ran riot while she thought of how to wreak her vengeance on Belle. The name plagued her and when she saw Ian striding along the lower road; it inflamed her even more.

Ian was her man. Belle had no right to take him away from her. And he wasn't the first. Before marrying Ian, Ellen had set her cap at his older brother Jimmie. Annie had encouraged the match and Ellen thought they would wed. That was before Jimmie brought Belle home as his wife. An incomer, a townser, whom none of the villagers welcomed. There was nothing Ellen could do, so she settled for Ian. But it hadn't been long before she noticed his eye straying to Belle. And even though Ian was second best in her eyes, jealousy had crept up on her, increasing every time she saw Ian look at Belle.

She clenched her fists around clumps of grass, tearing them out by the roots. Belle should have died in the fire, but she'd bewitched Ian, and he'd rescued her.

Curses spewed out of her mouth. She wasn't finished with Belle yet and if she didn't hang for setting the fire, she'd get rid of the bitch herself. But first, she'd have to find out where Belle was hiding. It was pointless to ask Ian to help her, but she knew who would. Rising from the ground, she stamped along the clifftop to the path wending down to the village.

As she slipped and slid down the path, a plan formed in her mind. For it to work, she had to be careful and hide her animosity towards Belle. She had to convince everyone her anger had subsided, and the fire was accidental rather than deliberate.

Reaching the end of the path, she stopped to gulp air. She needed to be calm. Gradually, the tumult in her mind lessened.

The scene before her was a familiar one. Men pushing boats from the shingle into the water, their voices and laughter mingling with the scrape of wood on stone and the subsequent splash. Fisherwomen kilting up their skirts and fastening the hems around their waists as they got ready to carry their men to the boats. Several of them nodded recognition to Ellen as she joined them, but others ignored her. Ellen bit her lip to control her temper and nodded back.

She knew Ian had talked to his mother. Hadn't she seen him with her own eyes leaving Annie's house and she wondered what he'd told her? If he had bad-mouthed her, would Annie speak to her?

Her eyes sought Annie among the gathered women. But Annie was already wading out to the Watt boat with James on her back, so she had no way of knowing.

Ian and her da were pushing their boat off the shingle into the water, so they didn't see her approach. She stood and watched for a moment, waiting for them to turn.

Her da turned first. 'You're back then,' he said. He was a man of few words, but his eyes reflected caution and a bit of suspicion.

'I couldn't see you go to sea wet,' Ellen said, with no further explanation.

Hector grunted in reply.

She kicked off her shoes. 'Come on, then. Get on my back. I can't be waiting all day.'

She glanced at Ian before stepping into the water and wading to the boat. After depositing Hector onboard, she had time to consider what to say to Ian while she waded back to the shore.

Her feet were numb from the cold water, so she didn't feel the stones and pebbles biting into her feet as she walked towards him.

He stood there, watching her, his face expressionless. She couldn't tell what he was thinking, but no doubt he remembered her violence and anger towards him earlier in the day.

Forcing tears into her eyes, she looked up into his face. 'I'm sorry,' she whispered. 'The anger got the better of me and I didn't mean what I said.'

Confusion swept over his face, and he hesitated for a moment. She thought he was going to speak but cut him off before he said anything.

'Well, are you going to get on my back and let me carry you to the boat?' Ellen turned her back to allow him to clamber on. Nothing more was said, but when she returned to the shore, she had difficulty repressing her smile of satisfaction. Ian was such a gullible fool, and he'd believed her.

18

Lachlan urged his horse into a gallop. There had been a time when he had been wary of Raven and the horse's power had intimidated him. But that time was now past, and he and Raven had become accustomed to each other. A thrill coursed through his body as the muscles of the powerful beast moved beneath him.

He bent low over the horse, urging him on, certain Belle was waiting for him in Invercraig. Confident of his ability to persuade her to accept his protection, he was sure she would not spurn him in her hour of need.

Oblivious to the muttered curses of those he passed, carters and suchlike, he urged Raven on, leaving a spray of filthy water and mud in his wake. Defiant glares followed his progress, but none dared to complain loudly enough for the laird's son to hear.

Raven's hooves thundered over the wooden bridge and Lachlan's spirits lifted as he glimpsed the ship lying at anchor in the harbour. The sails were furled, and the masts reached upward to the sky resembling trees stripped of their foliage. It rekindled his urge for life at sea under full sail, but he knew that was impossible. His father would never allow it.

He slowed the horse to a canter once they left the bridge. The road, still wet and muddy from the earlier storm, was busy. The cobbles rang with the sound of iron-rimmed wheels and the carters' shouts of encouragement to their tired horses while hurling abuse at the barrow boys. Boys pulled and pushed barrows loaded with odds and ends of merchandise, some of which looked no better than rubbish. Lachlan pulled the reins, guiding Raven past them.

Dismounting at the quayside, he tethered Raven to a railing before looking for his father's factor. He found Wullie McPhee tending to business at the harbour office.

The man laid his pen down and looked up from the ledger. 'If you're here to supervise the unloading, your da's boat isn't here yet. With a bit of luck and a fair wind, it'll be here tomorrow.' He returned his attention to the ledger.

Lachlan stiffened. McPhee's attitude never failed to rub him up the wrong way. The man never gave him the respect that was his entitlement.

'I am here to deliver my father's instructions to you. As his factor, you are required to oversee the rebuilding of the Craigden Inn.' Lachlan adopted a curt tone to emphasise his status.

'Aye, I heard the inn burned down during the night. Nasty business that.'

'We need you to start by hiring masons and joiners.'

He lifted his pen. 'I'll see to it once I've finished here.'

'I rather think you need to do it right away. The laird won't tolerate any delay.'

'Aye, if you say so.' Wullie refocused on the ledger. 'But the laird never tolerates sloppy record keeping.'

Lachlan left the office, smarting at the dismissive reaction to his orders. When he was laird, Wullie McPhee would have to smarten up.

19

Belle inhaled the sharp winter air into her lungs to quell the sick feeling in her stomach while she wondered if she could keep Gregor at arm's length long enough for her to sort her life out.

She stared across the river to the cluster of houses at Craigden. They'd been happy there for a time. The bairns loved the freedom to roam where the river was the only danger. But it was shallow on that side of the water. It was different here in Invercraig. The river was deep enough for ships to berth and far more dangerous.

A frisson of worry shivered through her. She'd instructed Sarah to look after the twins and keep them away from the inn, but other than that, she didn't know where they'd gone.

Several carts trundled along the road, heading for the bridge. Shouts of encouragement and the occasional whip crack floated in the air as the carters urged their horses on.

Her eyes followed them, but she knew Sarah would not have taken the boys that way unless she intended to return to Craigden. After last night, when they'd escaped the fire and the anger of the village women, it would be foolish to return. No, Sarah would have gone the other way towards the busy harbour, with its hum of activity and swarming population of workers and observers. A ship with its sails furled lay at anchor beside the jetty, and Davy and Jamie would have given their sister no peace until she took them to see it.

Belle turned in that direction, passing stevedores stacking barrels and lengths of wood in the dockyard. Close by, sacks of coal piled in untidy heaps waited for the coal merchant's cart to remove them. Nearer the river, longshoremen scurried up and down the gangplank of the ship, going up empty and making the return journey, carrying the ship's cargo. Wine bottles in the wooden boxes they carried, clinked, as several men passed her. One of them winked at her while his partner leered more lasciviously. Turning her face away from them, she hurried on, dodging between dockworkers and sailors, while her eyes searched for Sarah and the boys.

She breathed more easily when she reached the far side of the dockyard, and the crowd had thinned. Not that she feared the men working the docks. She knew how to handle men. Knew how to dodge their grasping hands and how to divert them. Her worry at the moment was how to find Sarah and the boys in time to take them with her to keep her appointment with Granny Mutch. Otherwise, she might lose the offer of a place to live.

After she passed a boatyard where men worked on the skeleton of a boat, she came to a huddle of dilapidated cottages. They straggled along the left side of the rough road, which followed the river's curve. Opposite, a single-masted boat bobbed in the water as the tide flowed out to the North Sea.

A shiver crept up her spine when she saw huddles of women on the doorsteps. It reminded her of the anger she'd encountered last night and made her reticent to approach them to ask if they'd seen her bairns. Averting her gaze, she marched past them but felt their eyes following her and was sure they were muttering among themselves.

A yard, stacked high with barrels, lay beyond the last house. The road narrowed into a footpath edged on the landward side by whin bushes and spiky marram grass. On her right, the river, bordered by sandy patches, tumbled seawards.

Beyond the bushes, there were dunes, the sea, and a sandy beach. A place she'd often come to with Jimmie. The place where they'd made love and where she'd conceived Sarah.

Tears pricked her eyes, and she stared out beyond the river mouth to the sea. The sea which had claimed her Jimmie. It wasn't fair. He should be with her now. If he had been with her, the women of Craigden would never have dared to burn them out of the inn.

Belle dashed the tears away. She couldn't change what had happened. She had to make the best of it. Make a new life for her and the bairns.

But where were they? Sarah wouldn't know the stretch of whin bushes hid a sandy beach. So, it was unlikely she would have attempted to push her way through the prickly plants with their deceptive yellow flowers.

Her hair whipped around her head as the wind changed direction. The river became more turbulent, sending spray to dampen her face and arms. She turned back. As she did so, the sound of children's laughter floated to her in the wind.

Unable to identify the source, she stopped to listen before pushing past overhanging bushes onto the footpath.

She pulled her shawl tighter, grasping it around her arms to protect them from the thorny twigs.

The path ended at a house the likes of which Belle had never seen before. A swirl of colour decorated the gable end of the house. White-topped waves and brilliant blues depicted a stormy sea underneath a hazy sun and glowering sky. A boat, similar to the Craigden boats, tossed in the waves. Whoever painted the scene had included the image of a man adrift in the sea. He struggled in the water with an arm raised in a desperate plea for help, to avoid being swallowed and taken to his last resting place in the cradle of the deep.

Catching her breath, she ran her hand over the painted wall, bringing it to rest on the figure of the drowning man as if by doing so she could save him.

Bitter-sweet memories of Jimmie invaded her mind. Was this how he died so far away in the Arctic seas?

The pain was unbearable. More than she could stand. Perhaps it was time to push thoughts of Jimmie from her mind. The past was the past, and she owed it to her bairns to stay positive and build a new life for them and herself.

Taking one last look at the painting and the words above it, '*Song of the Sea*', she turned her back, but not before thinking it was that song which lured so many seamen to their deaths.

Laughter and the sound of children's voices chased her thoughts away, and she remembered why she was there.

Following the sounds, she hurried around the side of the building, past the steps leading up from the sandy soil to a door inset in the middle of the house and then around the front.

She sighed with relief when she spotted her children playing on a sandy patch with the river running dangerously close to them.

'Sarah,' she shouted, 'what were you thinking of letting the boys play here? You know how dangerous the river is.'

'I told them we had to go back, but they wouldn't listen.'

'We were watching the ship.' Davy pointed to a ship entering the river mouth. 'Maybe my da's on it.'

Belle's heart sank. Jimmie was never coming back because his ship could never have survived the ice. But explaining that to her bairns was impossible. It hurt too much.

'Your da won't be on that ship and you need to come away with me now.' Her voice wobbled. She would give anything for Jimmie to be on board the ship and come rushing off it to fold her in his arms. But that was impossible.

She blinked away the tears and grabbed Davy, pulling him away from the river's edge.

'Aw, Ma,' Davy said, wriggling to get out of her grasp. 'I want to stay here.'

'No, we have to go.' Her voice was harsher than she intended. 'We have the chance to rent a house, but the owner wants to see you before she'll agree. That goes for Jamie and Sarah too. We can't lose the house. You'll come with me now if you know what's good for you.'

Sarah grasped Jamie's hand and led him up the bank. Turning her head, she said, 'Come on Davy.'

Still grumbling, Davy followed them as they made their way back to safer ground.

20

Bloody women. Gregor stood at the bottom of the stairs looking up and listening to the sounds of his sister moving around. He could tell from the creak of wood she'd slid the window up. With a bit of luck, she'd fall out. But when had he ever had much luck?

Life had been good until the two women arrived. He'd enjoyed being a bachelor again after the death of his wife. Bloody shrew, he was well rid of her.

Madge wouldn't be much better. Already she was nipping his head with her sharp tongue, and she'd made it plain she wasn't satisfied with an attic room. But he was the boss, and she'd have to accept his word was law.

Sisters were supposed to respect their brothers, but she'd been a bitch even when she was a bairn, always getting him into trouble with Ma. She could do no wrong. Even Da didn't see through her. It was just as well girls couldn't inherit property, so the inn had come to him when his father finally kicked the bucket. Madge hadn't been too pleased, but she'd set her cap at the innkeeper in Craigden and after his wife died, they'd wed. But what did she have now? A husband six feet under and an inn burned to the ground. She needn't think she was going to get her hands on his inn. He'd see her in Hell first.

His scowl deepened. He ignored the beer barrels and the tasks waiting to be done and strode to the door. Cold air seeped past him, and he shivered as his eyes sought the young woman with the tangle of curls streaming down her back. His fists opened and closed, and his muscles tensed as he remembered her taunting green eyes and the mouth that promised so much. She was ready for the taking and if anyone was going to tumble her, it would be him.

Madge surveyed the room. When she'd told Gregor she intended to stay, she'd sensed his reluctance and had to remind him she was his sister after all. But he'd dithered all morning, and it was only after Belle left he'd grudgingly agreed she could stay.

His mood hadn't improved when he led her up two flights of wooden stairs to the attics under the inn's roof.

Throwing the door open, he'd said, 'This is it,' in a take-it-or-leave-it tone of voice.

'I suppose it will do,' she'd said, 'although it's not as big as I'm used to.' She thought longingly of her previous large room with windows on two sides giving views of the village and the river.

'Not what you're used to then.' The sneer in his voice was unmistakable. 'But your braw inn is nothing but ash now, so you'll have to make do with this.' He turned around and stumped off down the stairs.

Madge sighed. Her brother had never been pleasant. He had grown from a discontented boy into a brute.

She looked around the room. The bed tucked into the slope of the roof looked comfortable enough. There was a chest of drawers for her clothes once she replaced everything she'd lost in the fire. The chair beside the bed looked like a hard wooden kitchen chair, but she'd soon replace that. She wandered around the room, testing the mattress, fingering the chair, and opening the drawers of the chest. She nodded with satisfaction. The room was larger than she'd first thought. Sloping eaves made it seem smaller than it was, but the window, set into the roof, gave her a view of the river. Leaning forward, she stuck her head out of the window. She could see as far as the lighthouse on her left and the bridge spanning the river to her right. Carts trundled along the street below while the shouts of encouragement to the horses and the crack of whips drifted up to her. A ship sat at anchor alongside the busy dockyard, where men scurried here and there, intent on their various tasks. Her initial dissatisfaction at being given an attic room dissipated. This place would do.

When she returned downstairs she found Gregor at the door, staring out into the road beyond. His clenched fists, stooped shoulders and habitual frown made him look intimidating. It was no wonder the place was empty. It would take a brave man to push past him.

He didn't turn when she came up behind him, although she was sure he'd heard her.

'I thought you'd be setting up the barrels. What are you looking for?'

'Nothing.' He turned and pushed past her.

'Is it Belle you're looking for?'

He grunted and scowled.

'I know you're taken with her.' Madge shot him a shrewd glance. It was easy to see Belle had worked her magic on him. 'But Belle could have anyone she wanted. Why would she give herself to you?'

'Why would I want her? I'm a man of property. I could have any woman I wanted.'

'Have you looked at yourself recently?'

'Mind your tongue, woman.'

Madge ignored him and kept talking.

'You're filthy, you smell. Your hair looks like a haystack. When did you last wash?'

'Still the same old Madge. Nipping my head with your nasty comments.'

I'm simply telling you the truth. You're going to have to smarten up if you want Belle to have anything to do with you.'

Gregor grunted and glared at her before turning away from the door.

'I have things to do and if you want to stay here, you'd best make yourself useful.'

Madge smiled to herself as she watched him grab a barrel and roll it behind the bar. She'd got under his skin. Gregor thought he was in charge, but she'd soon change that.

21

The wind caught the sails of the fisher boats as they sped out to sea on the outgoing tide. Ellen watched until they passed the lighthouse to enter the choppier waters of the North Sea. Only then did she turn and walk along the riverbank towards Annie's house.

She had to find Jeannie because the girl had accompanied Ian to Invercraig, so she must know where Belle had taken refuge. But Jeannie hadn't been at the shore when the boats launched.

When she reached the house, she hesitated. Annie could be fearsome when she was angry. She was likely to give Ellen short shrift over her involvement in last night's fire. But Ellen knew her anger was greater than Annie's and she wasn't afraid of her mother-in-law.

She braced herself. She had to face Annie, and she had to remain calm. Convince her she was repentant and hadn't meant for everything to go so far. Would Annie believe her?

The anger at her core stirred, and the turmoil in her mind increased.

The voices screamed.

Wind tore at the edges of her shawl, and she stepped into the gap between two of the cottages while she fastened it more firmly around her shoulders. She rested her head against the cold stone of the building and, after several deep breaths, the clamour in her mind quietened.

Stepping back onto the river path, she fixed her eyes on Annie's house further along. Her plan to wreak revenge on Belle could only succeed if she remained calm enough to convince Annie of her repentance.

Annie's eyes narrowed when she saw Ellen carrying her men to their boat. The memory of last night's madness was still fresh in her mind. Never would she forget seeing the women following her guid-daughter, brandishing their flaming torches, and shouting obscenities aimed at Belle. Nor did she have any doubts about who set the fire that razed the inn to the ground. The sheepishness of the women and the way they now turned their backs on Ellen was enough to confirm this in Annie's mind.

She determined to have it out with Ellen, but not now. Later.

Chilled to the bone, she hobbled back to her cottage on feet numb from their immersion in the icy waters of the river. Once inside, she perched on a stool and rubbed her feet with a rough towel until the feeling returned.

The smouldering fire gave out little heat, for they were on the last of their coal. If Belle's bairns had been here, they would have gone out scavenging for twigs and fallen branches in the nearby woods. But they were gone. Driven out by a mad horde of women led by Ellen.

Silence enveloped her. The house was quiet with the men gone, and Jeannie hadn't returned from her visit to the general store. She'd left earlier, telling Annie she meant to ask Wattie to extend their credit. Times were hard. The meal barrel was empty and there was little else in the house to feed the men when they returned. The women were used to pinched stomachs, but the men needed to be fed else they wouldn't be fit to take the boats out. If Jeannie persuaded Wattie to provide her with oatmeal and some potatoes that, along with the fish the men brought back, should be enough to tide them over. Annie didn't even entertain the thought of the boats coming back empty.

Her feet tingled as blood flowed back. Hearing footsteps, she went to answer the door, expecting Jeannie. But it was Ellen who stood on the doorstep.

Annie stared at her.

'You've got a cheek coming here after what you did last night. But I suppose you'd better come in.'

Ellen followed her into the house and, although Annie didn't offer her a seat, she pulled a chair over and sat.

'I expect you've come here to gloat now you've chased Belle and her bairns from the village. If I were you, I wouldn't be showing my face.'

Annie remained standing and looked down at Ellen with disapproval.

Ellen looked up at her with tears in her eyes. 'I'm sorry. I didn't mean it to come to this,' she said.

'What else could it come to when you set fire to the inn?' Annie turned her back on Ellen and stared out the window to mask the anger surging through her. She wanted to grab hold of Ellen and shake her until her teeth rattled.

'That was an accident. Someone dropped their torch, and the fire started before we could do anything.'

Annie snorted. 'Fine tale. I don't believe it for a minute.' She swirled around to face Ellen. 'You're a jealous bitch and you knew what you were doing. Mind you, I widnae see ye hang for it.' Annie paused to draw a breath. 'But I'll thank you to leave my house. I don't want to see your face again.'

'Will ye no listen to me,' Ellen said in a quiet voice. 'I've said I'm sorry and if I could go back and do things differently, I would. But I can't. What's done is done and I wish it wasn't.'

'D'you expect me to believe that?' Annie clenched her hands to stop herself from slapping Ellen. 'There's a blackness in your soul, Ellen Watt, and I'm ashamed you bear my son's name. Now get out of my sight and if you have any sense, you'll get out of the village.'

Ellen shrank back and a look of fear crossed her face. Without another word, she turned and slammed out of the house.

Annie sank into the chair while she struggled to get her breath back and quell the anger consuming her. An anger that had been enough to strike fear in Ellen's heart.

Wattie rested his hand on Jeannie's arm. 'Think about my offer,' he said.

'I'll speak to my ma and let you know.' She cradled the bags of oatmeal and potatoes in her arms. Wattie was a kind man, and she liked him. But she didn't know how her ma would react to his offer.

The shop doorbell tinkled when it opened, but Jeannie noticed it didn't tinkle a second time. Wattie must still be standing in the doorway.

Not wanting to embarrass him, she didn't turn her head to check. But it gave her a thrill of pleasure to think he was watching her walk home.

Her feet slowed when she heard angry voices coming from the house. It wasn't like her ma to shout like that even when her brothers were giving her grief. But Angus and Davie were at sea, so she couldn't be shouting at them. What was going on?

She stopped at the corner of the house, uncertain whether to interrupt or wait until the shouting stopped. The decision was made for her when the door was flung open. Ellen charged out on a collision course with Jeannie.

There was a wild look on Ellen's face and tears in her eyes. 'I only came to say I was sorry,' she said, 'but your ma won't listen.'

Jeannie might have believed her, but for the vicious way she spoke.

'I think she's upset. Maybe if you come back later, she'll have calmed down.'

'After she threw me out of her house?' Ellen's voice was as sharp as nails.

She spat on the ground and turned to glare at the closed door. For a moment Jeannie thought she intended to barge back inside to have it out with her ma. She placed a restraining hand on Ellen's arm but withdrew it when she felt the tightness of her muscles, which suggested she might lash out. Jeannie didn't relish being on the receiving end of a punch.

'I wondered where Belle went when she left the village. I wanted to say sorry to her and that the fire was an accident. We didn't mean to drive her out.'

Jeannie drew in a breath. Did Ellen expect her to believe that?

'Do you know where to find Belle?'

There was a hint of madness in Ellen's eyes that Jeannie didn't like the look of.

'Why would I know?'

'Because you and Ian went to see her this morning.' Ellen grabbed hold of Jeannie's arm and shook it. 'You must know.'

Jeannie wrested her arm from Ellen's grip. 'I don't know where she is. We didn't find her.'

Gathering up her strength, she pushed Ellen away and rushed into the house, slamming the door behind her and leaning on it to prevent Ellen from following.

Annie looked up in surprise.

'I think Ellen's had a brainstorm,' Jeannie said, 'and I didn't want her pushing in.'

'Ah!' Annie fumbled for her clay pipe and stuck it in her mouth sucking on the stem even though there was no tobacco in the bowl.

She stared into the dying fire. 'I must say, I agree with you. She was stroppy with me, and I had to tell her to leave before it came to blows.'

'I was outside, and I heard.'

'She asked me if I knew where Belle had gone. Said she wanted to apologise, but I didn't believe her. I think she means harm to Belle.'

'I think so too, lass. But I don't know what we do about it.'

With a sigh, Jeannie joined her mother at the table. 'I got some meal and potatoes from Wattie. He says it'll tide us over until the men return from the fishing.'

'He's a good man, Wattie.'

'Aye, he offered me a job in the general store, helping out and serving customers. I said I'd talk it over with you first.'

Annie removed the pipe from her mouth. 'I wouldn't have thought the store busy enough to employ an assistant.'

'He says he's finding it difficult to do everything himself because of his gammy leg.'

Annie was silent for a moment, but her eyes glittered with curiosity.

'I'm thinking maybe it's because he's taken a notion to you. You need to watch yourself.'

Heat rose from Jeannie's neck to her face, and she hoped she wasn't blushing.

'Would that be such a bad thing?'

Annie considered for a moment. 'I suppose you could do worse, although he's not a fisherman.'

'The fisher laddies aren't interested in me. They think I widnae be strong enough to carry them to their boats.'

'Maybe they're right. You've always been a bit on the weedy side.'

'I'm strong enough, though,' Jeannie protested. 'I cannae help it if I didnae grow as tall or as strong as the other lassies.'

'No lass, but they do say good things come in small parcels and there's no one better than you at baiting the lines.'

'But what good is baiting the lines when the weather's so bad the boats can't go out? At least if I accepted his offer, it would mean a wee bit of money when times are hard.'

'Ye're right, and Wattie's a good man. So, you have my blessing to take the job he's offered you. I reckon it will come in handy.'

Jeannie emptied the bag of oatmeal into the meal bin, but her mind was elsewhere, wondering what it would be like to work for Wattie.

22

They were within several yards of the tenement building when Belle knelt and faced the twins. 'It's up to Granny Mutch whether we get this house, so be good and do what you're told,' she said.

'Is she our granny?' Jamie widened his eyes and looked at her.

'Don't be daft,' Davy scoffed.

'No,' Belle said, 'that's her name. But we don't want her to think we're going to give her trouble, or she might not let us have the house.' She stared at Davy with misgiving. Why wasn't he as biddable as Jamie?

'I'll make sure he behaves,' Sarah said.

Belle nodded. Her daughter was wise beyond her years, although she showed little emotion toward her mother. Davy and Jamie were the only ones who made Sarah smile.

A dishevelled young woman carrying a bundle burst out of the tenement as they reached the door. She glared at Belle and spat on the road. Granny Mutch followed behind. 'And don't return until you pay me what you owe.'

The woman tossed her head, scraggly lank hair flying in the wind. 'Keep your damned house. Why would I want to come back to that hovel?' She spat on the road again. 'You're welcome to it.'

'You're lucky I didn't have you thrown in the Tolbooth as a debtor,' Granny Mutch shouted after the departing woman.

She turned to Belle and smiled. The harridan who had shouted after the woman vanished, and in her place was the smiling grey-haired woman Belle had met earlier in the day.

93

Belle shivered. She would have to remember to stay on the good side of this woman because underneath her pleasantness was a woman you wouldn't want to cross.

'These your bairns?' The woman's eyes narrowed as she examined them.

'Yes. The twins are Davy and Jamie, and this is Sarah.' She gestured towards them.

'I don't want trouble.' Granny Mutch stared at the two boys. 'Can't have my tenants complaining about bairns running wild.'

'They're good boys.' Belle drew them closer. 'They won't make any trouble.'

'What about when you're working at the inn? If I know Gregor, he won't want them under his feet.'

'That won't be a problem. Sarah is used to looking after them.'

Granny Mutch grunted. 'If there's a problem, you'll be out on your ear.'

She held out a key but drew it back when Belle reached for it. 'Money first,' she said.

Belle turned her back on the woman and, huddling close to the wall, raised her skirt to reach the leather pouch dangling from her waist. She teased the money from within, feeling the edges of the coins until she had the correct ones. She didn't want anyone to catch sight of the sovereigns.

'You're a careful one,' the woman said as she snatched the coins and handed over the key. 'The house is on the first floor. It's the first door on the landing.' She turned her back on them and retreated indoors.

'Wait,' Belle said. 'Aren't you going to show us the house?'

'What for? You've paid the first week's rent. If you don't like the house, that's too bad. Besides, I'm damned if I'll climb those stairs.' With that parting shot, she slammed the door.

23

Lachlan hesitated outside the factor's office. Wullie McPhee's response to his demands rankled. The man was only a factor. What right did he have to treat him in that way? The more he thought about it, the angrier he became. He stiffened and turned to go back into the office, determined to make the man follow his orders.

His hand was on the doorknob when the door swung inwards, pulling him with it. He stumbled on the step and struggled to maintain his balance. Wullie smirked down at him. Heat surged up through his neck to his face and his temper flared.

'Damn you, man. Take a bit of care.' He grabbed the door frame to steady himself.

'Sorry sir. But I thought you wanted me to make the arrangements to rebuild the Craigden Inn. You said you wanted it done right away.'

'Yes, of course.' Lachlan regarded the man with suspicion. Wullie didn't look sorry, and he detected a hint of insolence in his voice.

'Perhaps you'd like to accompany me to convey your orders to the builders?'

'That won't be necessary, but I will be here when you return, and I'll expect your report.'

'As you wish.' Wullie doffed his cap and strode off.

Lachlan stood in the doorway watching as McPhee weaved through the dockyard workers with the confidence of someone who belonged. Dockers nodded to him as he passed, and some stopped to speak to him. It was obvious everyone here respected him.

He suppressed a flash of envy. What did it matter that Wullie was respected here? He was only a workman. His father's factor. He didn't have the birth and breeding that was Lachlan's.

But he couldn't shake off the feeling something was missing in his life. He stared around at the busy dockyard. It swarmed with activity. Everyone had a purpose except for him. It made him feel useless. Not for the first time, he wondered what it would have been like if he'd been born a commoner. Would he have been any happier?

The sea had always pulled him, and he envied the sailors and fishermen their freedom and way of life. But there was no use thinking about that. His birthright was as the son of the laird. He owed a duty to his father and, whether or not he liked it, that was how it was and how it would always be.

Duty. It had been part of his life for as long as he could remember. Drummed into him from childhood. Forcing him to make decisions he never would have made otherwise. Like the decision to marry Clarinda. If not for that, he would still have Belle's love instead of her rejection after his marriage. It was that sense of duty that made him stay here, waiting for the factor to return instead of going to search for Belle.

The crash of breaking glass and wood splintering jolted him from his thoughts, and he wove through the crowd of workmen to investigate its source. Before he reached the scene of the accident, he smelled the brandy, a heady aroma that reminded him of days spent in the London clubs when he was wooing Clarinda. He pushed through the spectators, one of whom was sliding an unbroken bottle inside his jacket, clutching it under his armpit like a prize. Broken glass lay scattered, surrounded by the splintered wood of the crate. Amidst the wreckage, golden puddles trickled and formed pools on the ground while the intoxicating aroma of the brandy filled the air.

A docker dropped to his knees and lowered his mouth to a puddle before it dispersed while several others rooted through the wreckage, in search of unbroken bottles.

'Exciseman!'

The worker hid the bottle under his jacket before slipping through the crowd and out of sight.

Another two men turned to follow him, but the exciseman jerked the second man back with a hand on his collar. The man's face changed colour, and he gasped for breath.

'No, you don't, my lad,' the new arrival growled. 'That there brandy doesn't belong to you.'

'It was going to waste. I was only rescuing it. I weren't going to keep it.'

'Tell that to the Sheriff. It's the Tolbooth for you, my lad.' He kept a tight hold of his quarry while he turned to shout to his colleague standing at the rail of the ship. 'Best get down here, before any more of this stuff takes legs.'

Lachlan smiled to himself as the rest of the men slunk off. He reckoned they wouldn't want to risk being hustled off to the Tolbooth.

The exciseman wasted no time in summoning some dockers to clear the mess while he documented the unbroken bottles.

Lachlan wandered off, stopping at the quayside to admire the sleek lines of the ship at anchor. It was larger than his father's ships and he imagined it at sea with its sails blowing in the wind rather than being furled as they were now.

A group of sailors bounded down the gangplank, laughing and gabbling to each other. Their berets and striped shirts and dark blue pea coats labelled them as French. Several dockers followed them, each carrying wooden crates that clinked and rattled as they walked.

'May I ask what your business is here?'

Lachlan turned to face the exciseman who had finished inspecting the clear-up of the spilt brandy.

'I was admiring the ship.'

The man flexed his shoulders and puffed out his chest until Lachlan was sure the brass buttons of his dark blue jacket would pop off.

'I seen you loitering back there.' His eyes narrowed. 'Thought it suspicious at the time.'

'Suspicious?' Lachlan laughed. 'I presume you do not know who I am.'

'Makes no odds to me. I'm here to ensure none of this cargo of brandy ends up in the wrong hands. Just because you're a toff doesn't mean you don't indulge in a bit of smuggling.'

'May I suggest you check with your colleague when he returns from his current task? He will confirm my credentials and my right to be here.'

'Name?' the exciseman demanded.

'Lachlan Craigallan. Now, if you will excuse me, I have business with my father's factor at the harbour office.' Lachlan glared at the man, turned on his heel and strode off.

He clamped his lips and bulldozed past the workmen in front of him, ignoring their protests when he pushed them out of the way. Bloody exciseman. Officious bugger. What right did he have to question him? He was still simmering with anger when he entered the harbour office to await the return of Wullie McPhee.

24

Gregor swore as he positioned the barrel behind the bar. Bloody Madge. Who did she think she was, bossing him about like that? Women weren't important and sisters were only there to serve the men in the family. He was in charge now their da was dead and buried, so she'd have to toe the line else he'd throw her out.

'Don't think I'm going to listen to you cursing all day.' Madge leaned over the bar and glared at him.

Gregor glared back at her. 'You can't come in here and order me around. Da left me the inn, not you, so while you're here, you'll do what I tell you.'

'We'll see about that.' With a flounce of her skirts, she strode to the stairs at the rear of the room. 'I'm going upstairs. I'll come back when you're in a better temper.' The door banged behind her.

He waited until he no longer heard the clatter of her feet on the wooden stairs before he returned to stare out into the street. It felt like an eternity since Belle had left to find the bairns. But maybe she'd passed by when he was busy with the barrels.

Off to his left, the harbour buzzed with activity. Dock workers swarmed up and down the ship's gangplank, unloading its cargo. Gregor's eyes quickened with interest. The boxes and barrels signified a wine cargo. He stepped outside to see better and rubbed his hands.

A bunch of sailors wearing navy pea jackets and berets pushed past him. He recognised Frenchies when he saw them and his eyes glittered at the prospect of French brandy. Some of it would make its way into his wine cellars, provided Archie and his mate outwitted the excise men. Once there, he'd use Belle to keep their attention elsewhere.

With difficulty, he suppressed his urge to venture to the quayside and mingle with the longshoremen unloading the cargo. Although he couldn't see any excisemen, he was sure they were there with their ever-watchful eyes. Not much got past them. But Archie was an expert at evading the excise men and spiriting away cases of wine and brandy before they reached the warehouse. Which was just as well, because if they caught Archie, it would lead them to him.

He turned his gaze away from the harbour to mask his interest. The Frenchies had passed further along the road, swallowed up in the crowds hurrying about their business. A procession of carts rumbled past him, and the carters filled the air with curses as they urged their horses to go faster. Hooves clattered and wheels rumbled on the cobbles. Barrows wheeled by reckless youths added to the chaos as they darted through the steady stream of people going about their business. Cries of 'Mind how ye go?' rent the air when a barrow got too close to a hurrying workman.

The thud of something crashing to the ground, accompanied by the splinter of wood and the shattering of glass, drew his attention back to the quayside. That was when he spotted Belle dragging the two bairns along while the lass followed behind with a scowl on her face.

Pulling back into the door's shadow, he watched Belle stride past, her eyes fixed on the street ahead. He was sure she hadn't seen him. Once she'd mingled with the pavement crowds, he emerged from the doorway and followed her, making sure he stayed far enough back so she wouldn't see him.

If someone had asked him why he was following Belle, he wouldn't have known how to answer because he didn't know. But his fascination with her urged him on. The sight of her striding along the road with her gypsy hair blowing out behind her held his gaze. He wanted to run his fingers through those dark curls, stroke her skin and look into her eyes. But she would have none of him, and he knew she'd only been buttering him up when she looked at him with those inviting eyes and that smile on her lips. The promise in her eyes was a false promise.

He would have to think of a way to change that. Maybe he needed to do what Madge said and tidy himself up. It was worth a try.

He dodged into a doorway to watch her encounter with Granny Mutch. He'd have a word with the old witch later. She was partial to a drop of brandy, so he reckoned she wouldn't have a problem spying on Belle for him.

Gregor wasn't near enough to hear what they said to each other, but he didn't miss Granny Mutch's outstretched hand demanding payment. Nor did he miss the sight of Belle turning to face the wall and raising her skirts. Heat surged through his body at the sight of her leg, but the leather pouch forced him to concentrate on what she was doing. He watched her fingers feel around inside before drawing several coins out. His eyes glittered, and he sucked in his breath. She wasn't as destitute as he'd thought. Considering the fatness of the pouch and how low it hung; she had coins aplenty. He'd lay bets Madge didn't know about Belle's hoard.

After Belle entered the building, he emerged from his hiding place. It was time to have a chat with Granny Mutch.

She opened the door before he knocked. 'I saw you skulking in that doorway,' she said.

'Not much goes past you.' He leaned against the doorframe. 'Aren't you going to ask me inside?'

'Why would I want to do that?'

'I thought we might have a wee chat about your new tenant.'

'Interested in her, are you?' She beckoned to him to follow her inside.

Gregor sank into one of the armchairs. It was more comfortable than it looked, and he relaxed back, crossing one knee over the other.

'I find it pays to know about my employees. It's not good for business if I give a job to someone with a shady past or who doesn't fit in.'

'I thought a shady past would have been helpful in your line of work.' Granny Mutch eased herself into the other chair.

'Only if I know about it.'

Granny Mutch tapped her chin, and her eyes narrowed into a gaze that bored into him, seeking out his innermost secrets.

He uncrossed his legs to mask his discomfort. The woman was a witch; he was sure of it. What she didn't know, she would soon find out.

'You want me to spy on her? What's it worth?'

'A bottle of my best brandy.'

'Make it two,' she said, 'plus a daily supply of ale.'

'It's a deal.' Gregor stood. 'I'm expecting a fresh delivery of brandy tonight, so you'll have the two bottles in the morning.'

'Mind you do,' she said, 'else I'll have to tell Belle about our arrangement.'

'Bloody witch,' Gregor muttered as he walked back to the inn.

25

The chiming bells of Invercraig's steeple clock pealed four times before the factor returned.

Lachlan removed his feet from the desk and leaned forward in his chair when Wullie barged into the harbour office, slamming the door behind him.

'You took your time,' he said.

Wullie shrugged off his jacket and tossed his cap onto the desk. 'I've arranged for a builder to inspect the site in Craigden. Says he'll be there at eight in the morning to assess what's needed and work out a price for the rebuild. It'll need your father's approval.'

He hung his jacket on a hook in the wall and stood waiting for Lachlan to vacate his chair. When Lachlan didn't move, he continued, 'It might be best if either you or your father joined us, so there's no misunderstanding or delay to beginning the work.'

Lachlan stretched and flexed his shoulders before he stood. 'I'll talk to my father,' he said. 'Is there anything else I need to know?'

'Won't know what's involved until I've heard what the builder has to say.'

'That's not a lot to report. I thought you'd have had the matter in hand by this time.' He didn't say what a waste of time it had been for him to wait for the factor's return, but he implied it in his brusque tone.

Wullie McPhee shrugged, impervious to Lachlan's displeasure.

'I've done my best. It's up to the builder now.'

Once again Lachlan was left with the impression Wullie regarded him as a nonentity. Someone he had to tolerate rather than respect. It did nothing for his temper, which he suppressed with difficulty.

However, he refused to give the factor the pleasure of knowing his dismissive attitude affected him.

'I'll bid you a good day,' he said before leaving the harbour office.

The pale February sun had waned, and dusk gathered. In another hour, darkness would descend, and Lachlan hadn't yet traced Belle. He guessed she had sought shelter and employment in one of the many taverns and inns in Invercraig. She would have no trouble convincing any innkeeper of her experience as a barmaid.

From where he stood, the only tavern he saw was the Ship Inn, a few yards further along the road. He had never set foot in the establishment, which had a reputation for being a drinking den for sailors, dockers, and the rougher elements of the community. It was not a place he normally considered frequenting, but it was worth starting there.

Raven pawed the ground at his approach. 'Sorry boy,' Lachlan said. 'I'll leave you here. Don't want to risk tying you up outside the Ship Inn. You're safer here.'

Leaving his horse tied to the railing, he walked the few yards to the tavern.

The bar was no better than he expected. A large, gloomy room crammed with wooden tables and benches. The fire did little to relieve the chill as it smouldered in the grate and the man behind the bar added to the chill with his lack of welcome.

An old hag hunched over a mug of ale raised her head to give him a toothless smile before drawing nearer to the fire. The few other customers avoided his eyes. Lachlan couldn't help comparing it to the Craigden Inn, which was now nothing more than a pile of ashes. Madge and Belle had ensured a warm welcome to everyone who entered its doors. Not like this barren place.

He strode to the bar.

The man behind it stared at him with a glitter in his eyes that could only be greed. 'Flagon of ale, is it? Or are ye looking for something a mite stronger?' He ignored the tin mugs on the shelf behind him and placed a glass tumbler on the table.

Lachlan shook his head. The glass was greasy, and the hand grasping it was none too clean, with black dirt under the fingernails.

'I'm looking for a woman,' he said.

'Ye won't find one at this time of the day. But if ye care to wait awhile, I'm sure by the time you've had a couple of drinks there'll be plenty to choose from.'

'You misunderstand me,' Lachlan said. 'I'm looking for a particular woman by the name of Belle. She might be in the company of another woman named Madge.'

The man's eyes narrowed. 'Can't help you there. I know the names of all the doxies that come in here, but none of them are called Belle or Madge.'

Something in the man's attitude sent a shiver up Lachlan's spine. A sensation of menace he didn't understand crept over him, and he didn't feel safe.

The man leaned over the bar until his face was so close to Lachlan's he smelled the sour stink of his breath. 'What'll ye have to drink?'

'Nothing, thank you. I'll be on my way.'

Once outside, he didn't relax until he'd mounted Raven and was in the saddle.

Madge emerged from the shadows as soon as Lachlan left.

'What did he want?'

Gregor scowled at her before turning to replace the tumbler on the shelf behind the bar.

'Bloody waste of time. My drink wasn't good enough for him, so he left. Bloody good riddance.' He polished the bar top with a grubby cloth. 'That lot think they own the world.'

'Got under your skin, has he? I don't suppose it was because he was looking for Belle.'

'So, it's spying on me now, is it? You want to mind your own business.'

Madge stepped back as he thrust his face into hers.

'I don't need to spy. He was bound to come looking for her. Not that Belle will give him the time of day. She might have forgiven him for deserting her to go off to London. But she'll never forgive him for bringing back a wife.'

Gregor's eyes widened. 'You never said you knew him.'

'Oh, I know Lachlan. So does Belle. He's Sir Roderick Craigallan's son. I'm sure you know him.'

A thoughtful look passed over Gregor's face. 'What does someone like that want with Belle?'

Madge shrugged. 'They have a history together, although Belle wants nothing more to do with him. He keeps on trying, but Belle always sends him away.'

'What kind of history?'

'She's known him for nigh on nine years and I'd lay bets there's a possibility the twin boys are his. I wouldn't swear to that though, because she claims they are her husband's children.'

'He must have money, and if he is their father, why reject him?'

'You may ask. I wouldn't say no to him, but Belle's not that kind of woman. He won't find her easy to win over.'

Madge watched Gregor's hand tighten on the cloth. He dipped it in the bucket beside his feet, squeezed the excess water out and scrubbed furiously on the bar top. His mouth tightened and his frown deepened, etched into his forehead in angry lines. She'd seen that look before. It meant he was scheming something, and she would have given anything to know what.

26

Their footsteps clattered on the wooden stairs. The sound bounced off the walls and echoed upward in the stairwell while the gloom closed around them. Belle's breathing quickened as she fought the sense of being enclosed in a stinking tunnel of darkness. Her grip on the boys' hands tightened, and she continued climbing. As they went higher, the rank smell of human bodies and rotting vegetables increased. This was a lot different to the house she'd lived in at Craigden, where the air was fresh. Even the smell of fish when the boats came in was a pleasure compared to this. It made her wonder what kind of place she'd chosen to bring her children to. But what choice did she have?

The first door on the landing hung ajar, so she didn't have to use the key. She pushed it wider and was hit by the smell of urine and faeces.

'What the hell?' She covered her nose with the end of her shawl.

Jamie whimpered and hid his face in Belle's skirt.

'I don't like it here,' Davy complained.

Sarah stood behind him with an inscrutable expression on her face.

'Use your nose to find out where that smell is coming from,' she said to Sarah with a hint of exasperation.

Belle surveyed the room. A table and four chairs sat in the middle while a sideboard straddled the far corner, with the fireplace on the wall at its left and the door to the bedroom on its right. In the window space was a bench on which rested a tin basin piled high with dirty plates. Two tin pails sat on the floor beside it, one of which was half-filled with water.

The room wasn't too clean, but neither was it too dirty. Apart from the smell, it would do.

Sarah, holding her nose with one hand, emerged from the second room carrying a bucket. 'What should I do with this?' she said in a muffled voice.

Belle gagged as the smell increased. 'It'll need emptying. Put the bucket on the landing until we find out where to dispose of it.'

She strode to the window, heaving the sash up and leaning out to gulp in the fresh air. The wind ruffled her hair, and she held her face up, letting it waft over her, enjoying the whiff of salt and the aromas wafting from the docks. It was better than the fetid stink from the bucket Sarah had set outside the door.

Leaving the window open, she inspected the second room. It was bare apart from an iron bedstead and a sea chest. A threadbare shawl hung from one of the several hooks attached to the wall, probably forgotten by the previous tenant. Belle pulled a grimy sheet from the bed to expose a sack with the straw spilling from its side.

Her heart sank. She would have to spend precious coppers on fresh straw for the bed and some new bedding. It would make the place habitable for the time being.

'Hoi, you can't leave that here.'

Sarah darted inside but was unable to close the door and keep the owner of the voice out.

The woman advanced into the room and bent over to glare into Sarah's eyes. Her ample breasts jiggled and were in danger of spilling out of the low-cut lilac silk dress she wore.

Belle dropped the sheet to put a protective hand on her daughter's shoulder, ignoring Sarah's surprise.

'I don't recall asking you to come into my house.' Belle kept her voice polite, although inside she was seething.

'Your house, is it? Where's Morag then?'

'If you mean the previous tenant, she's gone.'

'Bloody Granny Mutch. I told Morag the old witch would put her out.' The young woman stood, considering, while she eyed Belle. 'I suppose you'll be the new tenant then.' She thrust out her hand. 'I'm Thelma. I live next door. You and me should stick together and not let the old bat get the better of us.'

Thelma pulled a chair away from the table and sank onto it. 'These your brats?' She pointed at the twins.

Davy and Jamie drew closer to Belle's skirt.

'Don't worry. I won't eat you.' Thelma laughed. 'I like bairns. Had none of my own. Well, not any I kept.' She laughed again. 'I don't mind keeping an eye on them when you're busy like.'

Belle wondered what she meant by being busy, but she could guess. By the look of Thelma's white-painted face and red lips, she could imagine how she kept herself busy.

'That's kind of you, but Sarah minds the boys when I'm not with them.'

'Whatever.' Thelma's eyes lingered on Sarah. 'She seems a capable lass, but the offer stands. Never know when you'll need it.' She looked around the room and tutted. 'Morag's left a mess behind her. But she never was too clean. Mucky besom. Never mind, I'll give you a hand to get things sorted.' She ran her finger across the table. 'This could do with a scrub. I wouldn't want to be eating off this. And before I forget, you need to get rid of that bucket outside your door. It's stinking the entire building out. You'll have Granny Mutch after your hide if you leave it there much longer.'

'I was going to get Sarah to empty it at the nearest midden.'

Thelma laughed. 'No need for a midden. Tip it into the river. The tide'll take it out to sea.'

'Sarah will do that while I get this place sorted.'

The afternoon passed in a flurry of activity. Thelma instructed Belle where to get the necessities. Water from the well two streets away, fresh straw from a nearby stable, and the location of the nearest general store.

There was no coal, so the fire remained unlit as they worked. 'Coalman comes day after tomorrow,' Thelma told her. 'You'll easy hear him, but it's one and threepence a bag. If you're sharp, you can get the spillage from the bags they've unloaded on the dock today before it gets carted to the yard. Best do it after dark. And make sure no one sees, else they'll throw you in the Tolbooth to rot.'

Belle nodded. She'd heard horror stories about the treatment of prisoners incarcerated within the Tolbooth. So, she'd do without the fire in the meantime, and it would have to be bread and cheese. They'd eaten worse, so the bairns wouldn't complain.

She was grateful for Thelma's help, although she still wasn't sure about her. Was the friendliness of the woman's smile genuine? Or did it hide some ulterior motive in the same way her painted face hid the ugliness of her profession? But if it hadn't been for her help, she'd never have found out where to dump the old straw. It was Thelma who had led her down the dark stair to the cellars in the bowels of the building into an even darker place that smelled of rot and decay. Water dripped down the walls and pooled in places. According to Thelma, the place flooded at high tide. She vowed never to venture down here again. Who knew what horrors lurked within these cellars?

Davy and Jamie were playing tag around the table when they returned while Sarah was washing some cups in the basin beside the window.

Davy gave Jamie a final push and ran to Belle as soon as she appeared in the room. 'I'm hungry,' he complained.

'I'll see to the bedding while you get the kids their tea,' Thelma said, vanishing into the bedroom.

It didn't take Belle long to slice the bread she'd bought from the baker for threepence. A scraping of lard and a slice of cheese completed their meal.

The town's steeple clock chimed five times, reminding Belle time was passing.

'I'll have to leave soon,' she told Sarah, so you need to mind the boys. 'But you'll be all right and I'll be home when the inn closes.' She turned to the boys. 'Be good and do what Sarah says.'

Thelma emerged from the bedroom. 'It's time I went. I need to tidy myself up.'

She didn't need to say for tonight's business, but Belle knew what she meant and knew the business she referred to.

'Aye, it's time I left as well,' Belle said as she nodded her thanks.

'I've finished stuffing the mattress with the fresh straw, so you'll sleep well tonight,' Thelma continued.

Thelma picked some straw from her hair and smoothed her dress. 'I'll be off then and don't worry about the bairns. When you're not here,

I'll look out for them.' The clacking of her heels on the wooden landing echoed in the stairwell as she crossed the landing to her own flat.

The smile slipped from Belle's lips after Thelma's door closed. How could she trust a doxy to watch out for her children when she wasn't here? She turned back into the room to grab her shawl. She'd made a commitment to return to the inn to serve Gregor's customers with ale and tend to their needs, and she always honoured her promises.

'Stay inside and keep the door shut,' she instructed Sarah before she left. 'Never know who's skulking on the stairs.'

But, as she hurried along the street to the Ship Inn, she couldn't shake off the premonition all was not right, and disaster loomed.

27

It was late when Lachlan returned home. Hunger pangs gnawed at his stomach. So, after leaving Raven with the stable boy, he entered the house by the back door and invaded the kitchen. Mrs Ross, the cook, had a soft spot for him and would make sure he didn't starve.

Sure enough, she slapped several slices of roast beef and potatoes on a plate for him, topping it off with lashings of gravy.

'Your father isn't best pleased you weren't here earlier,' she said as she laid the plate before him. 'Cursing and swearing he was. Your ma calmed him down though.' She fetched him a knife and fork. 'Best get that down ye before he sees you've come back. I've saved ye a slice of my clootie dumpling. I know how ye like the sweet stuff.'

Half an hour later, Lachlan went in search of his father. He knew if he sneaked off to his rooms without seeing him. It would make his temper worse.

He found him in the withdrawing room, lounging in a chair, smoking one of his favourite cigars.

Sir Roderick glared at him. 'Where have you been? As if I didn't know. Frequenting the fleshpots of Invercraig when you should be here tending to that wife of yours. It's time she provided you with a son and heir. You are failing in your duty, boy.'

Lachlan stiffened. When would his father realise, he was no longer a boy? He was a man with a man's needs and appetites. But how was he supposed to sire a son when Clarinda barred her door to him? Was he expected to break her door down and take her by force? The idea wasn't entirely repugnant to him, but Clarinda with her ice-cold beauty only had to look at him to turn him into a quivering wreck.

However, his father was obsessed with the need for him to sire a son, and Lachlan had no way of explaining to him how impossible that was.

'I was doing your bidding, sir, and it took longer than I anticipated.'

His father snorted. 'How so?'

'It took time to hire reputable masons to rebuild the Craigden Inn. The search for the innkeepers took even longer, but you were adamant they be found, so I investigated everywhere they might have gone.'

'I imagine that meant visiting every hostelry in Invercraig.'

Lachlan tensed. Why did he always feel he had to make excuses to his father? Would he ever measure up to his expectations?

'It seemed the logical thing to do.'

His father snorted again and stubbed his cigar out on the fender.

'So, did you find them?'

'No, sir.'

'And what about questioning the villagers in Craigden? Have you done that yet?'

'No, sir.' Lachlan wanted to add a lot more but held his tongue.

'I can't even trust you to do a simple task.'

'I don't think anyone could have done any better.' Lachlan struggled to hide the anger simmering inside him. How much did his father expect him to do in one day? After all, it was only last night the inn burned to ash.

Sir Roderick snipped the end from a new cigar, lit a taper from the glowing fire, and held it to the end. He didn't offer one to Lachlan.

'Wullie McPhee and the mason will be at Craigden in the morning to inspect the site of the inn. Permission will be required to approve the plan for the rebuild before it can go ahead. I imagine you will want to oversee this.'

His father contemplated the end of his cigar. 'You imagine wrongly. This is something for you to do. Can I entrust you with this task? At least if McPhee is there, he'll make sure we won't get robbed.' He waved his cigar at Lachlan in a gesture of dismissal. 'You may leave me in peace now.'

Lachlan moved to the door.

'And don't let me down this time.'

28

'Best ale, that is,' Gregor said as he slapped tankards of ale in front of the three sailors.

He had refused their request for brandy, and they had declined the offer of whisky. Frenchies, as a rule, didn't appreciate the peaty flavour of the latter.

Out of the corner of his eye, he observed the man at the next table. An exciseman, out of uniform and trying to pull a fast one. The list of duty-paid alcohol in Gregor's cellar was no doubt nestling in one of his pockets and while it was safe to provide ale and whisky to his customers, the minute he succumbed to serving brandy, he'd be nabbed.

Gregor sauntered over to Tam, sitting by the fireside, staring into his mug of ale. He bent over the table and wiped it with a cloth.

'That the new exciseman?' he whispered.

The old man nodded without looking up. 'Saw him parading about the quay when they were unloading the cargo. Brandy it was,' he said. 'Saw it and smelled it when Callum dropped a box. Waste of good brandy,' he mourned. 'I would've snaffled one of the unbroken bottles, but him over there was watching it like a hawk.' He spat in the fire. 'Bloody waste,' he said.

'Thanks, Tam. I'll get Madge to top your mug up.' He wasn't a generous man, but he had a soft spot for old Tam, who had sat on that stool to drink the inn's ale ever since Gregor was a child.

The old man slurped the dregs of ale from his mug before looking up. 'It'll be good to have a chat with Madge. I mind when the pair of ye were bairns, running around and getting in your da's feet. Mind you, she's grown into a fine-looking woman.'

'Aye, mind you don't keep her chatting too long. She's got work to do.'

A chill breeze blew around the tables as the door opened and closed.

'She's a bonnie one,' Tam said, nodding towards the doorway.

Gregor's pulse quickened as he followed Tam's gaze.

'Aye, that's Belle. You'll be seeing a lot of her now she's come to work here.'

A low whistle echoed around the room, and the French sailors beckoned to Belle. Gregor couldn't understand their shouted comments, but he guessed they were suggestive or insulting.

He strode to their table. 'We'll have less of that behaviour in here, lads,' he said. 'Belle is my barmaid. She's not a doxie and I'll thank you to treat her like a lady.'

'Belle,' they chanted, and their laughter rippled around the room.

'Je t'aime, Belle.' The sailor clasped his hands over his heart. He stood and beckoned to her, while his companions continued to laugh.

Gregor's hands tightened into fists.

A restraining hand grasped his arm. 'It's all right Gregor. I can handle this. I've dealt with worse at Craigden.'

The rest of the evening passed without issue. She was as good as her word, and Gregor watched with admiration as Belle fulfilled her promise. A sidelong look accompanied by an inviting smile, and a toss of her hair, was enough to have the drinkers delving into their pockets to replenish their glasses while she dodged groping hands with dexterity and good humour.

Gregor's doubts about hiring Belle vanished. He already anticipated his profits rising. All he had to do was make sure she stayed, and he hoped he hadn't jeopardised that by refusing to allow her to stay at the inn with her children.

'Time to go home.' Belle placed her hand on old Tam's shoulder. It felt thin and bony under her grasp, and she wondered what awaited him after he left the inn. Probably a cold and damp hovel by the looks of him. His clothes were shabby and in sore need of a wash.

'Do you have a wife waiting for you?'

'Naw. Whit woman would have me?' Tam looked at her with bleary eyes.

'Drink up, then, and I'll walk with you to the door.'

'Ye're a good lass,' Tam said, getting up.

He staggered, and Belle reached out to support him.

'Ye're a good lass,' he repeated.

She stood at the door for a moment to watch him lurch along the street. Poor man. She determined never to reach the depths he had. Her hand tightened on her leather pouch. The sovereigns it contained was her protection from that eventuality.

'That bugger would stay here all night if I let him. He's always the last to leave.'

Gregor leaned over her, his breath sour and hot. She squirmed and ducked underneath his arm, scuttling back to join Madge, who was clearing mugs and tankards from the tables.

'As soon as I find something better, I'm out of here,' she muttered.

Madge shrugged. 'You don't need to be afeared of him. You could wrap him around your little finger.'

'I'm not sure I want to do that.'

'You could do worse. Take Gregor on and you'd have all this.'

Belle surveyed the room. Dark and dismal and nothing like the inn Madge had run in Craigden. 'It's a dump.'

'Aye but think of the potential. We could make a wee fortune if we liven it up.'

'I'm not interested. I prefer to make my fortune by my own efforts.'

'And how do you plan to do that?'

Belle didn't bother answering, although a sly smile hovered on her lips. She gathered an armful of tankards and headed for the bar.

She busied herself tidying the tables and washing the surfaces while Madge raked out the ash from the fire before wielding a brush to sweep up. While she worked, Belle was aware of Gregor's dark eyes following her every movement.

The sooner she planned how to use the sovereigns to secure her future, the better.

After Belle left and Madge retired upstairs, Gregor carried his tankard of ale from the bar to the table old Tam had vacated. This was the warmest spot, even after the fire died down.

Silence enveloped the room, which only an hour ago had rung with voices and laughter as the drinkers tried their luck with Madge and Belle. However, the women's encouragement made the drinkers spend more, and Gregor was sure the evening's takings had increased.

He closed his eyes and thought of Belle, flitting between the tables, her hair a tumbled mess, that sly smile on her lips and the saucy glint in her eyes. It seemed second nature to her to flirt with the men while keeping them at arm's length. He shifted in his seat. What was there about her that stirred him? Every time she came near him, he had to fight his impulse to grab her, possess her, hold her, and make love to her. He was sure she was aware of his feelings, but she treated him the same way she did the drinkers in the bar, sliding past him and keeping her distance.

Gregor had never known a woman like her. His wife had been submissive, always ready to do his bidding, and he'd treated her with a disdain she accepted as her due. She had never stirred him like Belle did and when she'd died, the only thing he regretted was he no longer had a skivvy to do the work.

Belle was different. More independent. He reckoned she would never submit to any man's desire unless she wanted to. But that made her more desirable. It made him want to force her to his will, and he vowed to do that if it was the last thing he ever did. The problem he faced was how to take her independence away until the only person left to rely on was him.

As he brooded, his thoughts turned to the money pouch that hung from her waist. A woman who had money was unlikely to be beholden to a man. His eyes glittered. Without the pouch and the coins within it, she would be destitute and more likely to turn to him for help. But she kept it close to her body under her skirts, so separating her from her money pouch wouldn't be easy.

He swallowed the remains of his ale. He would sleep on it. Come morning, he was sure he would have the answer.

29

February 1840 - The next day - Wednesday

Still smarting from his father's comments of the previous evening, Lachlan hammered on the manse door. He would have preferred to question the villagers without the minister's presence, but he didn't want to annoy his father's order that the minister accompany him.

Murdo must have been standing behind the door because it swung open before Lachlan finished knocking. His black-robed figure hovered in the doorway like a predatory crow. Lachlan wondered if he ever removed his minister's garb.

The minister frowned. 'I have been waiting. Your father gave me to understand we were to question the villagers.' His eyes reflected his disapproval. 'I expected you yesterday.'

'I had more important things to do yesterday.'

Lachlan refused to be cowed by the minister's disapproval. He had no liking for the man and thought him a pompous idiot, full of his own importance.

'I will expect you to join me in the village square. As soon as I have discussed rebuilding the inn with the factor and stonemason, we will interrogate the villagers.'

'Rebuild the inn?' Murdo spluttered. 'It was God's will to destroy that den of iniquity. Rebuilding it will go against everything he stands for. It will invite Satan into our midst once again.'

'I don't think God had anything to do with it. It is more likely it was your will.'

Murdo stiffened and glared at Lachlan.

'In any case,' Lachlan continued, 'it is my father's decision to rebuild the inn and, as the laird, he has the final word.'

He swung himself into his horse's saddle and pulled on the reins. 'I expect to see you in the village square without delay,' he said before leaving the minister fuming at the manse door.

Ellen spent a restless night. She'd thought once she got rid of Belle, her life would improve. Ian would have more time for her. The village women would applaud her for ridding them of the temptress bent on seducing their men, and they would look up to her as their leader. But everything had gone wrong.

Ian blamed her for firing the inn and driving Belle out. She shivered, remembering the bitter words they'd both said. After he stormed out of the house fear had crept through her. Fear he would never return. Even now, a day later, she wasn't sure what he would do when the boats came back.

Her anxiety increased when she thought of the reactions of Annie and the village women. Annie had made her displeasure obvious and ordered her from her house. And instead of applauding her, the village women turned their backs on her. The few who acknowledged her refused to meet her eyes and scurried away as fast as possible.

It was all Belle's fault.

The sound of horse's hooves halted her pacing, and she strode to the door in time to see Lachlan galloping past on the track leading to the village square.

She grabbed her shawl and ran after him, leaving the door to the house open. Her stomach churned and her mind buzzed with plans of what she would say to him.

She'd see Belle hanged yet.

Thoughts of Belle flashed through her mind. Visions of her in her flashy silk dresses while she made eyes at the men. Ian panting after her. The other men slavering over her. Her boldness and arrogance.

Ellen's loathing of the woman increased. Belle was no better than a whore.

A memory from years ago rose unbidden in her mind and caused her feet to slow. It was a memory of Lachlan sneaking into Belle's house in the dead of night when Jimmie was away at the whaling.

Maybe accosting him was the wrong thing to do, when it was obvious he was another one who had been enslaved by her.

She stepped off the path onto the pebbles beside the river and stared into the water. If Belle was to hang, she would need a better plan.

Wullie McPhee and the builder were deep in conversation when Lachlan arrived at the village square. Wullie looked up and nodded before turning back to the builder.

Lachlan looped Raven's reins around the iron ring set into the wall beside the general store. From this position, he was too far away to hear their discussion, apart from picking up an odd word here and there. Words like foundations, stone, and timber, which meant nothing to him.

'Good boy,' he said, stroking the horse's neck before leaving him to join the two men.

He tapped his foot and slapped his whip on the side of his thigh to signify his impatience until he forced them to turn and acknowledge his presence.

McPhee raised his eyebrows.

Annoyance flooded through Lachlan.

'Your report, man,' he snapped. 'When will the building start?' He wasn't sure what else to ask because this was alien territory to him. Something the factor normally organised himself. But his father had been adamant he oversee it. And his father's word was law.

'Donal here,' Wullie nodded at the builder, 'reckons he can gather a squad of men and start the build at the beginning of next week.'

'Does he understand what is required?'

'Yes. The inn is to be built of stone and modelled on the previous building with the ale house at ground level and living quarters above.'

Lachlan nodded his grudging approval but, to assert his authority, added, 'Next week is too long to wait. I want the work started immediately.'

Donal, who up to now had been silent, said, 'Beg pardon, sir, but this be Wednesday and I'll need a few days to recruit the workers. Don't see how we can start before Monday coming.'

'I don't give a damn about what day of the week it is. You'll start as soon as you've gathered some workers together.'

He strode back to his horse.

McPhee and the builder muttered together for a moment before the factor left him to approach Lachlan.

'Well?' Lachlan demanded.

The factor hesitated before saying, 'Donal is the best stonemason and builder in Invercraig. He never wants for work, which was why I was at pains to agree to his starting date. He was reluctant to lower his price, but I persuaded him working for the laird would benefit his business.'

'Why should that concern me if you've struck the deal?'

'It's not yet signed and sealed and because he's a proud man, it is in our interests not to offend him.'

'Offended? A common working man? How is that possible?'

Wullie McPhee's lips tightened. 'Donal is a skilled artisan and, as I said before, a proud man. It is in our interests to remember that.' He strode over the rubble to rejoin the builder.

Lachlan fumed. His father's damned factor had once again succeeded in getting the better of him. He gathered Raven's reins in his hands.

As he passed the two men, he said, 'I'll leave you to continue making the arrangements. I have other business requiring my attention.'

Anger made Lachlan less observant as he left the village square. He stumbled over some debris left over from the fire and, imagining the eyes of Wullie and the stonemason boring into his back, he jerked his horse's reins. Raven, as if sensing his master's displeasure, nudged Lachlan in the shoulder, making him stumble for a second time. He looked back to the square, expecting the men's eyes to be on him.

However, they paid him no heed, as their eyes focused on the site of the inn and their voices rumbled on.

He stroked Raven's neck while he struggled to steady his breathing. The women were gathering on the foreshore, which made it an ideal time to question them about the fire. But he needed a level head to do that. Anger served no purpose in his search for the truth.

'Come on, Raven,' he whispered to the horse. 'We'd best get on with it.' He led the horse to where the path ran along the top of the foreshore.

30

Yesterday's rain had left a legacy of mud and puddles. Murdo picked his way between them as he headed for the path down the cliff face which was the fastest way to reach the village below.

Doubts formed in his mind when he observed the water trickling down the cliff path to form muddy pools in certain spots. Lifting the edge of his robe, he placed a tentative foot onto the path, but the mud squelched and sucked his boot in. He quickly withdrew it; the path was too treacherous to negotiate. There was nothing for it but to walk along the road at the top of the cliff until it sloped downwards to the lower road. Unlike Lachlan, he didn't have the benefit of a horse to speed him on his way, and if young Lachlan didn't like it, then that was too bad.

Wind caught the edge of his cloak, sending it whipping around his legs. He pulled it tighter before turning his thoughts to next Sunday's sermon. Sinners were everywhere, and it was his job to hunt them out. With Madge and Belle now gone from the village, he would have to turn his attention elsewhere. But where? And who?

What he needed was someone to sit on the sinner's stool. Lachlan was the ideal candidate for his sins were many. But Lachlan was the Laird's son and, therefore, untouchable. Such a pity.

He was still deep in thought when he arrived at the crossroads. The road to his left led to the Laird's castle and beyond that Dundee. In front of him, a small bridge connected the riverbank to the island where the water swirled as it flowed towards the inland basin during high tide. To his right lay the road he sought, the one leading to Craigden.

The noise of a cart and horse on the bridge interrupted his thoughts.

'Boats be coming in,' the carter shouted to him.

Murdo stared seawards. He saw nothing but the surge of the tide flowing upriver. The man must be mistaken.

'I fail to see them.'

'They be approaching the lighthouse. They'll be rounding it in a few minutes.'

The cart's wheels churned through a puddle, sending a wave of muddy water in Murdo's direction. He stepped back but wasn't quick enough to prevent the bottom of his robe and his shoes from being soaked.

Thoughts of his sermon vanished, and he scowled after the cart as it trundled along the village road. No doubt the carter wanted the boats to bring in a full catch. If so, it would be the first full catch this year, for the fishing had been poor over the winter months, and the villagers' bellies empty. With no money to spare, the kirk plate had more pebbles than coins which, as far as Murdo was concerned, was a disaster.

His thoughts as he trudged after the cart were not befitting that of a minister of the cloth. But no one had access to his thoughts, so it didn't matter. What mattered were the words he uttered, the sermons he preached, and his ability to influence his congregation.

Water lapped the shore in front of Ellen to spill over her toes, and she drew back further up the pebble foreshore. She'd been so intent on her plans for Belle's demise she hadn't noticed the encroachment of the tide as it flowed upriver to the inland basin.

Stumbling upwards to the path bordering the narrow road, rumbling wheels alerted her to the approach of a horse and cart. She waited for it to pass.

'Boats be coming in,' the carter shouted to Ellen as he coaxed his nag along the road.

'You sure?' She peered towards the river mouth.

'Aye, I saw them on my way here.'

Ellen hugged her body and pulled her shawl tighter. Her Ian was coming home, and she had to convince him she was the woman for him. Not Belle.

Anger tugged at her. Bloody Belle was always there, coming between her and Ian. But Ian was her man, and no bloody harlot was going to get him.

Her eyes narrowed when she spotted the minister walking towards her. He knew Belle was a harlot.

When he drew level, she stepped out in front of him. She had never addressed the minister before and wasn't sure of the proper way to do it.

Tentatively she said, 'It be a fine day minister.'

He stopped and stared at her, astonishment in his eyes.

'Aye, that it is,' he replied.

'And it was a fine sermon you preached on Sunday.'

'It is my duty as your minister to instruct you in the ways of our Lord. I expect you to pay heed to my sermons. Now, if you please, I will ask you to let me pass. I have an appointment to keep with Master Lachlan, who awaits me in the village square.'

Ellen bit her lip. She hadn't said what she wanted to say, so she didn't move.

'Aye, it was a fine sermon indeed, and the Lord God answered your plea for the flames of Hell to consume the Jezebels in our midst when he sent down the fireball. If it hadn't been for that harlot, Belle Watt, our Lord would not have sent fire to destroy the inn.' Ellens' excitement increased and she paid no heed to the minister's alarm at her words. 'Aye, it was a braw sermon you preached, and our Lord was listening.'

'What blasphemy is this you speak?'

Murdo's rough response grated on her ears and set her mind spinning.

'Tis no blasphemy. Your sermon was inspiring, and it was plain what God wanted.'

'You misunderstood. How can someone like you understand the word of God and what he wants?'

Ellen bit her lip. Had she misunderstood? Her mind whirled.

She stared at the minister. His face, no longer benevolent, was twisted with anger.

'But your sermon said the flames of Hell shall devour them. I heard it clearly.'

Murdo's voice quietened. 'That may be so,' he said. 'But God does not send fireballs, nor does he permit his flock to do this for him. When God indicates sinners will be devoured by flames, he means they will go to Hell when they die.' He stopped to draw breath. 'If there was a human hand in the fire that demolished the inn, it was not God's will that was acted on, but Satan's.' He glared at her. 'You must take care not to become Satan's tool.'

He pushed Ellen out of his way.

His words pierced Ellen's heart. Had she become Satan's tool? And if she had, would she be consigned to the flames of Hell when her time came?

No, she refused to believe that. She must make the minister see Belle was Satan's tool, not her.

Murdo brushed past Ellen. Damned impertinence of the woman accosting him in that way. She was like all of her kind. Oh yes, the fisherfolk paid lip service to him as their minister, but they lacked respect for him. He saw it in their eyes every Sabbath when they attended church. The farm workers were more respectful. They knew their place.

He ignored the patter of her feet behind him. But when she passed him and blocked his way, he had to stop. Annoyance surged through him. What did this woman want with him?

'Wait,' she said.

He resisted the temptation to push her out of his way. She was, after all, one of his flock. Perhaps she had a problem she wanted to discuss. Perhaps she sought absolution for a sin.

'If there is something you need to talk about, or you wish forgiveness for your sins, this is not the place,' he said. 'The time for that is after church on Sunday if that is what you wish.'

'It is not my sins I wish forgiveness for, but the sins of another.'

'The sins of another?' He raised his eyebrows.

'Yes, the sins of Belle Watt. You preached about her on Sunday.'

Ah, yes. He remembered Belle Watt. She of the black hair and enticing eyes. He remembered those eyes mocking him when he saw her with her skirts about her waist, dabbling her feet in the water at the lighthouse. She accused him of spying on her. Him, the minister. As if he would. And yet, the image of her kept returning to plague him.

He narrowed his eyes. Why was this woman concerned with the sins of Belle Watt when he'd observed her, only a few days ago, with a burning torch in her hand, inciting the women to set fire to the inn with Belle inside?

Curiosity overcame him. 'Why do you wish me to forgive the sins of another? Surely that is their responsibility.'

A sly look crossed Ellen's face. 'Belle does not consider she has sinned, but she is a harlot and must be made to see the error of her ways. If it were not for her sins, there would have been no fire. She is the one who is Satan's tool, as you foretold in your sermon.'

There it was again. The implication his sermon had been the match that lit the fire. He reached out and gripped her wrist.

'You are deranged. My sermon had nothing to do with the firing of the inn. Human hands were responsible.' He shook her arm. 'And those who held the burning torches to light the flames are to blame. Be mindful of that before looking for sin in others.'

He thrust her from him. She staggered and sank to her knees.

'Curb your tongue, else it leads you to the hangman.'

He strode away from her, still angry and wondering whether he had said too much.

31

The clop of a horse's hooves and the sound of wheels rumbling on the stony foreshore drew Annie to the window.

'Boats must be coming in. That's the first of the cadgers arriving. It won't be long before the rest of them are here.'

She grabbed her shawl and gestured for Jeannie to do the same before hurrying to the foreshore.

Maggie West acknowledged her arrival with a nod, but Jessie Cargill turned away to stare seawards. No doubt Jessie was still smarting from their previous encounter when Annie took them to task for their part in the fire-raising.

Lizzie McNab approached Cadger Wullie, who was sheltering from the wind behind his cart to smoke his pipe. Annie could swear Lizzie had an eye for Wullie. If her man found out, there'd be all hell to pay.

'You sure the boats are coming in?' she said.

He removed the pipe from his mouth and blew out a cloud of smoke. 'Aye, lass. You get a better view of the sea from Invercraig. They're heading for the river mouth and will soon sail past the lighthouse.'

'Daft besom,' Annie muttered to Jeannie. 'Everyone knows you can see further out when you're over there.' She nodded her head towards Invercraig.

Jeannie nodded and tucked her chin into the top of her shawl with fingers blue with the cold.

Poor lass, Annie thought, there isn't much fat on her bones to keep her warm. Why Jeannie was so wee and lanky considering the rest of the family didn't lack for brawn was a mystery to her. But if she got her paired up with Wattie, she wouldn't have to suffer the deprivations of being a fisher lass. She'd have to give some thought to that.

The chatter of the women's voices increased as the group grew larger. Annie scanned the faces but saw no sign of Ellen. The way the lass had been acting since the fire troubled her. She must speak to Ian. Ellen was his wife, and it was up to him to sort her out.

Annie heard the clatter of hooves and turned to watch Lachlan leading his horse towards them.

'The young master's heading this way,' she muttered to Jeannie. 'Best alert the others and remind them to hold their tongues. The least he knows, the better.'

She passed the word to the nearest group while Jeannie scuttled off to warn the others.

The women weren't daft, though. They had no wish to be turned out of their homes and the village. She wasn't so sure about Ellen. The grudge she bore against Belle made her less compliant. It was as well she wasn't here.

It was at that moment she looked along the road and saw the minister approaching, with Ellen not far behind.

Her heart sank. Would Ellen be the catalyst to deprive them of their homes and their living? Would they be under notice to leave the village by nightfall?

Lachlan's anger subsided as he drew near to the foreshore. The soft shush of the waves as they hit the pebbles calmed his nerves. In the distance, the first of the sails came into view as the boats entered the river's mouth. He wondered what it would be like to be on board. To be a fisherman and not his father's son. His affinity with the sea and the land was stronger than his wish to be a laird with all the responsibility that entailed. But his willpower was not strong enough to deny his father and his birthright. His life, mapped out for him at the time of his birth, was something he was powerless to change.

He tethered Raven's reins to a rickety fence before turning to consider the fisherwomen gathered on the foreshore. It would be better to question them before the boats landed, and they became engrossed in unloading the catch. His eyes roamed over the gathered women and among them, he spotted Jeannie Watt. After his return from London, Jeannie had been the one to tell him Belle was working at the inn. She would know where Belle had gone.

When the girl looked up, he beckoned to her. She said something to the woman standing beside her before approaching him.

'You're Jeannie. I remember you.'

Raven moved restlessly, and the girl stepped back, putting more distance between herself and the horse. Lachlan reckoned the only horses Jeannie came into contact with were the worn-out nags that pulled the cadgers' carts.

'He won't hurt you,' he said. 'He's restless because he's tied up.'

Jeannie nodded, but didn't move any nearer.

'Is there something you wanted, sir? I need to get back to the shore before the boats come in.'

Like all the fisherfolk, there was no hint of subservience in her voice. They were proud people who found it difficult to tip the forelock to those above them. But Lachlan preferred that to the veiled insolence in Wullie McPhee's voice.

'Yes, Jeannie. You helped me find Belle before when we met on the back road to the big house. I wondered if you could help me find her again.'

'There are folks who mean harm to Belle, so I cannot help you, sir?' She raised her eyes to meet his, and he saw defiance in her gaze.

'I mean no harm to Belle. I want to help her. It distresses me she is in need and if I can help, I will. If she sends me away, I will go.'

'I heard word the laird holds her and Madge responsible for the fire, and you're the laird's son.' She glared at him. 'But she weren't to blame and I wouldn't want to bring trouble to her door.'

Lachlan leaned forward and gripped her hand. 'I am not my father. I give you my word I will bring no trouble to her door. On the contrary, I will protect her even if she sends me away.'

'How do I know you're to be trusted?'

'Because I love Belle. I always have. Even though she does not love me in return.' There, he'd said it. He'd admitted what he knew in his heart. But how would Jeannie react to his admission? It was unheard of for men of his quality to fall in love with anyone from the lower classes, although it was common enough for the gentry to use them to meet their desires.

His anxiety grew as he waited for Jeannie's response. Would she divulge where Belle was?

32

Annie narrowed her eyes as she watched Lachlan tie his horse to the fence. Was he here to find out what happened on the night of the fire? She shivered. If he found out the truth, they would be homeless before nightfall. She surveyed the women gathered on the shore. They huddled in groups while casting anxious eyes at Lachlan. She had no worries about them sticking to the story they'd concocted. But what about Ellen? Her actions over the last few days had been unpredictable.

She stiffened when she saw Jeannie approach Lachlan. What did he want with the lass? Did he mean to question her again about what she saw on the night of the fire?

When he bent his head and gripped Jeannie's hand, her anxiety increased. She itched to stride over to him and demand he leave Jeannie alone, but he was the laird's son, and it would do no good to antagonise him.

Maggie West plucked at the edge of her shawl. 'What will we do? Ellen's on her way.'

Annie looked to where Maggie was pointing and said, with more conviction than she felt, 'Leave her to me. I'll talk some sense into her.'

The minister was several paces in front of Ellen, so Annie followed the river's edge. She shivered and pulled her shawl tighter as the icy February wind tugged at its edges and whipped her hair around her face. Sharp stones bit into her feet through the worn soles of her shoes, but she stayed on the foreshore until the minister passed her on the path above. She was sure the minister saw her, but he stared straight ahead and kept walking. He had never been a man to mingle with his congregation except to castigate them for wrongdoing. So perhaps he shared her reluctance for a confrontation.

She stood for a moment, staring after his flapping black robes, before clambering up the grassy bank to confront Ellen.

'What d'you want, Annie?' Ellen's scowl deepened and her pace didn't falter.

'Will ye stop for a minute?' Annie grabbed her arm. 'We need to talk.'

'What about?'

'What d'ye think? The fire, of course. If the laird finds out the women were involved and you were the one to incite them, then I fear for what will happen.'

Ellen turned to face her. 'It wasn't our fault. It was the fault of Belle and Madge, and I'll make sure the laird gets to know.'

Annie's voice lowered into a sibilant hiss. 'You and I know I have no great love for Belle, but she was my Jimmie's wife and the mother of his bairns. I'll not see her hang for something she didn't do. So, take care what you say lest you be the one to meet the hangman's noose.'

Ellen prised Annie's fingers from her wrist and glared at her. 'Belle may have been Jimmie's wife, but she's a harlot and deserves to be hanged. Besides, I'm in no danger. The women will back me up.'

'Don't be too sure of that. For if they back you up and are found to be lying, they'll hang too. And fine they know it. I've made sure of that.'

Annie turned away from Ellen and stared out at the river. The boats were near the shore now. Once they anchored, there would be no more time left to remonstrate with Ellen. She'd done her best; she could do no more. The fate of the village was in her guid-daughter's hands.

With a sigh, she turned to face her. 'You do what ye have to do. But be mindful, it will affect everyone in the village.'

Ellen's eyes were on the boats, and she made no response.

Her voice softer now, Annie said, 'I know you wanted Jimmie for yourself, and nothing would have given me greater pleasure if you had been his choice. But it was not to be. Belle took him from you and none of us approved of that. She was Jimmie's choice, though, and he loved her. There's no changing that.' Her eyes filled with tears at the memory of Jimmie, her eldest son. She blinked them away. 'When you wed my Ian, I was happy for you both, even though he wasn't your first choice. He's a good man, my Ian, and I thought he'd chosen a good wife.' Her voice faltered and her next words were barely audible. 'But now,' she paused, 'all I can say is I am disappointed in you, Ellen. I expected better of you.'

With that final remark, she strode away to join the other women to await the questioning that would decide their fate.

Ellen blinked tears from her eyes.

'I am disappointed in you. I expected better of you.'

The words lingered on after Annie left her. They stung more than anything said by Ian, her father, or even the minister whose words had only increased her determination to follow the path she'd chosen. The path that would lead to Belle's destruction. But Annie's words brought shame.

A chill wind blew around her, tugging at the ends of her shawl, but she didn't feel it. Nor did she hear the ripple of the waves and the clanking of anchors being dropped. Her feet were like lead, rooted to the ground, while her eyes fastened on the women on the foreshore. She watched as Annie joined them and saw several heads turn to stare in her direction. The minister, his black robes swirling around him, strode towards the Laird's son, who stood with his horse on the embankment above.

Her resolve wavered. She wanted to condemn Belle. But could she still do it? Annie's approval meant a lot to Ellen and to think her guid-mother was now disappointed in her was like a dagger in her heart.

She forced herself to walk towards the foreshore, where the women clustered around Annie. Heads turned as she approached, and several women moved further away, giving the impression her presence was unwanted. Their faces were grim and their eyes accusing. Ellen had never felt more alone. She found it difficult to believe these were the same women who had marched with her, carried their flaming torches, shouted her name and hailed her as their saviour. The realisation struck that if she carried out her plan, they would turn against her, and perhaps they already had.

Hatred of Belle burned in her mind and her body, and the thought of the harlot being hanged brought her satisfaction. But was the price worth it? Loss of her husband and her father was a great price to pay. But even worse was the disappointment expressed by Annie and the shame it brought to her.

The conflict raged in her mind as she drew nearer. Even Ellen did not know what she would do.

33

Maggie hurried over to Annie when she returned to the foreshore. 'Will Ellen hold her tongue?'

'I hope so. But you can do your bit by showing you don't support her.'

'Aye, I'll let the rest of them know.'

Annie watched her as she muttered to various women, wondering if their displeasure would be enough to convince Ellen to keep silent.

Jeannie stood near the water's edge, and Annie's curiosity rekindled. She walked over to join her daughter.

'What did the young master want?'

'He wanted to know where Belle had gone.'

'Did you tell him?'

'Aye. He would have found out anyway, and I didn't want him to be questioning anyone else, particularly when Ellen was here. It might have sparked something off.'

'Good thinking. I don't suppose it will do any harm.'

Annie glanced towards where Lachlan and the minister were conferring.

'Come on, let's join the others. If they're going to ask us about the fire, it will be easier if we're together.'

Maggie detached herself from the group and grabbed Annie's arm. 'What d'you think they'll ask us?' She nodded to where Murdo and Lachlan stood.

'They'll want to know how the fire started. Don't forget the laird found a burnt-out torch. He's convinced the fire was deliberate. It's up to us to convince him the villagers had nothing to do with it, so tell him what we agreed.'

The women gathered around Annie. 'But he's brought the minister with him.'

All eyes turned towards Murdo and Lachlan.

'Aye, that makes a difference. If we lie to the minister, we'll be damned.'

'And if ye don't, you'll be homeless and driven from the village. Mayhap some of ye might even hang.' Annie's voice was a sibilant whisper so the approaching men couldn't overhear.

A gloomy silence descended on the women.

'Aye, best be damned than meet the hangman's noose.'

Annie wasn't sure where the answering whisper came from, but a murmur of agreement rippled through the group. All that remained now was to hope her warnings to Ellen had been effective, otherwise, they were damned.

Murdo resisted the temptation to turn and remonstrate with the woman following him. What did she want from him? He'd already advised her to curb her tongue. Watch what she was saying. But her obsession with doing God's work and frequent mention of his sermon had bordered on madness, and he couldn't be sure she would comply.

A worrying thought crossed his mind. If she was unhinged, was she a danger to him?

He quickened his stride. The sooner he was with other people, the safer he would be.

Relief flooded through him when he saw the fisherwomen gathered on the foreshore and Lachlan standing on the bank above. He increased his pace because, despite his dislike of the young master, he didn't want to encourage his displeasure.

Lachlan turned to greet him, but his eyes lacked warmth. Murdo didn't care. He had no respect for the young whippersnapper; it was his father he had to impress. Sir Roderick was hale and hearty, so he gave little thought to Lachlan becoming the laird. It was of no consequence, although he ensured Lachlan never suspected his feelings towards him. There was no point in antagonising him.

'At last,' Lachlan said. 'You have kept me waiting.'

'My apologies.' Murdo gritted his teeth. 'The cliff path was treacherous, and I had to come by the road. It is longer that way and takes more time.'

'We have no time to lose. You must question the women while they are together on the foreshore. It will be easier than going from house to house.'

Murdo narrowed his eyes. 'I had thought you would prefer to question them.'

Lachlan glared at him. 'You may keep your thoughts to yourself. I have decided the villagers will respond more freely to you than they will to me. So, you ask the questions, and I will listen. As their minister, they will be obliged to speak the truth.'

Lachlan waited for Murdo to pass him.

'Make sure you find out whether the fire was set deliberately and, if so, the person responsible. My father will also want to know about the discarded torch.'

While they'd been talking, the small groups of women had merged into one larger group, and Murdo sensed their eyes on him as he walked towards them. He had never been at ease with the fisherfolk, finding them more intimidating than their farmer counterparts. During the Sabbath, as they gathered in front of the church, they never looked at him or the church. Instead, their eyes stared towards the horizon. It made him wonder if they worshipped the sea more than God.

Murdo's step faltered.

A vision of the fire arose in his mind. He'd seen everything from his vantage point in the alley bordering the square. The women brandishing their torches led by the madwoman who had accosted him on the river road. The image of her spurring them on with a crazed look in her eyes sent shivers through him.

It would be easy for him to condemn them. He only had to say the word.

But another memory intruded. That of James Watt and his veiled threats about Murdo's sermon and its effect on the villagers. But even worse, the man's premonition that when the laird banished the villagers, Murdo would lose his congregation. Finding another parish would be difficult at his time of life.

'What are you waiting for?' Lachlan's voice interrupted his thoughts. 'The first of the boats are dropping their anchors, and you'll miss the chance to question the women before the men arrive.'

A gust of wind swirled Murdo's cloak around his legs. His mouth was so dry he had difficulty speaking. Raising his voice, he said, 'I have come on behalf of the laird to ask you about the fire.'

'Aye, we thought that was what ye wanted.'

The fisherwoman who stepped forward stared into his face with a disconcerting boldness. Murdo didn't know many of their names, but he knew this one. She was Annie Watt, the wife of James, who had threatened him with the loss of his parish.

'But there's nought to tell. We were asleep when it happened. Isn't that right?' Annie looked around at the other women.

Nods of agreement and a rumble of voices confirmed her statement. Looking around the group to reassure himself there were no troublemakers, his heart jumped when he saw the madwoman who had accosted him. Would she be the voice who challenged the others? As he stared at Ellen, several women encircled her to imprison her in their midst.

'A burnt-out torch was found beside the remains of the inn. This suggests the fire was a deliberate action. The laird demands to know the identity of the person responsible.'

'Why would someone in the village start the fire? At least we knew where our menfolk were when we had an inn. Now they go to Invercraig and none of us know what they get up to there.' Annie's strident voice rang out, accompanied by a rumble of agreement from the other women.

Murdo would have drawn the questioning to a halt but with Lachlan at his back he felt compelled to continue.

'There is the matter of the torch, and if you protect the person responsible, the laird will be displeased, and you will incur God's wrath for lying.'

Annie laughed. 'We often use torches when we have a celebration. This one was likely left over from the Auld Yule celebrations welcoming in the start of the new year. Ye cannae say that because ye found a torch, someone must have set the inn alight. What good would that have done us? And as God is my witness, that is the truth of the matter.'

34

On his return from Craigden, Lachlan found his father poring over ledgers in his study.

He never understood why his father needed to do this when he employed a factor. However, Sir Roderick monitored everything to do with the estate and even his family. He made the decisions, expecting everyone to obey. It had even extended to choosing Lachlan's bride and what a mess that had turned out to be.

Given the choice, Lachlan would have preferred to avoid his father but knew that would inflame him.

Sir Roderick narrowed his eyes. 'Well, what news do you bring me?'

Lachlan quailed.

'The rebuild of the inn at Craigden is in hand. The mason has received instructions, and McPhee will be ready to discuss the costs with you by tomorrow.'

Sir Roderick grunted. 'I don't suppose it crossed your mind to bring them with you?'

'McPhee said he needs to get everything on paper before it will be ready for your inspection.'

'Learn to be more forceful. You'll never be able to run this estate if you let the workers dictate to you.'

'Yes, sir.'

'The fire. What about that? Have you found out who was responsible?'

'As you instructed, I have questioned the villagers.'

'Did you take Murdo with you?'

'Yes, sir.'

'So, what did you find out?'

'No information came to light to suggest it was anything other than an accident?'

Sir Roderick snorted. 'Accident? What about the torch we found beside the burnt-out building?'

'I have questioned the villagers, and they believe it was a torch used during the Auld Yule celebrations when they had a torchlight parade to celebrate the coming of the new year.'

'Fine story.' Roderick glared at him. 'What about the innkeepers? Wasn't there a suggestion they might have been involved?'

'I believe that rumour was started by a woman who disliked the two women who ran the inn. There appeared to be an element of jealousy towards the innkeepers among the village women. However, I fail to see how the innkeepers benefited from a fire which left them homeless and destitute.'

'This jealousy you mention. Is it possible the villagers set the fire?'

'I thought about that, but the fire has left Craigden without a tavern. The men have to travel to Invercraig to slake their thirst, which displeases the women. They prefer the men to do their drinking nearer home. No one has benefited from the destruction of the inn, which convinces me it was accidental.'

'I see. This information about the torch. Are you satisfied with it?'

'It seems the only explanation.'

'And does Murdo agree with you?'

'Yes, sir.'

'What about the innkeepers? Have you questioned them?'

'Not so far. There has been no opportunity because they have left the village.'

'Then you must find them and find out what they know about this unfortunate incident.'

'One of the village women informed me they sought refuge at the Ship Inn. I intend to visit the inn tonight and seek them out.'

Sir Roderick stared into space, pursed his lips and frowned while he mulled over the information.

Time stood still while Lachlan waited for his father's response. Would he accept the explanation about the torch? Or would his doubts remain? The villagers' explanations hadn't convinced Lachlan, but he abhorred his father's need for revenge on the instigators of the fire, whether that be Belle and Madge, or the village women.

His father turned his gaze on Lachlan. 'Most unsatisfactory business,' he said. 'After you've talked to the innkeepers, I'll have to talk to Murdo and think on it before I decide what to do.'

He flicked a hand at his son, dismissing him.

Lachlan left the room seething.

Why did his father have to discuss this with Murdo instead of accepting his son's word? Wasn't his word good enough? But one thing he was certain about was that he had no intention of taking Murdo with him when he went to find Belle and Madge.

Raven's hooves clattered on the wooden spars of the bridge as he galloped towards the town. At the river's mouth, the lighthouse's rotating light flickered, illuminating the masts of several ships against the night sky. But Lachlan paid no heed as he urged his horse onwards.

He pulled on the reins, bringing Raven to a stop at the Ship Inn. Oil lamps flickered in the windows and the sign over the door creaked in the wind. He shivered. His last visit had unnerved him and, remembering the landlord's hostility, he didn't relish making his acquaintance again.

Raven snorted and pawed the ground, sensing his master's hesitation.

'Easy,' Lachlan said, patting his horse's neck.

Despite his reservations, he forced himself to dismount. To find Belle, he would have to go inside. But not wanting to leave his horse to the tender mercies of revellers, he rounded the building and led Raven up the street to look for the back entrance.

Light filtered onto the street through the inn's side windows, allowing him to see a wooden gate which opened onto a backyard. Lifting the latch, he led Raven through the gate. The darkness of the yard, only relieved by the pale light of the moon, cast shadows over everything and it took a moment for Lachlan's eyes to adjust. A faucet with a drain below sat to one side of a back door, which Lachlan thought led into the inn. Outhouses and a stable lined the back wall, and to his right, an upended cart sat with its spars sticking upwards. A rustle of movement suggested the stable was occupied, so he looped Raven's reins around one of the cart's spars.

Making sure the gate behind him was closed, he walked across the yard to the rear door. It was unlocked, so he slipped through into a corridor with a door inset at one side, a stair leading upwards at the other and in front of him another door which he guessed led into the taproom.

Laughter, voices, the clinking of mugs and glasses, and the smell of ale mingled with smoke and unwashed bodies met him when he opened this door. Covering his nose and mouth with a silk handkerchief to blot out the stench, he surveyed the room.

A loud voice drew his attention to where a drinker was scowling up at Madge.

'I wanted to drink that,' he growled at her. 'Not bath in it.'

'You shouldn't have knocked my arm, then,' she retorted and slapped the mug down on the table. 'And you'd best mind your manners, or I'll have Gregor throw you out.'

'Aw, give over,' his mate said. 'It's time you had a bath.'

'I had one at Auld Yule,' the man grumbled.

'Aye, well, ye don't want to annoy Madge, else there'll be nae mair drink for you the night.'

A movement drew his attention, and his spirits lifted when he saw Belle emerge from the centre of the crowd.

She tossed her hair, flicked her skirts and flirted with her eyes, and the men responded by pushing others aside to let her pass.

The door at his back swished shut as he stepped further into the room to approach Belle. But a group of sailors blocked his way.

By the time he pushed past them, Belle was at the bar replenishing a mug with ale from a massive jug.

He reached out a hand to twine her curls in his fingers as he used to do, but at the last minute drew back. She'd rebuffed him so many times he didn't want to jeopardise his chances with her now.

'Belle,' he said. He had wanted to sound strong and forceful. A man Belle would respect and desire. But, instead, it came out in a choking whisper as his heart thumped in his chest.

146

35

Ellen ignored everything around her as she paced back and forth. Dirty plates left after the fish she'd cooked for Ian and her da littered the table. A sweeping brush lay neglected in the corner and the floor remained unswept. The fire in the grate smouldered but made no impact on her as the rage built in her mind.

Early evening darkness cloaked the village and the river, but Ian and her da were still outside washing out the boat. She glared out the window at their shadowy figures. Neither of them cared for her. That had been obvious when Ian placed a hand on her arm and admonished her with his eyes when she wanted to condemn Belle to the minister and Lachlan.

At the time, words of condemnation had seared her brain and trembled on her lips. So, why had she not given voice to them? Was it because of Ian's restraining hand? The sternness of the minister questioning her? The women's rejection? Or Annie's disappointment in her? Or was it the antagonism she saw in Lachlan's eyes? It was as if he guessed she wanted to malign Belle. And she knew exactly why he wouldn't want her to do that. She hadn't been blind when she saw him creeping into Belle's home all those years ago. It didn't take much brainpower to guess what they'd been up to.

She kicked a chair and sent it flying across the room. Bloody Belle. All Ian cared about was that harlot.

The sound of voices approaching the house compelled her to suppress her rage. It wouldn't do for Ian and her da to witness the depth of her hatred for Belle. She didn't want them to stop her from acting on her new plan. Maybe she'd failed to have Belle hanged, but there were other ways to rid the world of the harlot.

She forced a smile when Ian stepped over the threshold, but his eyes focused on the room's disarray, and he did not respond.

'I need to be away to talk to my ma.' His voice was gentle, but the troubled look on his face showed his concern.

Ellen bit her lip to prevent a torrent of anger from spewing out. Her previous outburst had done so much damage, and she couldn't afford to alienate him further. But neither could she allow him to leave her for Belle. If she wanted to keep him, she had to convince him her animosity towards Belle was gone.

'When will you return?' Her attempt to keep the abrasiveness out of her voice wasn't successful, and it had a sharp edge.

'I don't know.'

Ellen's shoulders slumped as she watched him stride along the village road. At least he was heading towards Annie's house, not to Invercraig, where Belle was ensconced. It didn't mean he wouldn't go there later, though.

The rage built again, and her face contorted.

'Are ye all right, lass?'

She'd forgotten her father was there and struggled to compose herself.

'Yes, but I'm disappointed Ian has gone to Annie when I wanted him here.'

'Ye cannae blame him after what ye said to him yesterday when he left for Invercraig with Jeannie.'

Ellen looked away from him. 'I was angry because he was going after Belle. I thought he was leaving me.'

'Aye, ye were angry. It was frightening to see. Ye were like a spitting cat. But he wisnae leaving you. He was checking to see if Belle and the bairns were all right after the fire. It was his ma sent him.'

'I know that now.' Ellen kept the doubt out of her voice. She mustn't let her father know her anger burned as bright as ever.

'I'm off to my bed, lass. It's been a busy day and if the weather stays fine, mayhap we'll take the boats out again tomorrow.'

Ellen stared at the door after it clicked shut. Not every house in the village was a but and ben. Many of them only had a single room and a net loft. But they were lucky. It meant she and Ian had the cosy box bed in the but room, which served as the kitchen and living area. The ben room where her father slept was smaller, with only enough space for his bed. But the box bed with its rumpled blankets lay empty, and she wasn't sure whether Ian would join her there ever again.

She waited until it became quiet, and the creak of the bedsprings signalled her father was in bed before she grabbed the gutting knife from the sink and sneaked out of the house.

Tonight, she'd put her plan into action. Belle would pay for everything she'd done.

Ian did not relax until he stood before his mother's house. Ellen's actions preyed on his mind, and he no longer felt comfortable in her presence. Her obsession and hatred of Belle had warped her to the extent he could no longer tolerate her mood swings.

Leaving her tonight was wrong. He was her husband. But the moment he'd stepped into the house, the tension inside swamped him, and he'd felt unable to stay.

Aware he'd spent several minutes staring at his mother's front door, he gave himself a shake, placed his hand on the knob and pushed the door open. The warmth meeting him had nothing to do with the fire in the grate. Contentment oozed from every one of the family, and Ian felt more at home than he'd done for a long time.

His da waved his pipe at Ian in a welcoming gesture. 'Come awa in, laddie. Ye look cauld.'

Annie, who was washing plates, looked up. 'Aye and close the door to keep the draught out.'

'I'm heading into the town soon with Angus to grab a pint. Want to come with us?' Davie was his youngest brother and a bit of a rogue with an eye for the girls.

'No, I'd best not. It'll only cause more trouble.'

'Trouble? What kind of trouble would that be then? Is Ellen giving you a hard time?'

'Come on, Davie. Let's leave Ian to talk with Ma.' Angus grabbed his jacket. He was quieter and more thoughtful than Davie.

Ian nodded his appreciation. He reckoned Angus had guessed something was up. He was a lot more observant than his younger brother.

Davie jumped up and headed for the door. 'Aye. Ye're right. The drink is going to waste while we sit here.'

'Ow,' Jeannie complained, 'you stood on my toe.'

'I didnae mean it.' Davie rumpled her hair.

Jeannie glared at him. 'You're a big careless lump.'

After the two brothers left, Annie turned to Ian. 'What's up, lad? Is it Ellen?'

'Aye. I'm at my wit's end to know what to do. It's like the devil has taken her over.' Ian slumped on a stool and leaned his elbows on the table.

'Was it Ellen did that?' Annie nodded to the inflamed scratch on his cheek.

He raised his hand and stroked it.

'Aye, it was when I went to Invercraig yesterday with Jeannie. Ellen flew into a rage. She's got it into her head I've been carrying on with Belle.'

'And have you?'

'Of course not. She was Jimmie's wife, and I'd not betray him.' He lapsed into a miserable silence.

James tapped his pipe on the fender. 'What d'ye plan to do?'

'I don't know.' Ian raised despairing eyes to his da.

Annie patted his hand. 'You know you have to go back to her.'

'Aye. I wed her for better or worse.' He blinked. 'But I didn't know it would come to this and I cannae bear to face her tonight.' He paused. 'I'll go back in the morning when it's daylight.'

Expressions of concern and doubt flitted over his mother's face. 'I suppose that will have to do,' she said. 'You'd best sleep in the net loft with Angus and Davie. I widnae want ye to sleep in the boat again.'

Relief swept over him, as well as confusion. How did she know he'd slept in the boat last night? But not much slipped by his ma, so he supposed it shouldn't be surprising.

Ellen's agitation increased the nearer she got to Invercraig. By now, the thoughts swirling in her mind convinced her Ian would be laughing and flirting with Belle. She imagined his arm around the harlot as he pulled her to him. Angry thoughts pounded through her brain, inflaming her with rage, and increasing her desire to punish Belle.

'The harlot will pay for her sins,' she screamed into the air as she left the bridge and turned onto the road leading to the Ship Inn.

The tide was on the turn and waves battered the harbour wall as it rushed out to sea. Spray spattered over Ellen, but she was too far gone to notice. Curses spewed from her mouth. Words she wasn't even aware she knew. Words only the coarsest of men used.

A group of sailors standing outside a tenement building nodded in her direction and sniggered. Ellen strode past them without a glance, oblivious to their crude comments and laughter. Sensing sport, the sailors followed her, although they were careful not to draw too near. If they meant to waylay her in the more isolated parts of the harbour area, then those hopes were dashed when she stopped in front of the Ship Inn.

Breathing heavily after her exertions, she stood in front of it, deliberating, unsure of what to do next. Her hand tightened on the gutting knife, anticipating the moment she sank it into Belle's flesh. But Belle was inside the Ship Inn and Ellen had never been inside a tavern. There was a name for women who frequented such places, and Ellen was not one of them.

Oil lamps flickered in the tavern's windows, casting shadows on the road outside. Ellen merged with the shadows and stared.

One sailor, bolder than his companions, sidled up to her.

'You looking for company, love?'

Ellen spun around. 'I'm not your love,' she hissed.

'Don't be like that,' he said. He cast a glance at his friends. Having come this far, he couldn't back off. That would be cowardly.

Her hand tightened on the knife.

Her aim was swift and sure, but the blade only skiffed his shoulder as he ducked out of the way.

'Bitch,' he said as he stumbled to his knees. 'I'll get you for that.'

Ellen leaned over him. 'Touch me and I'll gut you like a fish.' Her eyes glittered with madness, and her lips twisted, distorting her face.

'It's not worth it,' one of his mates shouted. 'She's mad. Besides, I know a house where the women are more welcoming than this one.'

He scrabbled backwards, away from her, glad of the excuse to return to his mates.

They helped him up and, turning away from Ellen, hurried back the way they had come.

Alone in the darkness, the flicker of the inn's oil lamps drew her towards the door. The voices and laughter inside grew louder and the thought of Ian with Belle tormented her.

She pushed the door open. The scene meeting her eyes resembled what Ellen thought bedlam must be like. Sailors, dockers, and work-men crowded every part of the room, standing in groups or sprawled at tables clutching their tankards and mugs. Unidentified smells mingling with the stink of smoke and beer filled the air, making her gag. A brute of a man stood behind the bar watching everything going on. Madge was close by, depositing tankards of ale in front of sailors sporting navy blue berets.

Sound hammered into her ears, making her head spin. Voices shouted over the din to make themselves heard, many of them speaking in foreign tongues, while raucous laughter rippled around the room, adding to the cacophony of noise.

Faced with this image of Hell, her courage seeped away, leaving her limp and wishing she were anywhere else but here. Paralysed with fear, she stood with her back pressed against the door. But the sight of Belle wending her way through tables close to the fire roused her out of her lethargy. She'd make the bitch pay, even if it meant venturing into this den of iniquity.

36

A cold draught of air swept through the room when the door opened. Old Tam shivered and drew nearer to the fire. The old man's frailty was even more obvious tonight, and Belle worried he might be ailing.

She filled a mug with ale. It would fortify the old man before he left for home, a dilapidated shack beyond the town's bleaching fields in a gorse-filled area of the links. A place where the wind from the North Sea whipped across the dunes and through every crack of Tam's home.

'Belle.' Lachlan's voice whispered in her ear.

'I'm busy,' she said.

'Sit with me. I need to talk with you.' His voice was insistent.

'I have no desire to talk to you, sir.'

He grasped her arm. Ale slopped from the mug onto the bar counter.

'Release me,' she snapped. 'I have work to do. A customer is waiting for his ale.'

Gregor, who had been tending to a cask behind the bar, stood up. 'Problem?'

'Nothing I can't handle.' She turned back to Lachlan. 'Gregor will serve you with your drink, sir. As you can see, I'm otherwise engaged.'

Gregor stood with narrowed eyes, studying the man. Belle smiled to herself. She knew Gregor was wondering how to separate this toff from his money. It served Lachlan right. He should never have come here.

She turned away from him to push past the mass of drinkers taking up every available space. The grasping hands of rowdy sailors reached for her, but she had grown accustomed to dodging them, as well as

153

ignoring their lewd comments. Reaching the table where Tam sat nursing the dregs of his ale, she sat on the bench beside him.

'I've brought you a mug of ale to sup before you go home. It's cold out there and it'll warm you up.'

Tam looked at the mug with greedy eyes. 'But I cannae afford another one. I've got nae coins left.'

'It's on me.' Belle patted his bony hand. 'Don't tell Gregor.'

He put a finger to his lips. 'Not a word,' he said, 'but I'd best get it down me before closing time.'

Belle looked up at the clock fastened to the wall above the fireplace. 'Ten minutes to go,' she said. 'I'll be glad to get finished tonight and see the back of that lot.'

She nodded towards a noisy group of sailors clustered around a woman. 'Damned Frenchies can't keep their hands to themselves.'

'Aye, I don't think that lass expected them to grab her.' He gulped a mouthful from the mug and wiped his lips.

'If she's a doxy, she'll be able to hold her own.'

'Not seen her here before, but she didn't look like one of them.'

Belle shrugged. She was too tired to intervene. But as she turned away, she glimpsed the woman. Shocked, she scrambled to her feet. What was Ellen doing here? And where was Ian?

Before she had moved a few steps, Ellen turned on the men.

'Touch me again and I'll gut you,' she hissed.

The largest sailor laughed and made a grab for the knife, but Ellen was quicker and with a slash, she slit his cheek.

'The next time I'll aim for your throat.' Ellen waved the knife at him.

'Merde!' He stared at her in disbelief as he backed away.

Blood dripped from his cheek, staining his tunic. He pressed the cut with his hand, but blood oozed between his fingers.

A faraway voice shouted for someone to fetch the watchman.

Across the room, Belle noticed Gregor leave the bar to push past the drinkers clustered in front of it. But she doubted he would get to Ellen in time to prevent her from doing further damage.

Cautiously she approached her. 'Ellen,' she said. 'You're safe. He won't touch you again.' She drew nearer. 'Give me the knife. You don't need it now.'

Ellen laughed. It resonated in the room, which had become much quieter. She held the knife aloft. 'This is the Lord's instrument. He has commanded I use it in His name,' she said. 'No one can harm me.'

The mutterings in the room grew louder and someone sniggered.

A movement drew Belle's attention to the French sailor creeping up behind Ellen. He reached for her arm with one hand while attempting to grasp the knife with the other.

Ellen whirled to face him, slashing his wrist to wrench her arm free. Blood dripped onto his hand and down his fingers. He grasped his wrist, trying to stem the flow of blood, quickly retreating when Ellen brandished the knife in his face.

'Bloody hell,' someone said.

Several other voices blotted out the moans of the injured men. Exhortations to take the knife from the mad bitch circulated, but no one else attempted to approach Ellen. She stood in her circle of space, glaring at everyone and swinging the knife around her body in a spiral of threatening strokes.

Worry combined with fear rushed through Belle, leaving her shaking. But she knew Ellen had to be stopped before she killed someone or hurt herself and if no one else was prepared to do it, then it would have to be her. Ellen was family, after all.

Lachlan sat on the end of a bench at a table close to the bar, nursing a tankard of ale and brooding about Belle's rejection of him.

He observed Gregor watching him, and it made him uncomfortable. Why this should be, he didn't know. The man had been attentive and obsequious. He'd pressured the previous occupant of the bench to remove himself and supplied Lachlan with a fine French brandy. He couldn't fault the man, but he didn't trust him and sensed his hostility.

Maybe it was because he'd been paying attention to Belle. It had been obvious Gregor hadn't liked that. Was it simply protection for an employee? Or was there something between them?

A disturbance caused him to look up. Fights were common in dockside taverns, but once they started, the trouble had a habit of spreading and within the blink of an eye, the place could become a heaving mass of battling bodies. Perhaps he should leave now before the fight escalated.

It was only after he stood, he realised the cause of the disturbance was a woman wielding a knife.

Voices resounded around the room, but her voice rang out over them. 'Touch me again and I'll gut you.'

Laughter greeted her statement, but it stopped when the blade flashed. The sailor muttered a curse and backed away from her, blood dripping from his cheek and running down his chin and neck.

No one else made a move. If it had been a man, a riot would have broken out, but it was a woman and despite the roughness of the area, men were hesitant to interfere.

As Lachlan watched, he saw Belle approach the woman. What was she thinking? The woman had a knife and had already used it. Besides, he'd recognised her. She was the madwoman he'd seen outside his home earlier in the day and then later at Invercraig. Belle wasn't safe.

His heart lurched. What if the woman used the knife on Belle? What if she carved her in the same way she'd done the sailor? It didn't bear thinking about.

'Drop the knife, Ellen.' Belle kept her voice low and non-threatening.

'You want it?' Ellen lowered her voice into a sibilant hiss. 'Then come and get it.'

Belle hesitated, alarmed by the glitter of madness in Ellen's eyes. Despite this, she knew she had to persuade her to hand over the knife.

Taking a deep breath, she took another few steps forward. 'Ellen, you need to give me the knife before you do any more damage.'

A hand grasped Belle's arm as she sidled closer to Ellen. 'Stay back, lass. I don't like the way she's looking at you.'

Belle turned in surprise. She hadn't been aware Tam had followed her. His wizened frame leaned towards her, and he pulled her back a few paces.

She patted his hand. 'It's all right, Tam. Go back to your seat. I know Ellen. She'll not harm me.'

'I widnae be too sure of that,' Tam said, but he released her arm and staggered back to the table.

'That's right, isn't it, Ellen? You won't harm me, and you'll give me the knife.'

Ellen kept her eyes fixed on Belle as she waved the knife to keep everyone away from her.

The drinkers pushed backwards away from Ellen, forming an impenetrable barrier between the two women and Gregor, who was trying to reach them. Lachlan was somewhere at the back of the room, although Belle couldn't see him. There would be no help from either of them.

Belle's heart thumped. She had to get the knife away from Ellen. The state the woman was in, she was liable to kill someone.

A flurry of cold air rippled around the room when a few men closest to the door slipped out, into the night. For the briefest moment, Belle wanted to follow them. But she held her ground, staring into Ellen's crazed eyes. What she saw in them was hatred mingled with madness.

'Let me take you home to Ian,' she murmured in a soothing voice, hoping to calm Ellen.

'Aye, fine you'd like that,' she grated. 'You think I don't know about you and Ian? First you took Jimmie from me, and now Ian. How many of our men will you tempt and seduce before you're satisfied? We know all about you. Harlot! Jezebel! Whore!' She stopped for breath. 'The knife is the Lord's instrument. You want it? I'll be happy to give it to you.'

Ellen raised the knife and lunged towards Belle.

The knife missed by a whisker as Belle twisted to the side, but Ellen wasn't about to be deterred and raised it again.

Fear rippled through Belle, and she jumped to the side as the knife whistled down again. Did Ellen mean to kill her?

'Ellen, you're not thinking straight. Ian is your man, not mine. He has never been mine.'

'Liar.' Rage suffused Ellen's face, making her appear more animal than human.

In desperation, Belle said, 'You mustn't do this. The Lord wouldn't want you to use his instrument in this way. Think of your immortal soul.'

Ellen's laugh sent chills rippling through Belle.

'It is the Lord's work I am doing. This knife has your name on it and the Lord will rejoice when I send you to Hell.'

Belle's mind whirled. Reared by her uncle, a minister of the church, her childhood had not been a happy one. But she recalled her uncle performing an exorcism on a woman afflicted by religious mania. Was this what Ellen was suffering from? She didn't know, but it was clear Ellen believed she was doing God's work.

Belle forced a laugh. 'Your knife is unclean. If you use it to do the Lord's work, you will accompany me to Hell.'

'You lie.'

'Look at it. It drips with the blood of men. Godly men from France.' Belle drew breath. 'If you use it on me, you will mix innocent blood with mine. That will not please God and He will punish you.'

Ellen's eyes turned to the knife.

Belle held her breath. Would her ploy convince Ellen? Or would she turn the knife on Belle yet again? She would never know because at that moment, Old Tam threw the remains of his ale into Ellen's face and then whacked her over the wrist with the empty mug. It sent the knife clattering to the floor.

'Don't think any of your fancy men will save you,' Ellen snarled, pushing the old man aside to get at Belle.

Belle backed away but lost her balance as Ellen's body collided with hers. Strong fingers gripped her throat and the last thing she heard before she lost consciousness was Ellen telling her she was on her way to Hell.

37

Lachlan tried to push through the mass of bodies to reach Belle but realised that would take too long. So, he turned and ran out the rear door into the yard at the back of the inn, down the street at the side and through the front door.

Three men coming out bumped into him.

'You don't want to go in there, mate. There's a madwoman running amok with a knife.' Taking to their heels, they headed for the ships in the harbour.

His breath came in gasps, and his heart thumped. He was too late. Belle lay on the floor with the woman straddling her. He ran towards them, expecting to see blood. Instead, the woman had her hands wrapped around Belle's throat. Was she dead or alive? He feared the worst.

With a howl of rage, he launched himself at the woman, tearing her away from Belle.

The woman screamed and lashed out with her fingernails, scraping them down Lachlan's cheek. His grip loosened, and the woman squirmed free.

But Lachlan's attack had broken the spell, and the men surged forward.

Ellen's eyes narrowed.

Lachlan, seeing his chance, lunged towards her. But instead of dodging out of his way as he expected, she raised her arm, clenched her fist and drove it into Lachlan's middle. He gasped and doubled over. The damned woman was as strong as any man. Before he caught

159

his breath, she'd whirled around to run for the door. Barging through it, she vanished into the night.

Lachlan, too concerned about Belle to give chase, turned back in time to see Madge flop down beside her.

He hurried to her side to help her revive Belle, but Gregor got there before him.

Annoyance rippled through him. The damned man had his hands on Belle. His Belle. He had no right.

Out of breath by the time he'd struggled through the men crowding the front of the taproom, Gregor was pleased to see Madge already at Belle's side.

He knelt beside her and whispered in her ear, 'I want you to get the pouch Belle wears around her waist.'

'Why?'

'Just get it,' he rasped. He looked around and spotted the gutting knife lying on the floor. He reached for it. 'Use this to cut the strap holding it around her waist.'

He bent over Belle. At least she was still breathing.

'Get the pouch before she comes to,' he muttered to Madge. 'She'll never know who took it.'

He grasped Belle's hand. He wanted that pouch, but he also wanted Belle and he'd been wondering how he would get it without her knowing. That problem was now solved.

'Remove your hands from her at once, you brute.' The loud demand drowned out the other voices in the room.

Gregor looked up. It was the damned toff who'd spoken to Belle earlier. Who the hell did he think he was, giving orders in Gregor's inn? The bugger should get back to where he belonged among his own kind.

'Make sure you get that pouch,' he whispered to Madge before rising to face the man.

'And who are you to demand I should not attend to my employee?' He glared at Lachlan and bunched his fists preparing for a fight.

The man smiled with amusement, although Gregor thought he detected a flicker of fear in his eyes.

'I am Lachlan Craigallan,' he said, 'an old friend of Belles and I'll not see her taken advantage of and have her virtue tarnished by any man.'

Gregor bristled. 'I have no intention of taking advantage, as you call it. On the contrary, I am concerned about my employee. I wanted to check her injuries.'

A gust of air wafted around the room as the street door slammed open. A large man stood on the threshold. The brass buttons on his black jacket glinted as he raised his lantern to survey the room.

Silence descended. It was a brave man, or maybe a foolish one, who pitted himself against the watchman. No one had a wish to be marched off to the Tolbooth.

The man's gaze settled on Belle and then on Gregor. 'I was sent for. What happened here?'

Gregor flinched. He was accustomed to being the one in charge and was unused to being diminished in this way. But the watchman's authoritative tone demanded submission.

'A madwoman assaulted my barmaid,' he said, resisting the urge to call the man, sir.

'Murder, is it?' the watchman tapped his heavy wooden baton against his leg as he stared down at Belle.

'She is breathing,' Madge said. She was crouched beside Belle but stood up when Belle moaned and stirred.

'Where is this madwoman now?'

'She ran off before you arrived,' Lachlan said.

'And you are, sir?'

'I am Lachlan Craigallan. My father is Sir Roderick Craigallan.' He paused as if expecting to see recognition in the watchman's eyes. When they remained inscrutable, he added, 'The laird.'

Gregor turned to Madge while the watchman's attention was on Lachlan. He raised his eyebrows in a mute question. Madge nodded and pressed the pouch into his hand. Gregor stuffed it inside his shirt. He would examine it later.

Belle moaned again, and her eyes fluttered.

Dropping to his knees, Gregor grasped her hand. 'Are you all right?' His heart thumped in his chest. 'Are you hurt?' That was a stupid question. Of course, she was hurt.

'My throat is sore.' Belle raised a hand to her throat and traced a finger over it, wincing as she did so.

'That woman tried to strangle you.'

'Ellen! Why would she do that?'

'For the same reason she set fire to the Craigden Inn,' Madge said. 'She wants you dead, Belle.'

A puzzled look crossed Belle's face. 'Help me up. I need to speak to her.'

Gregor, ignoring Lachlan's scowl, put an arm around her and helped her to stand. Then guided her to a bench beside the fire.

She looked around. 'Where is Ellen?'

'She's gone. You don't have to worry about her now.'

'Someone should tell Ian.'

'Yes, yes. All in good time,' Gregor said. 'But first we need to make sure you are safe, and Ellen does not hurt you again.'

The watchman turned his attention from Lachlan and focused on Belle. 'You know the woman who attacked you?'

'I'm sure she didn't mean it.' Belle winced and touched her throat.

Gregor snorted. 'Face up to it. She tried to kill you.'

'You have to tell him,' Madge said. 'This is the second time she's tried to harm you. First with the fire and now this. Next time she could succeed.'

A tear slipped down Belle's cheek. 'I can't,' she whispered. 'She's family.'

'If you won't, I will.' Madge turned to face the watchman. 'The woman who attacked Belle is Ellen Watt. She's the wife of Ian Watt, Belle's guid-brother.'

'You said this is the second attempt this woman has made on Belle's life.'

'Yes. The first time she set fire to my inn at Craigden. Belle worked for me and lived there. We barely escaped with our lives. And now, this attack.' Madge caught her breath. 'If Lachlan hadn't stopped her, she would have succeeded.'

Belle's eyes widened, and she looked beyond Madge to where Lachlan and Gregor stood.

'Attempted murder and fire-raising. These are hanging offences.' He scowled at Belle, as if blaming her for not providing the information. 'Once we find her, I'll make sure she's locked up in the Tolbooth until she's taken to court and sentenced.'

'No, you mustn't. That will destroy the family.' Belle struggled to her feet and grasped the watchman's sleeve.

He ignored her and turned to Madge. 'Where will I find this woman?'

'She lives in Craigden, but she was in such a state when she left here, I have my doubts whether she will have returned home.'

'I will find her wherever she has gone. There's nothing surer. Now, as there is nothing more for me to do here, I will take my leave.'

Gregor felt the tension decrease as soon as the watchman left. His eyes roamed the room. The injured Frenchmen had left, and the rest of the men had turned back to their drinks, ignoring the group gathered around Belle. The noise of their voices and laughter filled him with disgust. These men were only interested in how much ale they poured down their throats. They showed no concern over what had happened to Belle.

'Time!' he shouted over the din. 'Everyone out. We're closed for business.'

Grumbles and complaints echoed around the room, but ten minutes later the place was empty apart from Lachlan, who stubbornly refused to leave.

Gregor considered forcing him to leave, but it wasn't in his interests to invite the laird's anger by beating up his son.

After he locked the door behind the last straggler, he returned to where Belle was being tended by Madge and Lachlan.

She looked pale and the bruising on her throat had become more prominent.

'You'll stay with Madge tonight,' he said.

'No,' she croaked with an effort. 'I have to get home to the bairns.'

'It's not safe. What if Ellen returns? You might not be so lucky the next time.'

'If I'm not there, she might hurt the bairns. I could never live with myself if she did that.' She placed her hand on top of Gregor's. 'You do see that, don't you?'

Gregor's heart lurched at her touch. 'I will walk you home then, to make sure you are safe.'

'As will I.' Lachlan glared at Gregor.

Madge sighed. 'You two are behaving like bairns,' she said. 'We'll all go, and I will stay with you until morning. If Ellen returns, we'll be prepared.'

Gregor grunted, displeased because he hadn't got rid of Lachlan.

Outside, nothing stirred in the dark street. Lachlan held Belle's arm to support her. Gregor, with a scowl, grabbed the other. Madge walked beside them, smiling to herself.

Both men were reluctant to leave after they helped Belle into her flat, but Madge shooed them away.

Later, in the privacy of his room, Gregor examined the pouch Madge had removed from Belle's waist. He shook the coins out, onto his bed and looked at them in amazement. Where on earth had Belle acquired so much money?

<h1 style="text-align:center">38</h1>

Ellen raced down the road, but she was only halfway to the bridge when she saw the figure of a man come around the corner. His swinging lantern sent pools of light flickering back and forth over the road. She darted into a doorway and huddled into the shadows, pulling her shawl over her face. If the light struck her, he might think she was a pile of rags or a beggar.

As he drew nearer, the tall hat, the brass buttons on his jacket, and the swinging wooden truncheon hanging from his belt made her gasp. He was the night watch.

She shuddered. He wouldn't yet know she had killed Belle, so she was safe for the moment. But for how long? She shivered as she thought of the Tolbooth, a grim building beside the steeple church in the town's centre. Feared by everyone, it held all manner of ruffians. Once you entered the Tolbooth you didn't come out again except to meet the hangman.

She breathed more easily once he passed by, but she waited until he entered the inn before she scuttled along the road and onto the bridge.

Below her, the water churned as the river raced to the sea, sending spray upwards to dampen her skin. The wind, fiercer on the bridge, whipped her hair around her face, but she pulled her shawl tighter and kept her head down. There would be more shelter when she reached the island which lay between Invercraig and Craigden.

The smaller stone bridge over the stream separating Craigden from the island was in sight when she heard the thud of horse's hooves behind her. She darted behind the hedge bordering the track to the island's small graveyard to wait until the traveller passed.

He pulled the horse to a stop on the bridge, and she thought he must have seen her. However, after a few moments, he guided his horse along the road to the village.

She'd recognised him. It was the high and mighty laird's son. Lachlan, his name was. The one who lusted after Belle. She hoped his cheek hurt where she'd raked it with her nails. It was no more than he deserved.

But where was he going? What did he want in the village?

A grim smile twisted her lips. Of course. He was going to break the news to Ian that his beloved Belle was dead. She spat on the ground. It had been a good night's work.

Once Lachlan was out of sight she plodded on, but she didn't take the village road, instead, she followed the road leading to the church where she could spy on the village from the clifftop.

Lachlan pulled the reins, forcing Raven to stop at the intersection. Three roads stretched in front of him: one to his home at Craigallan Castle on the right, another leading to the church and cliffs straight ahead, and a third to the fishing village of Craigden on the left.

Home beckoned, but Belle's last words before he left her at Invercraig rang in his ears. 'You must help Ellen. You cannot let them incarcerate her in the Tolbooth and you must not let her hang.'

'But she tried to kill you,' he'd protested.

'She's family.' Belle's grip tightened on his hand. 'It was nought but a brainstorm. She needs help. Find Ian. Do not let her hang.'

His hands tightened on the reins. No one knew where Ellen went when she ran off and as long as she was at large, she remained a danger to Belle. If they caught her and locked her in the Tolbooth, Belle would be safe. His instinct was to do nothing and let matters take their course. But he had made Belle a promise and honourable men kept their promises.

Sleep evaded Ian as he lay in the net loft in his ma's house. It had been six years since he'd slept there, and he missed the bed with Ellen lying beside him. But Ellen had been strange since the fire at the inn. Her jealousy and obsession with Belle had driven reason from her mind.

He wasn't sure of the time. The sound of movement down below had ceased long since, and only his brothers' snores broke the silence of the night.

The memory of happier times flitted through his mind. Ellen sneaking off to the woods with him when they were courting, their marriage and wedding night, and the days and weeks following it. They had been happy. When had it changed? Was it after Ellen lost the bairn she was carrying? Or was it her lack of being able to carry another? He wasn't sure. But over the years, she had become sadder and quieter. Her swinging moods and the violence accompanying them were new. When did they start? Was it before or after the fire?

A hammering on the door interrupted his thoughts, and he shuffled over the floor of the loft to the top of the ladder to listen.

He heard his mother fumbling for her boots as his father's loud snoring continued unabated. Then the shuffling noise as she moved to the door. The man's voice was louder than hers, but he couldn't make out the words as the murmur of voices floated upwards.

The ladder shook as he clambered down, expecting to see Hector Bruce standing at the door. Ellen must be having one of her turns and her da had come seeking his help.

'What is it?' he said as he crossed the room. But when he reached the door, he stared in amazement at Lachlan. What on earth was he doing here, in the middle of the night?

'I am sorry to disturb you, but I promised Belle I would seek you out.'

'Belle? Why would she send you to me?' And why send the laird's son? Ian thought. He suspected Lachlan had an eye for Belle and had often seen his eyes following her before the Craigden Inn burnt down. Belle had never encouraged him, but the more she rebuffed him, the keener he got.

'It's about your wife, Ellen.'

'What about her?'

'I'm afraid she tried to kill Belle tonight, and she's now on the run. The night watch is out looking for her.'

Annie, standing at his back inside the room, gasped.

'Ye cannae let them take Ellen to the Tolbooth, Ian. Ye must do something.'

Ian's mind whirled. What could he do?

'There is some urgency,' Lachlan said. 'They are hunting for her in Invercraig, but they are bound to come here as well.'

'I need to get home. In case she comes back,' Ian said to Annie, turning to the fireside where he'd left his boots drying. 'I need to alert her da.'

Lachlan led his horse as they walked back to Ian's house.

'Hector,' Ian shouted the moment he was inside.

There was a movement inside the ben room. Ian banged on its door. 'Get up, Hector. Ellen's in trouble.'

The old man's tousled head peered around the door. 'What is it?' he mumbled. His eyes widened when he saw Lachlan standing in the but room.

'Sir,' he stuttered and then got stuck for words.

'The night watch is searching for Ellen.' The words spilled out of Ian.

'Why?'

'She tried to kill Belle.'

Hector's body sagged, and he leaned against the doorframe.

'I was afeared it would come to this,' he muttered. 'It's just like her ma.'

'What is?' Ian frowned. Hector had told him Ellen's ma was in the asylum but had given no other explanation.

'It's a long story.' Hector staggered over to a chair and sank into it. 'When Ellen was born, my Mary-Ellen lost her mind. She tried to hurt the bairn and when I stopped her, she turned the knife on me. I still have the scar.'

'What happened to her?' Lachlan had been silent up to now.

The old man turned his eyes towards him. 'She be locked up in the asylum,' he said. 'I go to see her now and again but she don't know me and the madness is still in her.'

He rocked in the chair. 'And now the madness has taken my Ellen.' A tear slipped down his cheek. 'There is no saving her.'

Despair flooded through Ian. He saw now he'd lost Ellen, but he still had a duty to look after her. She was his wife.

He turned to Lachlan. 'You said the night watch was searching for her.'

'Yes.'

'What will they do if they find her?'

'They'll take her to the Tolbooth and keep her there before sending her to Forfar for trial.'

'How long will that take?'

Lachlan shrugged. 'Weeks, months, or years. But that's not the worst of it. Madge told the watchman that Ellen set fire to the Craigden Inn, and that's a hanging offence, as is the attempted murder.'

Hector covered his face with his hands and groaned.

Ian's mind whirled, trying to work out how to save Ellen.

'And if she's committed to the asylum like her ma? Would they be able to do all that?'

Lachlan thought for a moment. 'I don't think so. My father is keen to see the perpetrator of the fire hang, but I could persuade him there would be no benefit to hanging a madwoman.'

'Better the asylum than the Tolbooth,' Ian said. 'Will you help us?'

'Of course, but only because Belle made me promise to save Ellen from the Tolbooth. But if the watch finds her first ...?'

Ian shuddered. Lachlan didn't need to continue speaking for Ian to know what he meant.

39

The chill from the damp grass seeped into Ellen's bones. Her teeth chattered, shivers engulfed her, and she yearned to go home.

From her vantage point on the cliff road, she had a clear view of her house. It was in darkness, and nothing stirred. She got ready to clamber down the slope. Ian and her da would protect her from the night watch. They wouldn't take much convincing to swear she'd been with them all night. After all, the village folks had little time for abiding by the law.

Voices and the clatter of a horse's hooves broke the silence. Alarmed, she lay back down in the grass and peered over the edge. Ian and Lachlan came into sight, walking together along the village road.

Bile rose in her throat. Lachlan was the one who tried to protect Belle. Too bad he was too late. But what was he doing here, and why was he with Ian? As far as she knew, they didn't know each other.

The two men reached the house and after Lachlan tied his horse to a nearby stump, they went inside. She couldn't risk going to the house now. Not while Lachlan was there.

Ellen lost track of the time as she waited for him to leave. But, as the time passed, and the chill within her bones increased, she realised he intended to remain there until she went home. He was there to trap her.

She struggled to her feet, shook the grass off her skirts and walked towards the church. It rose before her, stark against the night sky, but she felt comforted. The Lord would protect her. After all, she had been doing his work.

The heavy oak door opened at her touch. Her body relaxed as her anger and anxiety seeped away. God was waiting for her inside. When the door swung shut, peace swept over her. She muttered a prayer, walked down the aisle to the altar and knelt in front of it.

'I have done your bidding, oh Lord. I have cast the harlot into Hell where she belongs. No longer will she tempt our men with her flesh.'

She cast her eyes upwards and murmured the Lord's prayer. When she finished, she walked back up the aisle to a pew. She stretched out along the wooden surface, closed her eyes and slept.

The minutes felt like hours as they ticked past, but there was no sign of Ellen.

After a time Lachlan said, 'Perhaps we should mount a search for her.'

'If we do that, we'll lead the watch to where she is hiding.' Ian glanced over from the window. 'She will come home. She has nowhere else to go.'

'You are right,' Lachlan said. 'But waiting makes me restless.'

Hector struggled out of his chair by the fireside. 'She'll be hiding in the woods. That's where she went when she was a bairn. I reckon she won't come back until she's sure the watch has been and gone.'

He yawned and stretched before walking to the ben room. He paused in the doorway. 'I'm going to bed. I'm sure the watch will bang loud enough to wake the dead.'

'That's a good idea,' Lachlan said. 'We need to be alert if we want to help Ellen when she returns.' He looked around. 'Where can I stretch out?'

With a look of embarrassment, Ian pointed towards the box bed. 'Have the bed,' he said, 'but it's not what you're used to.'

'I've slept in worse.' Lachlan pulled the curtain aside, poked the mattress, and climbed in.

'I'll sleep on a couple of chairs pulled together,' Ian said.

Lachlan felt a modicum of guilt over depriving Ian of his bed, but his guilt decreased as he struggled to become comfortable on the straw-filled mattress. It reminded him of the times he visited Belle all those years ago. He hadn't minded the hardness of the bed when he had Belle in his arms. He tucked his heels into the grooves carved into the mattress by the previous occupant and, before he drifted off to sleep, thought it lucky he and Ian were of a similar height.

Loud banging and a voice shouting, 'Open up!' woke Lachlan from a restless sleep. He was stiff and sore and when he struggled to sit up in the confined space of the box bed, he banged his head on a wooden strut. By the time Ian opened the door, he had coaxed feeling back into his arms and legs.

Two men stood on the doorstep. One of them wore a tunic top with brass buttons and a high peaked cap. A wooden truncheon swung from his belt. The other looked more like the type of ruffian used to maintain order at some of the seedier establishments Lachlan occasionally visited.

'I am informed Ellen Watt lives in this house.' The first man didn't trouble to introduce himself.

'My wife is not at home.'

Ian staggered as the man pushed past him to enter the house.

'Search the place,' the man instructed his companion.

'You can't just push in here,' Ian protested.

'I am the town constable in charge of the watch. We can do anything we like.' He paused when he saw Lachlan emerge from the box bed.

'May I ask what authority you have to enter this man's house uninvited?' Lachlan wasn't sure whether the man recognised him, but his authoritative tone should show he was no common working man.

'I have a report from the night watchman that the woman Ellen Watt attempted to murder another woman last night and that she set fire to the inn here at Craigden. As such, I must arrest her.'

'And has the woman who claims Ellen Watt assaulted her made a complaint?' Lachlan was certain Belle had remained silent.

'I have still to question her.'

'I see.'

'But there is also the matter of the fire-raising.'

'And you have witnesses?'

'The night watchman will confirm the witness's statement, and I am sure there will be others.'

The second man returned from the ben room. 'She's not here,' he said. 'But that old bugger through there swore at me for waking him.'

'In that case, I suggest you both take your leave. You are not wanted here.' Lachlan kept his voice low and pleasant, but the authority in it was unmistakable.

'If Ellen Watt returns, I will expect you to report it,' the man said before beckoning to his companion and marching off towards the main road.

Ian closed the door and leaned against it. 'Do you think that will be the last we'll see of them?'

Lachlan shook his head. 'I doubt it.'

The reverend Murdo McAllan woke after a troubled sleep. When he'd heard sounds of someone outside in the early hours of the morning, he'd ignored it. He was not a brave man and had little trouble convincing himself it was his imagination. But now, with daylight streaming through the windows, he wasn't so sure. He had a duty to protect the sanctity of the church. That meant identifying any intruders and finding out their purpose.

Swinging his cloak around his shoulders, he fastened it at the neck and placed his black-brimmed hat on his head. There must be no misunderstanding. The intruder must recognise his authority as the minister of this parish.

While taking hesitant steps along the path from the manse to the church, he questioned the wisdom of what he was doing and considered turning back. But the massive oak door of the church stood before him, and it was his duty to see who had taken refuge inside. When he thought of refuge, his mind stilled. It had to be some poor soul seeking sanctuary, and who better than a minister to provide solace?

He turned the large brass handle and stepped into the church.

At first, he saw nothing. Perhaps the intruder had moved on when daylight came. If so, he had nothing to worry about. But, as he looked, a figure sat up in a pew on the left-hand side.

With a sense of dismay, he recognised her. It was the woman who blamed the fire on his sermon.

'What are you doing here?'

'Where else would I go now that I have done the Lord's bidding?'

A sense of dread passed over Murdo.

'What unholy thing have you done?'

'I have sent the harlot to her master, Satan. She is in Hell where she belongs.'

A chill ran up Murdo's spine. Surely that didn't mean what he thought it did. No, that was impossible. He refused to think of it. But the thought lingered, refusing to go away.

'I am sure that is not what God wanted you to do?'

Ellen turned to face the altar.

'The bible tells us a Jezebel who tempts men with the sins of the flesh must die.' A look of rapture crossed her face. 'It is God's will the harlot is no more, and our men are safe.' She turned her eyes towards Murdo. 'She is where she should be, in Hell with her master, Satan.'

Horror-struck, Murdo backed away from her. He turned and ran back up the aisle and through the door. Slamming it shut behind him, he turned the key in the lock.

What was he to do? He leaned against the door, panting to regain his breath. Should he go to the Tolbooth for the town's officers? Or should he fetch her husband?

He recalled her insistence the day before, that his sermon had instructed her to rid the village of the Jezebel in their midst. What if she repeated that? What if she cast the blame on him and the sermon he preached?

Even if she wasn't believed, the shadow of her accusation would stain his character.

He crept to the manse. He had to think about what he should do.

<h1 style="text-align:center">40</h1>

It had been more than an hour since the town officers had left Craigden and Ian's anxiety increased.

Where was Ellen? Why hadn't she returned home? The worry lines on his forehead deepened at the thought Ellen was suffering out there in the biting cold February wind.

He paced the floor, becoming increasingly agitated.

In vain, Hector and Lachlan suggested he sit and eat something to keep up his strength.

'How can I eat at a time like this? Until we find Ellen, there will be no rest for me.'

'Ach, laddie,' Hector said. 'What use will ye be to Ellen if ye dinnae maintain your strength?'

His face filled with sorrow, and he sighed as he walked over to the window.

'I don't know what use any of us can be.' Ian sank into a chair and buried his head in his hands. 'Ellen is damned, no matter what we do. It's the Tolbooth or the asylum. What else is there for her after what she's done?'

After a brief look outside, Hector announced, 'The minister is heading this way.'

'No doubt he's heard the news and is coming to offer his solicitations.' Lachlan joined Hector at the window. 'Be careful what you tell him. Murdo is a man of God, but I'm not sure he's to be trusted.'

Murdo was the last person Ian wanted to see at a time like this. No doubt he would expect them to pray for Ellen's soul. He staggered to his feet, crossed the room, and opened the door.

Today, the minister walked faster than usual, his black coat flapping in the wind.

'I must speak with you.' His breath came in short gasps.

Ian nodded and stood aside to let him enter.

Murdo stepped inside, his eyes widening when he saw Lachlan.

'What are you doing here?'

'I could ask you the same thing. Have you come to pray for a lost soul?'

Colour suffused Murdo's neck and face. 'I have come with news about this poor man's wife.'

Ian glared. He didn't appreciate being referred to as a poor man. If it had been anyone else but the minister, he would have retaliated.

Instead, he said, 'You have news of Ellen?'

Murdo turned to face him, ignoring the others in the room. 'Ellen is in the church. She told me she is communing with God.' He shuddered. 'I am afraid she has lost her wits, and she is saying dreadful things. Her soul is in jeopardy.'

Ian grasped Murdo's arm. 'We must get to her before she runs off again.'

'I locked the church door. I was afraid she would do herself harm if she left.'

'What has she told you?' Lachlan's eyes narrowed as he stared at Murdo.

'She talks in riddles, but I fear she has killed her sister-in-law, Belle Watt.'

'If she has told you this, what do you plan to do?'

Murdo drew a breath. 'I thought her husband should be the first to know.'

'And after?'

'I had not made up my mind.'

'That's not like you, Murdo. I would have thought you'd be scampering away to the authorities with the information and relish having her locked up in the Tolbooth to await her hanging.'

'You misjudge me. She is one of my parishioners. I would not wish to see her locked up in the Tolbooth.'

'No, and I suppose you wouldn't want her death on your hands, either.'

A look of anguish crossed Murdo's face. 'But what else is to be done when, by her own admission, she has killed?'

'You may rest easy. Belle lives, but it is no thanks to Ellen Watt she survived the attack.' Lachlan turned from Murdo to face Ian. 'Have you made your mind up? Is it to be the asylum?'

Despair gripped Ian. Ever since Lachlan arrived last night with the awful news, his mind had churned with desperate thoughts. It was a man's duty to protect his wife. But what Ellen had done was monstrous. To try to kill someone, not once, but twice. There was only one answer. She had lost her mind.

'Aye,' he said. 'I see no other way.'

Hector agreed. 'If the madness has taken her, the asylum's the best place for her to be.'

'I know. But it doesn't make it any easier.'

'Now you've decided it's time to make the arrangements.'

Lachlan's voice sent a sense of helplessness sweeping over Ian. Arrangements? How did he go about that? This was something outside of his experience.

He looked up in desperation at his guid-father. Hector would know what to do. He had committed Ellen's mother to the asylum.

'What do I do?' He hated the note of pleading in his voice, but he couldn't help it.

'I mind when they took her ma into the asylum, the man in charge said something about her being a risk to herself and other people. So, we need to tell him about how she's been acting and what she's done and ask him to admit her.'

'Will he believe us?'

'Perhaps if the minister agreed to come with us, it could help.' Hector glanced over at Murdo with a questioning look.

Murdo clasped his hands together as if in prayer.

'I think that's an excellent idea,' Lachlan said. 'A minister claiming one of his parishioners is suffering from madness will add weight to your request. What say you, Murdo?'

Murdo squirmed. 'If you think it would be helpful.'

'And if they refuse to take her, what then?' Doubts filled Ian's mind as he struggled to understand what must be done.

'It is up to you to convince the superintendent it is too risky not to admit her to the asylum. That she is a danger to others as well as herself. But we are wasting time discussing this. I think it best we set off for Invercraig without delay.'

They made an odd group as they strode towards the town. Ian and Hector walked side by side, while Murdo walked behind, trying his best not to appear to be with them. And Lachlan trotted his horse along the road, keeping pace with the walkers.

As they walked, Ian wasn't sure whether he was shivering from fear or the cold. In his mind, he rehearsed what to say. How to describe why Ellen needed to be admitted? But what did you say to a superintendent of the asylum? The very name, superintendent, made him quiver with nerves.

The asylum, a large grim-looking building, was situated several streets away from the harbour. It sat within spacious grounds, separated from the houses and streets nearby, and was a staggering five stories high. Towers attached to each corner jutted out from the main part of the building, which they framed within their grasp. Ian couldn't imagine living in such a place. Even the area of grass, trees and bushes in front did nothing to alleviate the air of despair this building evoked. He took several steps back from the imposing iron gates, imagining that once he passed through them, there would be no way back.

'You know this is the only way,' Lachlan said. 'It's this or the Tolbooth. Ellen will be safer here.'

He nodded, braced his shoulders and stepped inside the gate.

The lion's head knocker on the front door echoed eerily inside the building. Ian shuffled his feet as the minutes ticked by and he was raising his hand to the knocker a second time when the door creaked open. A young girl stood framed in the doorway. Her sparkling white pinafore covered a black dress which was too big for her.

She stared at them for a moment before speaking. 'What might you gentlemen be wanting?' The white mob cap on her head sat askew and wobbled when she spoke.

Ian detected a trace of nervousness in her voice. It was as if she didn't know how to address them. He supposed it was because he and Hector were not gentlemen, although Lachlan and Murdo were.

Lachlan took over. 'We wish to see the superintendent.'

'Best you come in then while I try to find him.'

Doors lined the long gloomy hallway which continued the length of the building, ending at a flight of stairs which led upwards into realms unknown. The smell of disinfectant nipped Ian's nose and there were other smells which he couldn't identify.

'Wait here,' the maid said before scuttling off down the corridor.

Several minutes later, she reappeared with a burly man dressed in a white tunic.

'Maisie here says you want to see the superintendent,' he said. 'May I ask your business with him?'

Ian closed his eyes in despair. It was clear the superintendent did not wish to see them.

Lachlan laid a hand on his arm.

'Mr Watt's wife is in crisis. At the moment, we have her locked in the church to keep her safe. It is imperative we consult with the superintendent as to how we may handle this situation and help the poor woman.'

Lachlan's voice was crisp and authoritative, and it had the desired effect.

'If you will wait a moment, sir, I will inform the superintendent you wish to see him.' Respect tempered the note of resentment in the man's voice.

He returned in a few moments. 'This way, sir.'

The superintendent sat at a polished mahogany desk. Cabinets lined the walls, and several leather chairs completed the furniture in the large room. Light streamed in the narrow window behind him, which looked out to the garden area at the front of the building.

'Please be seated.' He waved to the chairs. 'I am Dr Browne; the medical superintendent of Invercraig Lunatic Asylum and I understand you wish to consult me about Mr Watt's wife.'

Ian, struck mute by the opulence of his surroundings, nodded.

'I take it you must be Watt.'

Ian nodded again.

'Well, speak up, man. Tell me what is so important you require to consult me about your wife?'

'It's like this, sir. She be having brainstorms. Twice she's tried to kill my brother's wife and I'm afeared next time she might succeed.' Ian's shoulders slumped. He didn't know how best to describe Ellen's state of mind, and he looked at Hector for help.

'Aye, that's right,' Hector said. 'She's my daughter and it pains me to admit she's going the same way as her ma. She's been here in the asylum for over twenty years now.'

'You believe her condition to be hereditary.'

Ian nodded, although he didn't understand what the doctor meant.

'I'll need more details.'

Lachlan leaned forward. 'I witnessed the most recent murder attempt, so perhaps I can explain the circumstances leading to where we are today.' He described the events of the previous night, adding this was a second attempt, the first being when Ellen set fire to the Craigden Inn. He finished up by saying, 'The Reverend McAllan discovered Ellen in his church this morning and thinks she may be suffering from religious mania. She believes Mrs Watt is dead and by killing her, she has done God's work. When she discovers Mrs Watt survived the attack, we fear she will try again. Not only that, but the innkeeper, Madge, is at risk, as well as Mrs Watt's children. They were meant to perish in the fire.'

'I see.' Dr Browne leant forward. 'When did this behaviour start and does she exhibit violent traits all the time, or do they come and go?'

Ian thought he understood what the doctor was asking, although he was unfamiliar with his choice of words.

'I'm not too sure when they started. She's always been a bit moody, but I noticed after the fire she got a lot worse. She flies into rages for no reason.' He pointed to the angry red scratch on his cheek. 'She did this when she was in one of her brainstorms. It made me wary of her even when she's calm.'

'I see. From what you've told me, I feel she needs an assessment to ascertain her state of mind. The normal procedure is that you apply to the parish for their agreement to refer her to me.'

A wave of despair flooded through Ian and his shoulders slumped. What did they do now? If they had to apply to the parish, Ellen would be in the Tolbooth before they came to a decision.

'I fear we do not have time on our side.' Lachlan's voice was urgent. 'We cannot keep Ellen locked in the church indefinitely. If we set her loose, I fear someone will die.'

Dr Browne adjusted his spectacles and stared at Lachlan.

'This is all very irregular,' he said.

'I am sure my father, Lord Craigallan, in his role as a magistrate for this county, will be able to assure the parish an emergency admission at this time is wholly appropriate.'

'In that case. I will admit her for assessment.'

'How soon?' Lachlan demanded.

'I will arrange for the wagon to set off for Craigden Church as soon as possible. Perhaps the Reverend McAllan could accompany the attendants in order to open the church for them. Now I have some papers I will require Mr Watt to sign before we can get started.'

41

'Your wife will be safe here,' Lachlan said, 'and there is no further need for me to stay. So, I will take my leave of you.'

'I thank you for your help, sir, but what do we tell the town constable when he comes looking for her again?'

'After she is admitted it will do no harm to say she is in the lunatic asylum. He will need a court order to remove her, and I doubt the court will grant that without Belle's evidence.'

Ian frowned. 'But Ellen tried to kill Belle. What is to stop her speaking out?'

'Have faith,' Lachlan said. 'Belle has no wish to harm Ellen by speaking out against her. When she finds Ellen is no longer a risk to her, she will say nothing.'

A frown creased Ian's forehead, and Lachlan saw doubt in his eyes. Sympathy for the man invaded his mind, because during their time together since last night, a bond had sprung up between them. Discovering he cared about what happened to Ian and his family astonished him.

He tightened his grip on Ian's arm. 'I will inform Belle she is safe from any further harm from Ellen. In the meantime, go home and get some rest. You have acted in your wife's best interests and there is no more you can do.'

Lachlan left his horse in the Ship Inn's backyard. Finding the rear door to the inn locked, he strode down the street and around the corner to the front entrance.

The place was empty apart from two men sitting on a bench beside the fire. Lachlan supposed it was too early for most folk, although Old

182

Tam seemed to be a fixture in the place. Tam looked up and nodded when Lachlan entered the taproom, but Gregor, sitting beside him, met Lachlan's eyes with a glower.

'What brings you here?' There was no welcome in Gregor's voice.

'I'm looking for Belle.'

'Well, she's not here. She don't start work until five of the clock.'

Lachlan nodded and left the inn. He'd felt the innkeeper's animosity the evening before and had no wish to argue with him.

Remembering Belle's determination to return home to her bairns last night, he strode along the street to the tenement where they'd taken her.

'I know you're in there,' he said when his knock went unanswered. 'Open up, Belle. We need to talk.'

The door opened a crack, and Belle peered out. Her face lacked colour, while her uncombed hair tumbled around her shoulders. The bruises on her neck stood out, bluish-purple against her pale skin.

Lachlan caught his breath and reached out for her, but she backed away from him.

'What do you want?' Her voice was flat and unwelcoming.

He followed her inside and closed the door behind him.

She gestured for Sarah to take the two boys into the bedroom. 'Stay there until this man leaves,' she said, before turning back to face Lachlan.

'I came to tell you Ellen is being admitted to Invercraig Asylum today. You no longer have to fear her.'

'The asylum?' Belle sank into a chair. 'I would not wish that on anyone.'

'It was that or the Tolbooth.'

'I would not wish her there either.'

'I know.' Lachlan knelt beside her and clasped her hand.

'Is there no hope for her?'

'Her only hope is to remain in the asylum. I will ensure I have some-one to speak for her to prevent her removal. I am sure the court will agree an insane woman's confession is worthless. The only evidence against her is the attack on you.'

'I said nothing to the watchman. Ellen is family.'

'Madge spoke out.'

'I will talk with Madge and make sure she agrees with me.'

Belle tugged her hand free from Lachlan's grasp and turned her face away from him.

'I think you should go now. I need to rest. If the bairns will let me.'

'Ah, yes, your children.'

Thoughts Lachlan had repressed over the years surfaced in his mind. Belle had never forgiven him for leaving her without a word of goodbye six years ago and, in her eyes, his subsequent marriage to Clarinda was a betrayal. Belle's passionate nature blinded her from seeing that the marriage between him and Clarinda had been arranged by his father when they were children. He was duty-bound to marry her.

Belle walked to the door. Holding it open, she said, 'Please leave.'

But the thought that had plagued him for six long years wouldn't leave him alone, and only Belle could provide the answer, which would give him peace.

'Belle.' He gripped her shoulders. 'I need to know. Are the twins my children?'

She stared at him with a blank expression on her face.

'No,' she said in a harsh voice. 'They are not your children.'

His hands dropped from her shoulders, and he turned away from her.

The thud of the slamming door echoed up through the empty stairwell. The echo died away, leaving only the sound of a muffled sob coming from inside the flat.

Had Belle spoken the truth? The doubts returned to plague him.

Ian stared through the iron bars of the asylum gate. Before the day was out, Ellen, the woman who had shared his bed and his life, would be locked inside. How on earth had it come to this? He shuddered and gripped the gate. The bars were a symbol of Ellen's future life. Isolated and imprisoned within this bleak building.

'Come away, laddie,' Hector said. 'Ye cannae change things and once she's inside, she'll be safe from the hangman.'

His voice shook and Ian realised the older man was near to tears.

He turned his back on the gate. 'Aye, ye're right.'

Silence cloaked the streets leading from the asylum and it was only when they drew nearer to the harbour that the bangs and thumps of cargo being unloaded from a ship penetrated their gloomy thoughts. They followed the sound until they turned the corner onto the busy riverside road leading to the bridge.

Unlike the deserted streets surrounding the asylum, it seemed as if all humanity was there. Labourers, burdened with crates, barrels, bales of cloth and all manner of goods, swarmed on the quayside. Darting between the ships' gangways and the wooden warehouses in the harbour area, they hardly seemed to have time to breathe.

Ships bobbed on their moorings and bumped against the harbour wall, caught by the wind sweeping downriver from the inland basin and the hills beyond.

Carts and barrows trundled along the street while men and women went about their business. Children and ragamuffins gathered at street corners, throwing abuse at each other.

Turning his eyes away from this mad throng, Ian's heart lightened as he looked over the water to where the cottages of Craigden glimmered in the pale February sunshine. The only place he felt at home. His steps lengthened. He disliked the bustle of the town. It was time they left Invercraig.

The clatter of horse's hooves and the rumble of wheels on the cobbled road behind them added to the general noise. He pulled Hector closer to the harbour wall and watched as carts and barrows hastily moved to the side to make way for the large wagon with its barred window slots.

He glimpsed three men inside, recognising the black-clad outline of Murdo as one of them.

'That'll be the asylum wagon on its way to collect Ellen.' Hector's voice was mournful.

'Aye.' Ian choked on the lump in his throat, unable to say anymore. A vision of Ellen being manhandled into the wagon filled his mind. Guilt consumed him. What had he committed her to?

Ian ignored the gusts of wind blowing through the spars of the bridge, for this was where Invercraig ended, and home was little more than a mile away. The road stretched in front of him, empty apart from a solitary cart. The asylum wagon had long since vanished out of sight.

It rumbled past on its return trip when they were crossing the smaller Inch Bridge, which spanned the narrower part of the river encircling the island.

Despair washed over Ian. He turned to watch the progress of the wagon until he could no longer see it.

'What have I done?' he said.

Tears sprang to his eyes, and he leant on the bridge's parapet to stare into the water below.

'Don't fret, lad. Ye did the right thing.' The gruffness of Hector's voice suggested he wasn't far from tears himself.

'Aye,' Ian said again. But all he could think of was that to save Ellen from the Tolbooth and the hangman he'd sentenced her to a life in a madhouse.

42

It was midafternoon before Lachlan headed homeward and even the wind blowing from the inland basin through the spars of the bridge failed to energise him. His meeting with the town constable had been wearing. The man was obstinate, but at last, he'd seen sense and called off the search for Ellen.

'I expect you're right,' he'd grumbled. 'If the witnesses won't provide evidence and if the court decides the woman's confession is the ramblings of a madwoman, then there's little hope of a conviction.'

By the time Lachlan slid off his horse in the stable courtyard, he'd made his mind up to avoid his father until he slept off his exhaustion. He wanted his wits about him when he informed him of all that had happened since yesterday.

Alfie, the stable boy, rushed over and grabbed Raven's reins. The lad usually grinned at Lachlan and murmured to the horse, but today his face was sombre, and he wouldn't meet Lachlan's eyes. Old Hamish emerged from the stables as Alfie led the horse away.

'Ye're needed inside,' he said in his usual taciturn voice.

Lachlan's heart sank. His father was looking for him. He closed his eyes and groaned. He was too tired to cope with his father's disapproval. But he knew better than to avoid him.

The smell of roasting beef filtering from the kitchen reminded him he hadn't eaten since yesterday. But it wouldn't do to keep his father waiting, so he ignored his craving and sped along the corridor into the main part of the house. As he hurried along, it didn't strike him the house was too silent. No maids getting under his feet and no rumble of voices from the rooms adjacent to the corridor.

His father wasn't in the room he used as an office, nor was he in the library or any other room he habitually used. Stranger still, his mother wasn't in her sitting room.

A faint rumble of voices on the upper floor of the house led him to his father's bedroom.

He turned the knob and eased the door open, even though he knew his father didn't appreciate anyone invading the privacy of his bedchamber.

Inside, closed window curtains shut out the daylight. In the dim interior, shadows danced around the room from the glow of the fire and the light of an oil lamp. His mother, Clarinda, and Aunt Beattie were among those clustered around the four-poster bed blocking his view. He frowned. Why was Clarinda there? What had tempted her from her room?

His mother, hearing him enter, turned to face him.

'You've returned,' she said. 'We have been searching for you every-where.'

He strode forward and approached the bed.

'What has happened?' His voice didn't sound like his own.

'Your father is unwell. The doctor,' she gestured towards a portly man, 'has been in attendance since earlier today.'

She stood aside to make room for him at the bedside.

His father moaned and his eyes flickered as the doctor plucked a leech from his chest. The puncture wound oozed blood. From the many red and swollen marks on his father's skin, Lachlan could see the bloodletting treatment had been extensive.

Questions raced through his mind as he watched the man place the swollen leech in a glass container, along with several other leeches. However, he waited until the doctor placed the jar in his black leather bag before he sought answers.

'What have you diagnosed?' he demanded.

'Sir Roderick has had an attack of apoplexy which has affected his left side and his speech.'

The doctor snapped his bag shut.

Lachlan's limited knowledge of apoplexy made him struggle to understand the implications.

'How serious is it?'

'Very serious indeed. Sir Roderick has lost the use of his left arm and leg and is exhibiting considerable confusion.'

'Will he recover?'

'He will live, but it is doubtful how active he will be. The paralysis of his left side means he may never walk unaided. Apart from that, his mental capacity is impaired.'

'Your treatment,' Lachlan gestured to the leech marks on his father's chest, 'will it help?'

'Bloodletting is the usual way of treating apoplexy. It reduces the volume of blood and relieves pressure on the brain. It is not a cure.'

'I see. And what other treatment have you prescribed?'

'I administered a purgative prior to the bloodletting. That will remove any toxins from Sir Roderick's blood, and I have advised the use of warm baths and cold compresses. You must keep him in a quiet, dark room so he gets plenty of rest and to help the brain recover. I would also advise you to ensure his head is elevated with the use of pillows. This will reduce blood flow to the brain. Apart from that, there is little that can be done.'

'I see.' Lachlan stared at the shell of his father lying on the bed. 'As I understand it. What you are saying is my father will never recover fully and will be an invalid. Am I right?'

The doctor sighed and picked up his black bag. 'Yes, you are right. There is nothing anyone can do to make your father the man he once was.'

After the doctor left, Lachlan accompanied his mother to her sitting room. 'What will we do if father never recovers?'

His mother grasped his hands and looked into his eyes. 'It is up to you now, Lachlan. You must take charge. The business we run, the estate, the ships, the house. It must all continue to operate as normal. It is time to face up to your responsibilities and ensure that happens. Your father would expect no less of you.'

43

It was a week before Lachlan returned to Invercraig. During that week, Belle became even more despondent. Most of the time, she sat staring out the window.

The children, sensing her mood, became subdued. Meanwhile, Sarah, despite only being in her tenth year, kept the household going. She cooked, cleaned, and made sure the twins didn't annoy their mother.

Belle, although aware of Sarah's worried sidelong glances at her, had no energy left to console her child.

Instead, she watched the river with its ever-changing moods. There were days when it was a raging torrent matching the conflict in her mind. Then there were times it was calm, but always it flowed. Upstream to fill the inland basin to turn it into a vast lake. Then downstream to flow seawards when the tide changed, emptying the water from the basin and leaving muddy flats behind.

It felt as if her life was on the same trajectory. She had thought her life was getting better. She'd had hopes of becoming independent, reliant on no man, and just when her future had seemed so bright, everything had crashed around her. The loss of the gold sovereigns Lachlan gave her all those years ago, which she had guarded until now, removed that hope. Once again, she must depend on others to survive. Like the river's outgoing tide, everything had ebbed away, leaving her desolate with no future to look forward to.

Mixed in with the depression consuming her, was guilt. When Lachlan told her she was safe because Ellen was in the asylum, she'd felt such a surge of relief. But it hadn't taken long for her relief to be replaced by shame.

Was it her fault they locked Ellen up in the asylum? Had she provoked Ellen's jealousy by encouraging Ian?

She didn't think so, but if she had, she hadn't meant to.

Working as a barmaid, she had to be pleasant to men while serving them with drink. Now she wondered if she'd gone too far. Had she given the impression she was willing to provide them with more than ale?

A knock on the door disturbed her rambling thoughts. She pulled her silk scarf higher around her neck to hide the yellowing bruises and nodded to Sarah to open it.

Her eyes widened when Lachlan entered the room.

'I didn't expect you to return.' She kept her voice flat and unwelcoming.

'I wanted to make sure you had recovered from your ordeal.' Lachlan hesitated before continuing, 'I would have come earlier, but there has been trouble at home.'

'There is no need for you to concern yourself.' Belle adjusted her scarf, pulling it higher.

'There is something I wished to discuss with you.' He raised his eyebrows and glanced at the children.

'Very well.'

Belle gestured for Sarah to take Davy and Jamie into the bedroom. After the door closed behind them, she turned to Lachlan. 'If it is the same question you asked me the last time you were here, the answer is still the same.'

Lachlan dropped to his knees and grasped her hands. 'Ever since we first met, I've never stopped thinking about you.' His voice shook. 'So, I have decided to offer you my protection.'

Belle laughed without mirth. 'Your protection? What makes you think I need that?'

His grip tightened on her hands. 'I'm offering to take you away from all this.' He gestured to the room they were in. 'You deserve better.' His voice continued in a rush. 'I will set you up in your own house or flat, whichever you prefer, and I will take care of your expenses. You could have anything you desire and will want for nothing.'

Anger surged through her.

She'd given this man her love and her body and thought he loved her in return. But, six years ago, he'd left without a word and married another.

'You think you can come here and make me an offer to become your whore? I am nobody's whore, sir, so I suggest you leave and return to your wife.'

'No, Belle, not a whore, never that. I love you but cannot offer marriage, as I already have a wife. As my mistress, you will be wife to me in all but name.'

'You take me for a fool, sir? When you deserted me, you had no wife. Your professed love did not prevent you from bringing one home with you.'

His eyes saddened, and a look of misery crossed his face.

'Ah, Belle,' he said. 'You do not understand how much pressure my father exerted on me to marry Clarinda and fulfil my duty to my family.'

'And what about your duty to me?'

'You had a husband, and our lives followed different paths.'

Belle flinched.

He was right. Her Jimmie had still been alive then, and she remembered how conflicted she had been between the two men. When Jimmie was away to the sea, she'd thought she loved Lachlan, but when Jimmie returned, she never doubted her love for her husband. Besides, she'd known Lachlan would never wed her. However, that did not excuse him for leaving her without an explanation or a goodbye.

Her anger lessened, and she suppressed the bitter retorts hovering on her lips.

'You may plead as much as you like, but I have no wish to accept your offer. I suggest you return to your wife and seek your pleasures there.'

'As you wish.' He rose. 'I still love you, Belle,' he said before he left.

Belle stared at the closed door until she could no longer hear the sound of his feet clattering down the stairs.

Had she made a mistake by refusing him?

After all, what did her future hold now she had lost her money pouch? A life working at the Ship Inn and dodging Gregor's advances? Or a life as Lachlan's whore?

Neither of these choices boded well for her desire for independence.

44

February 1840 - The Arctic

A gust of icy wind whipped over the ice field, breaking the silence of the Arctic night. It sent flurries of snow around the two men crouched over blow holes. The only other sound was Jimmie's heels scraping on the ice as he adjusted his position on the fur pelt.

The stark white of the landscape glittered with a silver sheen in the moonlight. Jimmie narrowed his eyes, straining to see where the ice stopped. Out there lay the remains of his ship, along with his former companions.

A few yards away, Nukilik crouched over a blow hole with his eyes fixed on the ice, waiting for signs of movement in the water underneath. Movement meant they would have fish for their next meal. Sighing, Jimmie turned back to his own blow hole. He wasn't as adept as Nukilik, but he was learning.

So much had changed since the man who crouched next to him had rescued him from an icy death several months ago. He owed Nukilik his life and, because of that, he did his best to follow his lead so he would fit in and be accepted by the community.

But adjusting to life here had been difficult. It was so different from the life he'd known in Craigden. Here they had to hunt and fish to make sure they ate and survived. Back home, life had been hard but simple, and he missed the companionship of his father and brothers as they sailed the Scottish coast to bring home fish to provide a living for the family. Most of all, he missed Belle and the bairns. He wondered what they were doing now and hoped life would be good for them.

So much time had passed since he'd woken from the sleep where death beckoned, but the memory of the warmth cocooning his naked body below the mound of furs was still fresh in his mind. That warmth had come from the bare flesh of two women who nestled close to him, wrapping him in their arms, sharing their body heat with him. In his dream state, he'd thought Belle was lying beside him, but there couldn't be two Belles.

Forcing his eyes open, he'd found himself in the strangest place. Shadows flickered off skins and furs lining the walls of a peculiarly shaped room. He'd had the impression he was in a giant-sized ball. Only later did he realise the houses in this strange land were constructed from ice blocks. The pelts were there to keep the occupants warm and safe from the bitter cold.

In his struggle to make sense of it, he'd wondered whether he was dead and whether this was what heaven looked like. While he'd been trying to figure out where he was, a man had emerged from a tunnel at the room's rear. He'd grunted when he saw Jimmie's eyes were open and said something unintelligible. Motioning with his hand to his mouth, he'd made a chewing motion.

It had taken a moment before Jimmie realised the man was asking him if he wanted food, and he'd nodded.

After vanishing back through the tunnel the man reappeared a few minutes later, carrying a bowl.

'Imerpoq,' he'd said.

Jimmie hadn't known what he meant, but he'd grasped the proffered bowl containing a thick red liquid which looked like blood.

'Thank you,' he'd said, hesitating momentarily before raising the bowl to his lips with trembling hands.

'Imerpoq,' the man had repeated, reaching out with his hand and tilting the bowl towards Jimmie's mouth.

Jimmie had closed his eyes and gulped.

This seemed to please the man who had smiled and nodded before turning to a heap of skins and furs piled in a corner of the room. He selected some of them and placed them in front of Jimmie.

'Quarliik,' he'd said pointing at one skin and gesturing towards his legs. Then he'd patted his upper body and pointed to another skin. 'Atigi.' This skin resembled a jacket with a hood.

Jimmie had wriggled free from the mound of furs covering him and he'd donned the garments. At first glance, they'd appeared cumbersome, but to his surprise, he'd found them light and warm. Uncertain how to communicate with this man, he'd nodded his thanks and smiled.

The man had smiled back. He'd slapped his chest and said, 'Nukilik.'

Jimmie's bewilderment must have shown on his face because the man had repeated himself once again, slapping his chest.

Guessing that the man had been telling him his name Jimmie had slapped his own chest before saying, 'Jimmie.'

The man's smile had broadened, and he'd repeated, 'Jim-mee.'

Nukilik had then put his hand on the older woman's shoulder and said, 'Kanguq.' He'd followed this by touching the young girl and saying, 'Quamnanic.'

Jimmie had thought he would never remember these strange names, and his jaw ached from smiling.

The man had nodded with satisfaction, lifted the empty bowl and, once again, vanished down the tunnel. Returning a few minutes later, he'd thrust the refilled bowl into Jimmie's hands. Pointing to his mouth he'd said, 'Nerivoq, Jim-mee.'

The chilled meat in the bowl had gleamed red in the dim light, and Jimmie had suspected it was raw. He recalled his repulsion at the thought of eating uncooked meat, but the man had kept on smiling and nodding at him, obviously expecting him to eat it.

He'd lifted a piece to give it a closer inspection and found he hadn't been mistaken. At least it wasn't warm and dripping blood.

The man, as if sensing his hesitation, had taken one piece of meat from the plate and crunched it. He'd nodded to the plate and then to Jimmie and said, 'Nerivoq.'

Jimmie had guessed the word meant eat, so he'd selected a piece and bit into it. The taste wasn't as bad as he'd expected, although he would rather have had it cooked.

Since that time, he'd become accustomed to eating raw meat and fish and drinking blood. He'd regained his strength after a short time and now felt stronger and healthier than he'd ever been.

Over the months that followed, the icehouse had become his home and its inhabitants, his friends. Communication had been the major difficulty as neither spoke the other's language, but at least he now remembered their names.

When he'd first ventured outside, he'd discovered the icehouse he had woken in was one of many. An entire village of these strange dome-shaped structures made of compacted snow and ice. Many of them with connecting tunnels linking them together. And a community of squat men, women and children, so swathed in furs it was difficult to tell the difference. They'd smiled and peered into his face with undisguised curiosity. It felt strange and intrusive at first but not threatening and soon he'd grown used to them and they to him.

Life was simple here, although the landscape was strange. Jimmie did his best to fit in and even learned a few words of their language. Not long after his arrival, the days shortened until there was no daylight at all. Darkness prevailed. There were nights, or was it days, Jimmie had no way of telling, when only the moon and the stars glimmered in the sky. But on other nights, the sky was lit by a panorama of colours. They swirled across the sky in dancing lights of green, purple, pink, and red. It was the strangest thing Jimmie had ever seen. And he wished Belle was here with him to see it.

Time passed slowly during the dark time. Snow and ice predominated, and the cold was more bitter than anything he'd ever experienced. Blizzards were common and while they raged, no hunting was done. Everyone huddled inside their icehouses until the weather calmed.

A slap on his shoulder jolted him out of his thoughts. Nukilik stood before him. He beckoned and pointed to the dog sled. Jimmie sighed and gathered up the few fish he had caught before following in Nukilik's wake.

It was time to return to the icehouse, which was now his home, here in this frozen wasteland where the sun never shone.

45

April 1840 – Invercraig

February, with its snowstorms and blizzards, slid into a blustery March. The days marched relentlessly on, while Belle and her children settled into their new way of life. But the bairns were restless, with no woods or seashore to explore. The streets of Invercraig were no replacement for the fun they used to have in Craigden, and Belle didn't like them roaming the docks. Yesterday's howling gale had seen March out with a last parting shot from winter.

The wind had dropped by the time she left for work and a hint of warmth in the April sunshine lifted her spirits.

A babble of voices and raucous laughter greeted her when she entered the Ship Inn.

Madge met her with a curt, 'Thank goodness you're here. The place is hotching with sailors and I can't keep up.'

She clattered two mugs of ale on a nearby table and scuttled back to the bar where Gregor was filling tankards. Gregor looked over at her with a frown and gestured for her to hurry.

The next few hours passed in a haze of activity. Drink flowed, money changed hands and Belle dodged grasping hands with a dexterity she'd learned through experience.

After working at the Ship Inn for seven weeks, Belle had grown accustomed to handling seamen from various countries. She'd even picked up a few words of French and Spanish, although the Norwegian language had proved more difficult. Tonight, with three ships in the harbour, the Ship Inn was rowdier than usual. Dutch, Spanish and Norwegian sailors crowded inside, demanding alcohol.

As the evening wore on, trouble brewed. Tempers frayed and curses in various languages echoed around the taproom. It wasn't long before the first punches were thrown.

Bottles and tankards flew through the air, and only the solidity of the benches and tables prevented them from following suit.

Madge and Belle crouched behind the bar when the fighting was at its worst, while Gregor skulked at the back of the room. As the ruckus increased, the regular drinkers sneaked out of the door and fled.

The battle raged for a long time before the last of the fighters staggered outside, leaving several bodies lying on the floor.

Madge heaved a sigh and pulled herself up to survey the damage. 'This'll take a bit of clearing up.'

'Give me a hand up,' Belle said. She had been jammed in the corner between the bar and the wall, and her legs had cramped.

Outside, the sound of running feet and curses grew less as the sailors returned to their ships. Belle shivered, hoping they would be long gone when it was time for her to walk home.

'Are you two going to stand there doing nothing?' Gregor walked over to the bar. 'This place is a mess.'

'Aye, where were you when the fighting started? If you'd thrown them out before it worsened, the bar wouldn't be in this state.' Madge glared at her brother.

'None of your damned business,' Gregor snapped. 'Your job is to clear it up.' He kicked one of the prone sailors. 'Start by getting rid of these bodies.'

Madge squared up to him with her hands on her hips. 'How d'you suggest we do that?'

Gregor pushed his face close to hers. 'I don't care how you do it. Just do it,' he snapped. 'Drag them out onto the street and leave them to sober up. Surely the two of you can manage that.' A malicious smile tugged at the corners of his mouth. 'I want them out of here.'

By the time they'd done everything, it was midnight, and Belle was exhausted.

'I have to go,' she said to Madge. 'I need to get back to the bairns.'

The full force of the smell when Davy got up from the bucket made Sarah wrinkle her nose.

'Did you have to do that in here? Why didn't you go outside to the lavatory during the day?'

'I was desperate, and it's too dark to go outside.' His eyes pleaded with her to understand.

Sarah stared at the slops bucket. Then she looked out the window into the darkness.

'I suppose I'll have to empty it,' she said. 'Can't have it stinking the house out.'

She bent and grabbed the handle.

'Ma says we have to keep the door locked and we're not to go out at night.' His voice was muffled as he snuggled beneath the blanket in the bed he shared with his brother Jamie.

'You should have thought of that before you used the bucket.'

She unlocked the door and peered out onto the landing. No one was there, although a sliver of light showed beneath Thelma's door, and she thought she heard a male voice.

Sarah tiptoed out and crept down the stairs. The building's front door creaked when she opened it, and she paused for a moment on the doorstep to inspect the street. When she was sure no one was around, she hurried over to the low wall separating the road from the river and tipped the contents of the bucket into the rushing water below.

Her task completed, she darted back across the road and into the tenement. She crept back up the stairs, taking care not to let the metal bucket clank on the wall. With a sigh of relief, she grasped the doorknob. It was at that moment Thelma's door opened.

The large man who stood on the threshold narrowed his eyes as he looked at Sarah.

'Come.' He advanced towards her.

'Leave her be,' Thelma said, appearing behind him.

He turned his head and slammed his fist into the side of her head. She crumpled to the floor.

Fear thumped in Sarah's chest. She didn't like the look in this man's eyes or the way he smiled at her.

She twisted the doorknob and pushed the door open, preparing to slam it. But he was too quick for her. He grasped her arms and bent over her before running a grubby finger down her face.

The touch of the seaman's finger was rough and unwelcome on Sarah's cheek. She shrank from the sour smell of him; a smell that was a strange mixture of whisky, tobacco, and oakum. He pushed her further into the room. She felt the wall press on her back as she jerked her head, banging it on the wooden mantel shelf.

Her eyes darted towards Thelma, but she lay where the man had thrown her.

'Ah! Is gute! So pretty.' The seaman's breath enveloped her. His finger stroked down her cheek and neck in one motion, stopping at the neck of her skimpy chemise before continuing its downward journey.

A shiver of revulsion went through Sarah. She tried to pull further back and away from his groping fingers, but there was nowhere to go.

'Leave the bairn alone.' Thelma's voice was strident as she struggled to her feet.

The seaman paused in his fondling to pull a money pouch from his pocket. 'I pay.' He breathed heavily, his eyes not moving from Sarah's small, slim body, and worried eyes.

Sarah froze. What would Thelma do? Everyone needed money.

'She's only a bairn. She's too young.' Thelma's voice softened, 'and if it's needing that pouch lightened ye are. I'm sure I could oblige ye.'

'You I have had. Her I want.' The seaman shook the leather pouch, making the coins clink together.

Thelma crossed the room and laid her hand on the seaman's shoulder. 'Come. I'll give you a better time. What d'ye want a bairn for?'

'I want! I pay!' The seaman pushed Thelma from him with one swipe of his huge, rough hand.

She sprawled across the floor, her dress riding up to expose her thighs. 'You'll pay for this. See if you don't,' she shrieked. 'And keep your hands off Belle's bairn.'

The seaman spat on the floor and kicked Thelma in the head. 'What you do, woman? You whore.' Turning to Sarah, he dragged her into the room.

Sarah dug her heels into the floor, but she felt helpless and alone. Her mother hadn't come home yet, and Thelma was lying in a heap on the floor, unconscious. The twins who were peering from behind the bedroom door were only six. What could they do?

As if in answer to that, a whirling dervish of a six-year-old launched himself at the seaman's shoulders while the other laid into him with a poker.

'Run Sarah!' Davy's voice was urgent. Sarah needed no other telling. The seaman's hands had loosened as he tried to defend himself. Tearing herself free, Sarah slammed out of the door.

She clattered down the stairs to street level and out of the tenement's back door. Outside, the night was dark and moonless, and the wet grass deadened her footsteps.

The heavy thuds of the seaman's feet pounding down the stairs set her heart thudding. She crossed her fingers and hoped he thought she'd fled out the front door onto the street. The sound of his feet faded, and she breathed a sigh of relief. It was short-lived and her breath caught in her throat when she heard the thump of his feet returning.

What if he looked out here? Even without a moon, he was bound to see her. Fear engulfed her, and she ran to the row of washhouses and sheds bordering the drying green. She tugged at the latches with fingers numb from the cold. The first few were locked, but eventually, she found one that opened. Holding her breath, she pulled the door, trying not to make a noise, and once inside, she crept into the dark corner between the boiler and the wall.

She pulled her knees up to her chest and wrapped her arms around them before staring wide-eyed at the door. Was she safe here? Or would he find her?

<h1 style="text-align:center">46</h1>

Belle glanced nervously along the street before she ventured outside. The darkness was unrelieved by moonlight, for the moon was hiding its face in the clouds. No sign of the rioters from earlier in the evening remained, apart from several broken bottles littering the road. A burst of laughter from the ship nearest to the inn echoed along the street, making her nerves tingle. The only other sound to break the silence was the rushing of the water and the bumping and grinding of ships at anchor as they bounced against the harbour wall.

Water buffeted the wall separating it from the street and spray dampened the air as the tide rushed out to sea. The sound reminded Belle of her life in Craigden, which had been so simple compared to how she lived now. If only Jimmie hadn't insisted on joining the whaling ships, he wouldn't now be lost to her. A tear gathered at the corner of her eyes. Ah well, no use dwelling on what couldn't be changed.

A man's rough voice and a child's wail greeted her when she pushed open the tenement's door. Her heart skipped a beat. It sounded like Jamie. She broke into a run and stormed up the stairs to where the door of her house gaped open.

The flickering candlelight revealed a sight that horrified her. A large man dressed in the rough clothes of a seaman held Jamie aloft while Davy hammered ineffectually at his legs. Over to their left, beside the fireplace, Thelma lay sprawled on the floor. Unconscious? Dead? Belle wasn't sure. A sudden flare from the smouldering fire illuminated Thelma's face. Her eyelids flickered and a small moan escaped her lips.

Belle shifted her gaze away from the stricken woman. She didn't have time to help her. Rescuing the twins was more important.

'Leave Jamie alone.' Davy's small fists continued to thump the man's legs with no more effect than a bothersome fly.

The man kicked out and shook Davy off without taking his eyes off Jamie.

'Where she go?' the sailor demanded, shaking Jamie again. Jamie's head rocked back and forth, and he squealed.

Davy's shrill voice combined with Jamie's squeals tore at Belle's heart. 'Take your hands off my bairn,' Belle screamed.

He turned to face her, still holding on to Jamie.

'I said, take your hands off my bairn.' Her voice was lower this time and more menacing.

He dropped Jamie, who landed on the floor with a thud.

'You pretty lady,' he said. His eyes glittered as he looked at her.

'Ma.' Davy tugged at her dress.

She reached down and lifted Jamie from the floor before pushing him to the door.

Davy tugged at her dress again. She patted his head but didn't look at him.

'Take Jamie and go to Madge,' she said. 'You'll be safe there.'

'But Ma.'

'I said go, and make sure you look after your brother.'

'Come on Jamie. Ma says we're to go to Madge.' His voice broke and Belle knew he was near to tears.

Belle backed away from the man, edging towards the door. His eyes followed her movements, and his beard quivered as his lips stretched into a smile.

Waiting until she heard the door of the building clang shut, she turned to flee.

A massive hand closed around her arm while the other pawed at the neck of her dress. She struggled, punching him with her free arm and kicking his shins. But it was hopeless. It was like kicking a rock. She twisted her head from side to side, trying to escape the foulness of his breath.

He laughed and pulled her closer. If she'd been a lady, she would probably have swooned. But Belle was no lady, and she swung her knee into his groin.

His face twisted with pain, his eyes closed, and the roar from his lips sounded like a wounded animal.

When his grip loosened, she tore herself free and rushed for the open door and the stairs that would lead her to safety.

With another roar, he pounced on her, pulling her back inside the room and throwing her against the wall with enough force to make her head spin.

She lay on the floor, stupefied, as he advanced towards her with a gleam in his eyes and a savage look on his face that did not portend well.

Her heartbeat quickened and her breath wheezed from her lips, but she was damned if she would show her fear of him. Defiantly she glared at him. She couldn't stop him, but she would make sure her nails left their mark.

The aroma of whisky, oakum, and a multitude of offensive smells from the seaman's body turned Belle's stomach.

He bent over her. 'Pretty, so pretty.'

She twisted her head to the side, but he grabbed her chin and forced it back. Unable to escape, she gathered all her strength and spat in his face.

A globule of spit rolled down his cheek and onto his beard. His eyes flared with anger and bunching his fist, he slammed it into her face.

Belle's head rocked back, hitting the wall with a thud. Her teeth punctured her lip, and she tasted the saltiness of blood on her tongue.

With one massive hand, he grasped the top of her gown and ripped her bodice open. Throwing her to the floor, he straddled her.

His beard scraped her face, and she gritted her teeth. There was nothing more she could do to save herself. At least the bairns were safe.

He collapsed on top of her and lay unmoving. She wriggled, but he was a dead weight. Belle didn't believe in God, but she sent up a prayer of thanks. The seaman had passed out. Now, all she had to do was get him off her.

She pressed her hands to his chest and pushed while she wriggled some more. That was when she sensed another pair of hands pushing from the side.

He was heavy, and it took all her strength to escape from beneath his body. Exhausted, she lay back on the floor to regain her breath.

'Are you all right? Has he hurt you?'

Thelma's voice trembled. She sank to her knees and reached for Belle. 'I tried to protect the bairns, but he was too strong for me. And then, when he attacked you, I didn't know what to do.' Tears streamed down her face.

'Whatever you did, I thank you,' Belle said, gathering Thelma into her arms.

Thelma raised her tear-stained face to stare into Belle's eyes. 'But I think I've killed him.'

47

Thelma's words rang in Belle's ears and, horror-struck, she stared at the seaman's body. Was he dead as Thelma said? Or was he unconscious? She stretched her leg towards him and nudged him with her foot. He didn't move, but that didn't mean he was dead.

'Are you sure he's not just unconscious?'

'I killed him.' Thelma's voice was little more than a whisper.

Belle stared into Thelma's tear-stained face. The woman was shaking. Obviously, she hadn't recovered fully from the blow to her head, which made it difficult for her to believe Thelma had enough strength to kill a man.

'How did you kill him?'

Thelma shuddered. 'With the fire iron. My head ached after he hit me, and everything went black for a time. I'm not sure how long I was out, but when I came to, I saw him attacking you. I knew I had to do something.'

Belle tightened her arms around Thelma's body. 'I'm glad you did. It might have been me lying there. But how on earth did you manage? When I came in and saw you lying on the floor, I thought you were dead.'

'My head was spinning, and I couldn't see straight but I pulled myself up and walloped him on the head with the fire iron. It didn't take much strength.'

Belle's relief at being rescued from the seaman's clutches dissipated as the horror of the situation swept over her. What were they to do? If the man was dead, they had a problem. Damn it all, it was more than a problem. It was a catastrophe.

Visions of the Tolbooth filled her mind. Would they lock her and Thelma up in that horrible place? Would they hang?

Fear crawled up her spine.

'What do we do about the body? We can't leave it here.'

'I don't know.'

'If anyone comes in here, they'll see it. We need to put him in the bedroom while we think of what to do.' Belle struggled to her feet.

Thelma grabbed the table and pulled herself up. 'He's too heavy for us to move.'

She swayed, and Belle thought she was going to collapse. But this was no time to feel sorry for Thelma. They had to move the body out of sight.

'Come on,' she said through gritted teeth. 'You take one leg, I'll take the other, and we'll drag him.'

Unable to keep a grip on the man's boots, she grabbed his knee. But no matter how much both women pulled, they only moved him a few inches nearer to the bedroom door. Exhausted, Belle shuffled away from him, distancing herself from the foul smell of his body. The dirt-encrusted cloth of his breeches had left her fingers sticky, and she rubbed her hands on the tatters of her dress to clean them.

'It's no use,' Thelma said.

'We'll try again in a minute.' Belle took several deep breaths. They couldn't give up now. They had to get the strength from somewhere. But even if they got him into the bedroom, what then?

'Did you hear that?' Thelma's whisper was barely audible.

'What?'

'The downstairs door. I'm sure I heard someone come in.'

'I didn't hear anything.'

Belle crawled across the floor to Thelma and grasped her hand. Had Thelma imagined it, or had someone entered the building while she was concentrating on her breathing?

'Footsteps,' Thelma whispered, 'on the stairs.' She turned anxious eyes towards Belle. 'What will we do?'

The footsteps were getting nearer. Belle stood and snuffed out the candle on the mantelpiece before crouching and pulling Thelma underneath the table.

'The door,' Thelma whispered.

'No time. Stay quiet. Maybe they'll continue upstairs.'

The footsteps paused before they reached the landing. Belle held her breath.

Soundlessly, she prayed. Keep going up the stairs. Don't stop. But it was useless. Whoever was there mounted the last few steps and entered the room.

Someone stopped in the doorway. She heard a sharp intake of breath and then the person crossed the room to where the seaman's body lay.

His feet were inches from where they hid and Belle tightened her grip on Thelma's hand, but it wasn't enough to prevent her slight moan of fear.

'We're closed. Go away,' Gregor shouted in response to the banging on the door. He'd had enough of drunken sailors for one night.

Scowling, he poured himself a whisky, although he reckoned it would take more than one drink to forget the contempt he'd seen in Belle's eyes when the trouble broke out. What did she expect him to do? Wade in and break it up? But he'd seen his share of fights over the years and had no regrets about staying out of the way. Belle probably thought he was a coward, but he knew better than to intervene when a battle was at its height. It would be a foolish man who confronted a horde of enraged seamen.

The banging on the door continued as if both hands and feet were pummelling it. Not satisfied with that, they knocked on the window.

'I said, go away.'

He slammed his glass on the bar counter and strode to the window with his fist raised in a threatening gesture. But when he peered out, a child's face stared back at him. It only took a moment for him to recognise one of Belle's bairns. What was he doing here at this time of night? Was Belle with him? Or was she in trouble?

The boy mouthed something but, unable to hear what he was saying, Gregor hurried to the door, pulled the bolts back and swung it open.

Gregor stood back as the boys rushed inside. He stared along the road before closing the door.

'Where's your ma?'

The boys huddled together and looked at him with scared eyes.

'Ma said we'd to come here and Madge would keep us safe,' one boy said. Gregor wasn't sure whether it was Jamie or Davy. He could never tell which boy was which.

'What do you mean?' Fear crawled up Gregor's spine. What did they need to be kept safe from? And where was Belle?

'She said to come to Madge,' the boy repeated, shrinking back from him.

Although Gregor was desperate to find out what the boy meant, he resisted the urge to shake the information out of him.

The boy trembled and backed a few steps more, his eyes focused on Gregor's clenched fists.

Realising he was scaring the lad; he hurried to the staircase.

'Madge,' he shouted, 'I think something's happened to Belle. Her bairns are here, but they won't speak to me.'

A few moments later, Madge appeared.

'What's happened?'

She staggered as both boys launched themselves at her. Jamie hid his face in her skirts and Davy pulled at her arm.

'Ma said we'd to come to you and you'd keep us safe.' Tears shone in his eyes, and he blinked to stop them from rolling down his cheeks.

Madge knelt and pulled both boys into her arms. 'Why do you need to be kept safe?'

Jamie, his face wet with tears, lifted his head from her skirts. 'The man,' he said, 'he's hurting her.'

Gregor's heart thumped. Belle was in trouble. He needed to go to her.

'You stay with the bairns,' he said. 'I'll see to Belle.'

Without waiting for Madge to respond he rushed out of the inn. Leaving the place unlocked was the least of his worries.

Oblivious to the rising wind and the spray whipping over the road, he raced to Belle's tenement house. The sense of doom he'd experienced after Jamie's words increased with each step he took.

The building loomed up in front of him. He expected Granny Mutch to show up at the doorstep, but her windows were dark like the others in the building.

Silence met him when he pushed the street door open. Without hesitation, he stepped into the lobby. The door swung shut behind him. Darkness enveloped him. He paused for a moment to allow his eyes to adjust. But no light penetrated this dark tunnel leading to the stairs, where the only sound was the soft patter of tiny animal feet. He shuddered. Rats were everywhere in this part of town, and he loathed them.

Placing his hand on the wall, he felt his way to the stairwell. A glimmer of moonlight blinked through the window halfway up the stairs to relieve the stygian blackness from which he emerged. It was enough to let him see the stairs. One flight led down to the cellars and the other up to the houses within the tenement. A wrong turn and he would have been down among the rats and the stinking water which seeped in when the river was high.

His footsteps echoed upwards as he climbed the stairs. It was an ominous sound, and he didn't like it. The silence bothered him. What if something had happened to Belle? What if he was too late?

The door of Belle's flat was open, but nothing stirred. Pausing for a moment, he tightened his grip on the rickety banister and listened. Something wasn't right. His throat tightened, and defying his initial instinct to be cautious, he climbed the last few steps until he reached the doorway to Belle's home.

The glow from the fire was enough for him to see the body sprawled on the floor.

Madge grabbed Davy's collar as he tried to follow Gregor from the inn.

He wriggled. 'Leave me be. I have to go back.'

She tightened her grip. 'Your ma sent you here to be safe. Gregor will see she's all right.'

'But ...'

'No buts. Your ma won't be pleased if you defy her wishes. She'd want you to look after Jamie and you can't do that if you leave here.'

Davy stopped wriggling to swipe away a rogue tear trickling down his face. 'You sure Gregor will help her?' His voice was quieter now.

'I'm sure. Gregor's a big man, a match for anyone, even that sailor you told me about. He'll make sure your ma is safe.'

'Don't leave me.' Jamie tugged at Davy's hand.

Madge gathered the boys into her arms. Jamie's body quivered as the child gave way to tears and he buried his face in her bosom. Davy, the stronger of the two, fought the tears, but even he clung to her.

She had no children of her own, but as she felt the two small bodies pressing into her, a rush of maternal feeling took her by surprise. Her arms tightened around them. 'Come on, boys. You can sleep in my bed tonight and in the morning, you'll find Gregor has sorted everything out.'

Jamie nodded and allowed her to lead him upstairs. A reluctant Davy trailed behind.

Madge sat beside the bed until both boys fell asleep and waited until she was sure they wouldn't wake again. After a time she left the room, closed the door quietly behind her, and returned downstairs to wait. There would be no sleep for her tonight. Not until Gregor returned.

48

Belle stared at the man's feet and prayed silently. Please, please don't let him hear her. But it was no use. The man bent to look under the table.

'Belle,' he said. 'Is that you?'

It was too dark to see his features, but Belle knew the voice.

'Gregor?'

'Aye, lass, it's me. The bairns told us there was trouble.'

His hand closed over hers and she crawled from under the table, although Thelma remained crouched underneath.

'We've been so scared, and we didn't know who was coming up the stairs.'

'No need to be afeared of me.'

He reached out to pull her into his arms, but she shrank back. Damn, why did she do that? If she wanted his help, she couldn't risk alienating him.

'I'm sorry,' she whispered. 'But it's so dark and after what's happened, my imagination is running riot.' She turned from him and reached for a spill from the jar perched on the fender. 'I'll light a candle. Maybe that will help me cope better.'

Her hand shook as she held the spill to the glowing embers of the fire before transferring it to the candle on the mantelpiece. The flicker of light reflected off Gregor's face. His usual glower had gone, replaced by a look of concern. For the first time since they'd first met, she felt she could trust him.

'You'd best tell me what's happened.' He lifted the candle and held it over the seaman's body. 'And who this is?'

'I don't know. I came home. He was hurting my boys and Sarah wasn't here. I don't know where she is.' Tears slid down her face. 'Then he attacked me.' A strangled sob shivered through her lips, and she shook as she remembered the horror of it.

Gregor straightened. 'You killed him?'

'No, no. That was Thelma.'

Belle bent and peered under the table. 'It's safe to come out now, Thelma. Gregor won't hurt us, and if we tell him the story of what happened, maybe he'll help us.'

Gregor turned and closed the door. 'Don't want any nosy neighbours seeing what's in here,' he said.

Thelma stood and straightened her skirt. 'The folks living in this tenement won't want to know. That's why their doors have stayed shut. They'll know something's been going on, but they won't want to be involved.'

Gregor listened while Thelma related what happened, starting with the seaman threatening Sarah and the girl's escape, ending with the attack on Belle.

'I didn't mean to kill him,' she said, 'but I was afeared for Belle. So I swung the poker at his head to get him off her.'

Belle watched him. His face had remained expressionless while Thelma was speaking, and she did not know what was going on in his mind.

'It's a rum do,' he said when Thelma finished speaking. 'If the town officers get wind of it, you'll both end up in the Tolbooth.'

'Bloody hell,' Thelma said. 'We wouldn't last a week in that rat-infested hellhole.'

Belle shuddered. As long as the seaman's body remained here, they were done for. They hadn't a hope of moving it themselves. And what if some of his mates came looking for him? Her mind whirled, panic tightened her throat, and she struggled to breathe. There was only one thing she could do to get them out of this mess. She would have to appeal to Gregor to help them.

Her decision made, she laid her hand on top of Gregor's. 'We need to get rid of the body before anyone sees him. Will you help us?'

After a moment's thought, he said. 'I have no more wish to end up in the Tolbooth than you do.'

'I'd be in your debt forever if you help us.' She stroked the back of his hand to emphasise her meaning. It was an unspoken promise that hung in the air between them, for she knew Gregor desired her.

Her eyes held his, and she saw the indecision on his face. Would he help them?

'Please,' she said. 'I have no one else I can turn to.' And then she held her breath, waiting for his answer.

Every sound in the flat magnified as Belle waited for Gregor's decision. Wind and rain rattled the window. She heard her own breathing. Thelma whimpered beside her. And a mouse scurried behind the skirting boards.

When Belle saw the scowl return to Gregor's face, she sensed he was wrestling with his desire for her and his need for self-preservation. She could tell he was wavering and getting ready to leave them to fend for themselves. But she couldn't allow that to happen.

It wasn't difficult to force tears to her eyes, for she knew left to their own devices, she and Thelma had no chance of getting rid of the seaman's body. They didn't have the physical strength. Gregor, used as he was to handling beer barrels every day, had that strength.

She reached for him, holding her body close to his and lifting her tear-stained face to look into his eyes. 'Please Gregor, I don't want to hang for this,' she whispered. 'You are the only one who can help me.' She deliberately refrained from mentioning Thelma so his focus would be on her alone.

His hands tightened around her. 'For you, Belle.' His voice was husky. 'Anything for you.'

He kissed the top of her head and held her close. The several moments they stood together felt to Belle like hours and her instinct was to pull away. But instead, she laid her head on his chest and leaned into him. If he was willing to sacrifice his safety and risk the hangman, she could do no less than acquiesce to his need for her.

49

Gregor, weighed down by the body slung over his shoulder, stumbled after Thelma as she headed for the stairs leading down through the darkness of the building.

'I'll lead the way to open the doors,' Thelma had said. 'You two follow on with him.'

Fear rippled through Belle as the lower they went, the darker it became, and she hoped the arm she'd slung around Gregor's waist would steady him. Getting the seaman into an upright position and onto Gregor's shoulder had been difficult enough. It would be disastrous if he dropped him. And it would only take one stumble or a missed stair for that to happen.

Belle tested the edge of each step with her foot, whispering to Gregor each time in case he overbalanced by looking down.

'This is the last step,' she whispered when they reached the bottom. 'Turn to your right.'

She guided him along the darkened lobby, feeling her way with one hand on the wall while the other continued to support him.

The door to the street creaked open, and they stood still for a moment, but nothing stirred.

Thelma stood in the open doorway, a grey shadow against the night sky. She bent to peer outside and, after a moment, whispered, 'It's all clear. No one in sight.'

Belle left the building first, then turned to guide Gregor down the doorstep. 'Be careful,' she whispered, 'the rain has made the step slippery.'

Wind whipped down the street, forcing Belle to remove her arm from Gregor's waist to grasp her shawl and secure it. Without her supporting arm, he staggered when a gust caught him, and the fire iron embedded in the seaman's head clanked off the doorpost.

Belle grabbed him, and her eyes darted to Granny Mutch's window, expecting to see a light. But it remained in darkness. She let out her breath with a sigh of relief. This was not the time for her landlady to poke her nose in.

'I'll stay here and hold the door open,' Thelma whispered, her eyes wide with fear as she glanced back into the lobby.

Not a sound emanated from the building. If any of the inhabitants had heard what was happening, they were keeping their heads down. No one wanted to get involved, not like Craigden where you couldn't move without everyone knowing.

Buffeted by the wind, Gregor and Belle staggered across the road. As they approached the other side, the rush of the water, mixed with the howl of the wind, battered their ears.

Gregor balanced the body on the low wall bordering the river and stood for a moment to gather his breath.

'What are you waiting for?' Belle hissed.

'I need you to pull out the poker,' he said.

'Why?'

'Because if they fish his body out of the sea and the poker is still there, they'll know it was foul play and it will lead them back to you. If you take it out, clean it and put it back where it belongs, it can't be proved your poker did the damage. The fishes will get him before he's found, and they'll think he fell in the water and drowned.'

Belle shuddered. She didn't want to touch the fire iron, but she'd always faced up to anything life threw at her, even the most unpleasant tasks. So she steeled herself and grasped the metal shaft. The hooked end had embedded itself with such force in the man's skull it took every bit of her strength to pull it out. At last, it came free.

Gregor let go of the seaman, but the body swayed and was in danger of toppling back on top of them. However, after a moment, it lurched forward and vanished over the wall, landing with the faintest of splashes in the water below.

'The tide will take him out to sea,' Gregor said. 'If we'd been much later, it would've been on the turn, and he'd have landed up in the basin.'

Belle looked upriver to the bridge silhouetted against the night sky but, although she heard the torrent of water rushing between the bridge pillars, she was unable to see it. Soon the inland area of water known as the basin would become mud flats until the tide turned to refill it again. If the body was swept there, it would only be a matter of time before it was discovered.

A burst of song, echoing from a ship in the harbour, drifted to them on the wind.

'Best we get away from here.' Gregor grabbed Belle's hand and hustled her across the road to where Thelma waited for them in the doorway.

'What took you so long?' Her voice echoed up the lobby.

'Shh.'

Thelma burst into tears at Gregor's sibilant response. Belle sensed the woman was on the point of a breakdown and reached out to hug her. But Thelma let go of the door she was holding and scuttled into the darkness of the building. Belle followed, to quieten her before she roused anyone.

Behind her, Gregor caught the door and eased it shut to prevent it from slamming against the doorpost.

As Belle hurried after Thelma, she was conscious of even the smallest of sounds. The pad of their feet, the swish of her skirt, and Thelma's gasps when the stairs creaked. Belle, although her anxiety levels were just as high, reached out a hand to calm her.

Once they reached the safety of Belle's flat, Thelma, after peering into the darkness of the stairs leading upwards, insisted they lock the door.

'We're safe now,' Belle said in a soothing voice.

'But what if someone comes? What if they see this?' Thelma gestured to the stain on the floor and the upturned chairs. Her eyes widened with fear. 'They'll know what we've done.'

'Then we can't let anyone see it,' Belle said. 'We need to get cleaning.'

Gregor nodded in agreement while he heaped sticks and coal on the dying embers in the grate. 'Fill some pots with water, ready to place on the fire once it takes hold.' He blew on the flickering flames to encourage them to burn. They would need as much heat as the fire could muster to provide enough hot water to scour the stains from the floorboards. While he waited, he cleaned the poker and replaced it in the fender.

After they scrubbed the floor and tidied the flat, Thelma was a lot calmer.

'I need to go home now,' she said, 'back to my own house.'

'Will you be all right?' Belle was still worried about her.

Thelma nodded. 'It's just next door. If I get scared, I'll come back.'

After she left, Belle huddled into a chair and stared into the fire. 'D'you think she'll be all right and hold her tongue about what happened tonight?'

'She'd be a fool to talk,' Gregor said. 'She was the one who killed him.'

'But we helped get rid of the body. So, we're just as guilty.'

They both lapsed into silence. After a time, Belle said, 'What now?'

'You need to get some sleep. You're exhausted.'

Belle hesitated. Did that mean he wanted to bed her?

As if sensing what she was thinking, he said, 'You can leave the bedroom door open if you want or close it. I'll stay here and sleep in the chair.'

She paused before entering the bedroom. 'I don't know where Sarah is. What if she comes back?'

'I'll wake you.'

Belle nodded and tumbled into bed, but did not sleep. Guilt plagued her. Why hadn't she given thought to Sarah before? She tried to excuse herself. A lot had happened over the past few hours. It was no wonder she'd given little thought to her daughter. But, if she'd been a good mother, she would have worried more about Sarah. She wouldn't have rested until she knew what had happened to her and made sure she was safe. With that thought, she closed her eyes but still sleep evaded her, and every minute seemed like an hour.

50

Sarah sat scrunched in the corner of the washhouse all night, afraid to move, afraid to go back to the house. Afraid the seaman would still be there. Afraid of what she would find.

The night seemed endless, and she dozed off and on. In between the snatches of sleep, she watched the tiny square window lighten until dawn came, but still, she did not move.

The creak of the door set her heart thumping, and she pushed herself further back into the corner. She screwed her eyes shut, afraid of what she might see.

A hand grasped her shoulder, sending a shiver through her. She recoiled.

'What's wrong, lass?' the woman's voice was rough but friendly. 'Don't tell me ye've been here all night. Have ye nowhere else to go?'

Sarah turned frightened eyes up to the woman who stood there. She looked massive and alien in her rubber apron and boots, and it was a moment before Sarah recognised a neighbour who had come to the washhouse to do her washing.

'Why it's Belle's wee lass, isn't it?' The neighbour tightened her grasp and pulled Sarah from her corner. 'And ye're frozen. What are ye doing here anyway? Has tha' Ma thrown thee out?'

'No!' Sarah gasped. 'I was hiding.'

'Why are ye hiding, lass? What's to hide from?'

Sarah saw the curiosity in the woman's eyes, so she scowled and shook her head.

'Ye'd better get back home then, hadn't ye?' and with a slight shake, the neighbour turned her round and pushed her out of the washhouse door.

Sarah stumbled across the grass, afraid the woman would call her back.

Faint light filtered through the window before Belle lapsed into a troubled sleep. She tossed and turned, fleeing from the unknown. Harsh voices and clutching hands peppered her dreams. She reached for Jimmie, but of course, Jimmie wasn't there. He'd never returned from his last voyage to the Arctic, where he slept in an icy grave. The cries of the twins filtered into her consciousness. Crying out for her. Crying out for Sarah.

Belle groaned and blinked her eyes several times. She had the strangest feeling her head was floating above her body and couldn't remember where she was. She moved her arm, gasping as the rough blanket rubbed against the bruises, and was suddenly fully awake.

The door in the next room banged open.

Two voices in unison demanded, 'Where's Ma?'

At least the twin's voices weren't leftover remnants of her dream. They were real. But that didn't answer the question lingering in her mind. Where was Sarah? The last time Belle had seen her was before she left for work the previous day.

The low rumble of Gregor's voice answered the twins, and they bounded into the bedroom and onto the bed.

Belle winced, and ignoring the pain from her bruises, pulled herself up to wrap her arms around them.

Gregor stood in the doorway. 'I couldn't keep them out. They wanted to know if you were safe and if the bad man had gone.'

'Is Sarah not with them?'

'No, it's only the boys. When you sent them to the inn last night, Madge kept them there, but Sarah wasn't with them.'

Belle's arms tightened around her boys. At least they were safe. But where was Sarah?

Davy wriggled in her tight grasp. 'We wanted to come back and help. But Madge refused to let us. She said Gregor would protect you.'

'Madge was right. You're only little, and Gregor is a lot bigger. If you'd stayed, you might have got hurt.'

'I'm not too little,' Davy protested. 'I'm six now.'

'But you also had another job, and that was to keep Jamie safe. He's not as brave as you and when Sarah's not here, it's your job to look after him.'

'I suppose,' Davy said.

Jamie lifted his head from the crook of Belle's arm. 'We thought ye were dead.' His voice trembled.

'Well, I'm not. Gregor looked after me just fine,' she said. 'But I'm worried about Sarah. She's not here and I don't know what happened to her.'

'She ran off,' Davy said, 'when me and Jamie belted the sailor man.'

'That's right,' Jamie interrupted, 'and look, I've got a black eye. The sailor mannie whopped me because we let Sarah get awa.'

'My,' Belle said, 'aren't you the brave ones.'

She held them close, her two boys so alike no one but she and Sarah could tell them apart, so like their da it was painful to look at them. She tightened her grasp and tried not to think of Jimmie, who had sworn never to leave her.

Davy was the first to wriggle free from her grasp. 'Ye're hurting me,' he protested, his face red with the exertion.

Belle relaxed her grip on him. Davy had never enjoyed cuddles as much as Jamie did. He was too independent and had a tough image to maintain. Both he and Jamie had run wild since they came to Invercraig, and she didn't know what he got up to when she wasn't there. She hoped he never got caught.

Jamie remained in her arms, and she stroked his hair absent-mindedly. He was the sensitive one, always concerned about her, and about Sarah. As if sensing her thoughts Jamie looked up, his eyes brimming with tears, 'Where's Sarah? D'ye think she's all right?'

'I hope so, Jamie. I surely hope so.'

She shivered as she remembered last night's events. The fear when the sailor held her by the throat. Had he done the same to Sarah?

And had she felt the same fear? Sarah was only a child and shouldn't have to experience such things. Belle had never been maternal, but she realised it was up to her to protect her children.

In Craigden they had been safe, but here in Invercraig, it was different. Dangers existed here that affected all of them. They weren't safe here. She would have to do something about it.

Belle loosened her hold on Jamie. 'I'm aching all over,' she said, dangling her feet over the side of the bed before she attempted to stand up. Tears pricked her eyelids. She wasn't sure whether this was because of Sarah, or because of her aches and pains. It had been a long time since she'd shed tears. She'd cried a lot after she lost Jimmie, but she'd resolved never to cry again, so she blinked and refused to allow the tears to flow.

'I'm going to find somewhere else for Sarah to live,' she announced to the twins. 'It's not safe for her to stay here.'

'What d'ye mean? Where else can she live but here?'

Belle avoided Jamie's eyes. 'Just what I said. I need to know she's safe. After what happened to her last night, I know she's not safe here.' Belle clasped her arms around her body and rocked in her chair. 'Now off you go and find Sarah and tell her to come home.'

Her eyes were bleak. She'd never given much thought to Sarah, and the wrench in her heart surprised her.

Sarah slid to a halt at the back door to the tenement. The urge to remain outside and hide was strong, but the neighbour who had discovered her hiding in the washhouse now stood with folded arms, watching her. With a final despairing look at the woman, Sarah slipped into the lobby of the building.

The stairs, gloomy in the dawn light, yawned above her, leading to the unknown above. Her reluctant feet climbed upwards. What awaited her in the flat upstairs? Would the sailor still be there? And what would she do if he was? Her feet slowed at the top. She paused to listen. Hearing nothing, she advanced to the door and pushed it open the merest fraction.

The sight of a man standing in the living room caused her to gasp, and she took a step back, ready to flee. But the man turned, and she saw it was Gregor from the inn. But she didn't trust him any more than she did the sailor.

'Wait,' he said. 'Your ma's been looking for you.'

But Sarah was already running down the stairs.

'Madge, run after her and tell her it's all right.'

His voice floated down the stairs after her.

Madge caught up with Sarah at the front door. She grasped the girl's arm.

'There's no need to be afraid. Gregor didn't mean to frighten you. He's only there to protect your ma.'

'The sailor,' Sarah gasped.

'He's gone and won't be returning. Not while Gregor's there. Come home, lass. Belle's been worried about you.'

Sarah doubted that. Her mother had never worried about her in the past. She'd never wanted a daughter and only ever loved the twins. Sarah often thought her mother would be glad to see the back of her, even though she made herself useful by caring for Davy and Jamie.

Reluctantly, she followed Madge back upstairs to the flat. It was the only home she knew.

51

After Gregor and Madge left, leaving Belle alone with the children, she had more time to think. She had wanted to take time to tell Sarah her decision, but the twins pre-empted her.

'Ma says you can't stay here. You have to go away and live somewhere else.'

'Why?' Sarah turned puzzled eyes to Belle

'It's not safe for you here.'

'It's not safe for any of us.'

'I know. But you are still a child, and my job is to protect you.'

Sarah fell silent and looked away from her mother to stare into the fire.

Belle wanted to reach out and hug her. Tell her it didn't mean she wasn't loved, but she couldn't bring herself to do it. Sarah wouldn't believe her anyway, because Belle's jealousy of Jimmie's love for his daughter had prevented a bond from developing between them.

'It's for your own good.'

Sarah turned away to remove a pot from the fire. She poured warm water from it into a basin at the sink, then wiped a wet flannel over Davie's face.

The boy wriggled in her grasp. 'I don't need my face washed.' Davie had an aversion to water and wasn't as compliant as Jamie.

'I'll be glad when you're not here,' he said. 'I won't need my face washed.'

Sarah scrubbed harder, and Belle thought she saw tears in the girl's eyes.

Sadness encompassed Belle. What would she do without Sarah's help? But after last night she knew Sarah wasn't safe here, and she had to do something.

Doubts filled her mind. How would she cope with the boys on her own? She loved them, but Sarah had always been the one to attend to their needs. At ten years old, her daughter was more of a mother to them than Belle was. And how would the twins react without Sarah in their lives?

Conflicting thoughts raced around her mind, but she could find no simple answer. She knew the twins, left to their own devices, would run wild without Sarah to curb their excesses. There was no knowing what kind of mischief they'd get up to.

She gathered the twins into her arms and hugged them.

'You're hurting me.' Davie struggled to free himself, but she tightened her hold.

'How would you feel if you went with Sarah?'

Davie stopped wriggling. 'D'you mean send us away, like Sarah?'

Sarah dropped the wet flannel into the basin and stared at her mother.

'Where would we go?'

'Back to Craigden. I'm sure Annie would make room for you. And you'd have Jeannie for company.'

'What about you?'

'I'd have to stay here to earn enough money for our keep.'

The doubt left Sarah's eyes, and she looked at the twins. 'Would you like to go back to Craigden?'

Davie wriggled out of Belle's grasp. 'Yes,' he shouted. 'Craigden's better than here.'

Jamie, after a glance at his mother, nodded his head.

'That's it settled then. I'll go to the fish market tomorrow and talk to Annie.' Belle's voice broke, and she turned away to avoid letting them see her tears. Her heart was breaking at the thought of losing her boys.

The morning started fine and sunny, spring was in the air. But, as the day wore on, clouds gathered, obliterating the sun and darkening the sky. Belle sat by the window, listening to the wind whistling up the river as the storm increased, and angry waves turned the river into a torrent. If it carried the sailor's body far away, there would be no link back to Invercraig.

She was so deep in her thoughts she didn't hear Sarah the first time she spoke.

'Will the sailor come back?' Sarah repeated her question.

'No,' Belle said. 'I don't think he will.'

Her children were unaware of what had happened after they left. The only thing they knew was the sailor had been in their house and had threatened them.

'If he comes back, I'll save you again.' Davie squared his shoulders and clenched his fists. 'Like I did last night.'

'You're very brave,' Belle said, 'but you're too wee, and I wouldn't want anyone to hurt you.'

'Is that why we have to go to grandma?'

'Yes. I want you to be safe.'

'Will you come too?' Jamie had been quiet up to now.

'No, I have to stay here and work, so we have money to live. I'll need to give grandma some money to take care of you.'

'But grandma is always working. She won't have time for us.'

Sarah crossed the room and folded the boys into her arms. 'Don't worry,' she whispered. 'I'll look after you. I've always looked after you.'

Belle flinched. Sarah was only a child herself, but she was more of a mother to Davie and Jamie than she was.

The rest of the day passed in an uneasy silence while Belle brooded on the catastrophic events of the night before. Similarly, the boys were subdued, whispering to each other, and Sarah, hunched on a stool beside the fire, appeared to be lost in her own thoughts. Belle could only imagine what those thoughts might be and how the sailor's attack affected her.

The steeple clock chiming five reminded her it was time she left for the inn. Indecision rippled through her. After everything that had happened, how could she leave the children? But she needed to work.

She would need every penny she made to ensure their safety in Craigden. Annie wasn't rich and couldn't be expected to feed extra mouths without Belle providing for their keep. Besides, she didn't want to risk Gregor's anger. He relied on her to be there because she was popular with his customers. They bought more ale when she served them. He wouldn't understand her need to protect her children from further harm.

She rose from her chair and sank back down again.

Sarah, as if sensing her mother's reluctance to leave, said, 'Don't worry about us. I'll look after Davie and Jamie, and I'll make sure I keep the door locked.'

Belle opened her eyes and stared at her daughter. Sarah's solemn eyes stared back at her. It was as if she were the grown-up, and Belle was the child. Had Sarah ever been a child? Even from her earliest days, she'd had this serious nature combined with a sense of responsibility far too old for her years.

'I'm afraid to leave you alone.' Belle's voice quavered.

'But you need to give grandma money, and you won't have any to give her unless you work.'

What Sarah said made sense, but it didn't make it any easier for Belle to leave.

'Lock the door and put a chair under the doorknob,' Belle said before she left. 'And don't open it for anyone but me.'

She waited until she heard the click of the lock, a chair being dragged over the floor, and the clunk against the door as Sarah manoeuvred it into position.

By the time she reached the Ship Inn, she wasn't sure whether her face was wet with tears or the rain.

With a last glance back along the street, she pushed open the inn door, pasted a smile onto her face and made ready for the longest night of her life.

Belle shook the drips out of her hair and wiped her wet face with the edge of her shawl after the door clicked shut behind her. A few men propped up the bar while old Tam, cradling a mug of ale in his hands, huddled in his usual seat beside the fire. Give it another hour and the place would be heaving with sailors from the three boats in the harbour. No doubt the place would be rowdy before the night was out.

Madge looked up from pouring a mug of ale when Belle deposited her shawl behind the bar. 'You're late,' she said.

'I was getting the bairns settled. They're a wee bit upset after last night.' Belle found it difficult to explain her reluctance to leave them.

'Aye, I had a bit of trouble with your boys last night. They wanted to go back home, but I put them to bed. Thought it best, so they didn't get in the way.' She laid the full glass on the bar top. 'Gregor get it sorted then?'

Belle wasn't sure how much Gregor had told Madge. 'Aye,' she said, 'he persuaded the sailor to leave.'

Madge laughed. 'I'll bet the sailor has a sore head this morning.'

'Yes, I expect he does.' Belle shivered as the memory of the poker lodged in the man's head flashed across her mind.

'You look scared. Are you worried he'll return when you're not there?'

'I don't think he will, but there are always others. The bairns aren't safe in Invercraig.' Her eyes filled with tears. 'Oh, Madge,' she said. 'I've decided to ask Annie to take them back to Craigden with her. That's where they were happiest, and they'll be safe there.'

'Are you sure that's the right thing to do?'

Belle brushed the tears from her face. 'There's no other way. I can't look after the boys and they're running wild. Sarah does her best, but she's a bairn as well.'

Madge wrapped her arms around Belle. 'Then maybe it's for the best,' she murmured.

Gregor strode over to the bar. 'What's up with you two?'

'Belle has decided to send the bairns back to Craigden to live with their gran, and she's upset.'

'There's more than Belle upset. There's a man over there moaning you're taking too long to bring him his ale. You'd best get over there and sweet talk him.'

After Madge flounced off, Gregor turned to Belle. 'You're sending the bairns away?'

'They'll be safer in Craigden,' her voice broke when she thought about losing them.

'Aye, that they will.'

Gregor leaned his arms on the bar. 'And how safe will you be when you're in that house on your own?'

Belle shrugged. 'I can take care of myself.'

'Like you did last night?'

The memories returned, and a shiver of fear crawled up her spine. There were always men visiting the tenement to see Thelma, and she wasn't the only woman there who entertained the sailors.

She narrowed her eyes and looked at Gregor. 'What other options do I have?'

He sidled closer to her. 'Move in here.'

'With you?' Belle glared at him. 'I'm not a whore. I don't bed with men I'm not wed to.'

Gregor wouldn't know she'd bedded Jimmie before they wed, nor that she'd allowed Lachlan to share it. The less Gregor knew, the better.

'Ach Belle, I didnae mean that. You could share Madge's room for the time being.'

'What do you mean?'

'Until we get wed.'

Belle caught her breath and moved away from him. 'I'm already married.'

He moved closer until he'd backed her into a corner behind the bar. 'Not anymore,' he said. 'Your man is dead like all those other poor souls on the *Eclipse*.'

Tears rolled down her cheeks. 'My Jimmie was a good man.'

'I'll be a good man to ye as well. You need me, Belle. I'll protect you and if we're wed, they can't make either of us give evidence against the other.' He gripped her arms. 'We need each other, Belle.'

Belle stared at him as the full horror of what he was saying hit her. The awful events of last night bound them together in a secret so terrible it must never see the light of day.

Slowly, she nodded her head. She needed to ensure Gregor's silence. What better way to do that than to marry him?

He released his grip. 'We'll be good together, Belle. With you by my side, we can make this inn the best one in Invercraig.'

'What about the bairns?' Surely, he couldn't refuse to let them join her if they were wed.

'This is no place for bairns, fine ye know it. They'll fare better with their grandma, and ye can see them from time to time.'

Belle's last hope of keeping her children with her vanished. Gregor wanted her, but he didn't want the encumbrance of her bairns.

The rest of the night passed by so slowly, Belle thought it would never end. She laughed and flirted with the customers as usual, but her actions were mechanical, and her smile forced. Nothing seemed real except for Gregor standing behind the bar, watching her every movement.

What had happened last night had changed her life forever. It would never be the same again.

52

On market day there was much to do, and Annie woke early. She pushed the rough blanket aside, opened the doors enclosing the box bed, and swung her legs over the edge. The stone slabs chilled her feet and, shivering, she fumbled for her shoes.

She blinked in the semi-darkness. The mound in the truckle bed where her daughter slept didn't move, and only the top of her head showed.

'Up you get,' she said, prodding Jeannie in the back. 'There's no time to waste today.'

Jeannie, rubbing her eyes, emerged from below the blanket.

Annie pulled her clothes on over her shift, which she never took off until the weather improved. She wore it all winter and much of the spring.

'I'll get the fire going and the porridge pot on while you see to the beds.'

Jeannie grunted a response, and within minutes she was pushing the truckle bed underneath the box bed.

The fire didn't take long to kindle because it was easier to revive dying embers than to start a new fire.

She mixed the oatmeal and hung the pot on the sway hook before moving it over the flames.

Jeannie grabbed a broom and hurriedly swept the floor. Once that was done, she laid bowls on the table in readiness for the return of the men.

'Ye'll make someone a braw wife someday, Jeannie.'

'The fisher lads aren't interested in me.' Jeannie didn't look up from her task. 'They want lassies strong enough to carry them to the boats.'

'I wisnae thinking about the fisher lads. I've seen the way Wattie looks at you.'

Annie watched with interest as Jeannie's cheeks reddened. She hadn't been mistaken. There was something between the two of them.

'Havers,' Jeannie said, but there was no conviction in her voice.

Annie slopped porridge into two of the bowls before moving the sway hook away from the fire.

'Get that down ye. We won't have time to come back here once they land the fish.'

The sun was rising when they left the house, and although it was early, Annie thought she detected a bit of warmth in the rays. Maybe spring was coming at last, and April would be better than the March storms.

Annie and Jeannie joined the other women on the foreshore and, like them, they strained their eyes looking seawards. Waves battered over the rocks at the river mouth, but as yet, there was no sign of the boats. But Annie knew her James was out there, heading home as fast as possible with the wind in *Bonnie Annie*'s sails. It was a feeling she couldn't describe, but she knew it within herself, and she was never wrong.

They hadn't been waiting long when cadger Wullie's cart drew up alongside. Wullie came from Invercraig, and he usually set off when he spotted the boats far out to sea, long before the villagers caught sight of them.

Sure enough, moments later, the first of the boats swung around the lighthouse and into the river mouth. With full sails, they scudded up the river until they were close enough for the men to leap off.

Annie fixed her eyes on James and her sons as they pulled and pushed the *Bonnie Annie* shoreward until the boat rested on the pebbles. She waited, thankful she didn't need to carry them on her back to the shore when they were homeward bound. It was different when they were heading out to the fishing grounds. A fisherman's wife would be ashamed to send her man to sea in wet clothes.

Cadger Wullie drew his cart up alongside the *Bonnie Annie*. James had an arrangement with him, and Wullie was always on hand to transport the excess fish to the Dundee market.

Annie strode to the boat. 'Come on Jeannie, best get our fish before Wullie gets started.'

Angus grinned at her. 'As if I'd let that happen.'

'Mind and fill a creel for taking home with ye.'

'I'm not daft Ma.'

Angus laid fish in the skull, the round basket which sat on top of Annie's creel which already held the tools of her trade. The gutting board and knives, weighing scales, and paper for wrapping the fish.

Meanwhile, Davie filled Jeannie's creels. They were smaller and differently shaped because she only needed to carry fish for her deliveries to the big house and other customers.

'That's your creels full, Jeannie. I'll help you strap them on.'

Davie lifted one of the baskets and lifted its strap over her head, then did the same with the other one so both straps crossed over the front of her body. The weight of the fish caused her to stagger, and she readjusted the straps to better balance the creels on her hips and reduce the pain in her shoulders.

'The fish are wee, so mind you give good measure.' Annie wiped her hands on her skirt.

'Aye, Ma.'

'And if you've any left when you finish your round, bring them to the market.'

Jeannie nodded and staggered up from the foreshore. She regained her balance once she got to the path leading out of the village and took off at a trot.

Annie watched her go. The lass was keen, but she wasn't strong. Even Belle, with all her faults, had managed the creels better. She'd carried them with a flair Jeannie didn't possess. She turned back to her creel with a sigh.

Angus had finished packing fish into the skull, and it lay at her feet full of gleaming white fish, the harvest of the line fishers. Craigden hadn't yet succumbed to using nets, although they said there was good money in the herring fishing. But it wasn't for them. The Craigden fishers regarded herring much the same way they did the red fish; the name they gave salmon. For no self-respecting fisherman would let that name cross his lips.

James and Angus were busy helping Cadger Wullie load his cart, but Davie hung back to help Annie.

'Are ye ready for your creel?'

'Ay, lad. But it's best we do it up on the road, so I don't have to climb from the foreshore with it.'

'You go on up, I'll bring the creels.'

Davie hoisted the creel up to feed the leather strap over Annie's head before positioning it across her shoulders. He scurried back to the foreshore for the skull of fish.

'You ready?' he said on his return.

When he placed it on top of the creel, Annie braced herself in readiness for the weight increase. She took several deep breaths and stood up straight. It was a long walk to Invercraig, and she would need all her strength. But Annie was strong, and the creels, although heavy, were no heavier than her man's weight when she carried him to the boat.

'I'll be off then. No sense in wasting time if I want to get one of the better spots at the market.' She waved to her men and strode off, leaving them to attend to the rest of the catch.

Selling fish at the fish market was something Annie took in her stride, but it had been a hard winter with a lack of good catches. Today's catch had been better, and Annie's creel was full. But competition at the market was fierce, with each fishwife trying to outdo the others.

The wind mocked her as she battled against it when crossing the bridge into the town. Would she make enough sales at the market to pay her bill at Wattie's general store? Or would she have to stay later, trudging around the big houses in the town to sell the leftover fish?

Thoughts of Belle didn't intrude, and she had no way of knowing that before the day's end, she would face a decision she hadn't expected to have to make.

53

Belle tossed and turned most of the night before falling into an uneasy sleep as dawn was breaking. She woke with a start, her cheeks wet and her pillow damp. Today was the last day before her children left. And then there was Gregor. What would her life with him be like?

Yesterday had been a disaster, and she'd been on edge since her decision to send the children to live with their grandparents. Her need to keep them with her was strong, but their safety was more important. In her anguish, she'd kept pulling the boys into her arms while Sarah looked on with big sad eyes. She wanted to hug Sarah as well, but the barrier between them was insurmountable. Belle realised she should have loved Sarah more, but it was too late now.

Belle parted the curtains of the box bed. No sound came from the adjoining bedroom, but she suspected Sarah was awake.

Last night's storm had passed, and the early morning sun glinted through the window. Padding over to it she looked across the river, but the ships in the harbour blocked her view of Craigden. They swayed and bumped against the quayside wall reminding her of the sailor. She shuddered. Would he be missed? Would they look for him?

Today, the tide was flowing up the river into the inland tidal basin. But when they tipped the sailor over the wall and into the water, Gregor had said it was in full flow, rushing out to sea. She hoped he was right, otherwise they would be in trouble. Anything the ingoing tide took into the basin remained on the mud flats when the tide turned. If they found the body? She shuddered. It didn't bear thinking about.

Footsteps on the landing and a knock at the door set her nerves on edge. She gripped the windowsill. Who could it be this early in the morning?

The knock came again. 'It's me.'

The low voice was barely more than a whisper.

Belle opened the door and peered out.

Thelma stood there clutching a carpet bag. 'I couldn't leave without saying goodbye.'

Belle opened the door wider. 'You're leaving?'

'Yes, I thought it for the best.'

'But where will you go?'

Thelma's cheeks reddened. 'I'm going away with one of my men friends. He's waiting in the street with his cart.'

'Will you be happy with him?'

'I don't know, but it's better than being thrown into the Tolbooth. And better than the hangman's noose.'

'Good luck,' Belle said.

Thelma laid her carpet bag down, leaned forward and hugged Belle. 'I'll miss you and the bairns.' The plume on her hat wobbled when she pressed her wet cheeks on Belle's face.

She released her arms and clattered down the stairs.

Belle watched her go with a heavy heart.

Annie staggered as the wind, whistling down river from the inland basin, caught her creel when she crossed the bridge. Lowering her head, she strode on, eager to reach the road on the other side. Once she reached its shelter, she stopped in front of the new infirmary to catch her breath and adjust her creel.

A line of carts rumbled past her, heading for the markets at the town centre. Friday was market day, where buyers and sellers came together for the produce on sale. Some carts would head for the meat market beside the town's steeple church. Others to the vegetable market further along the street. Not forgetting the fish market where Annie was going.

As she walked up Bridge Street, she couldn't help wondering about the grand houses lining the west side. What were they like inside? Were the folks who lived there as happy as she was in her wee cottage?

Life in Craigden was hard, but James was a good husband, and she had her family. There was nothing more important than family. It made her think of Belle and the children. How were they faring since leaving Craigden? The thought made her uneasy. She should have done more to help them. The bairns were, after all, sired by Jimmie, and were all she had left of him.

Lost in thought, she reached the end of Bridge Street and turned the corner into Castle Place. From there, the road split into Invercraig High Street on the left and Upper George Street on her right. She turned right.

The fish market lay halfway down the street, sandwiched between a tenement house on one side and the two-storey Eagle Inn beyond. It huddled between the two, a squat ramshackle structure which housed the town's fish market.

A holler from a carter forced Annie to stop before she reached the wide doors leading inside.

'Don't want to run you down,' the carter said, 'but if I stop Nellie,' he gestured to his tired-looking horse, 'I'll never get her to start again.'

He shouted a warning to those inside as he guided his horse into the gloomy interior.

Annie followed close behind. Voices echoed in the long hall to mingle with the clatter of hooves and the rumble of wheels. Annie's spirits sank while her eyes scanned the wide stone shelves lining the walls. If she couldn't find a space, she'd have to squat on the floor and sell her fish from there.

'Annie!'

A voice sounded above the clamour coming from the gaggle of fishwives crouched over the shelves, setting up their wares.

'I've saved you a space beside me.'

She peered to see where the voice was coming from, and when the horse and cart moved further along, she spotted Lizzie McNab waving to her. Ever since the fire, Lizzie had been currying favour with the

Craigden fisher folk. But Annie couldn't forget the hand she'd had in it.

'Thanks,' Annie said. 'You must have run all the way to get here before me.'

'Ye have to be quick to get in now the fishwives from Johnshaven are coming here instead of Stonehaven.'

'Their fish are not a patch on ours. Line caught fish are the best.'

'Aye, well, some folks seem to like the herring.'

Annie snorted. 'I widnae feed herring to a dog, never mind my family.'

She marched to the pump at the rear of the room. 'Lazy bugger,' she muttered under her breath as she refilled the bucket sitting beside it. Everyone knew the last one to use it shouldn't leave it empty.

The metal arm creaked as she pumped water. It was old and stiff and made her arms ache. Once the bucket was full, she massaged her arms before filling the dipper and carrying it back down the fish hall.

She poured the water over her portion of the stone shelf before returning the dipper to its place beside the bucket.

Her shoes squelched on the wet cobbles and dampness gathered around her toes. It would take a few more good catches before she could pay a visit to the cobbler.

Sighing, she selected some of the larger fish and laid them on the slab. This early in the year the fish were still on the wee side. However, she reckoned the smaller the fish, the tastier they were, although the townsers liked bigger fish. But what did townsers know about fish?

A flurry of activity at the door drew her attention. The group of newly arrived fishwives paraded up and down the fish hall looking for a space, but they were too late. They'd have to push amongst the crowds and sell their fish from the creels hanging from their waists.

'Haven't seen them here before.' Lizzie glared at them. 'Damned coasters think they'll do better here. But they're taking trade away from us.'

'We have our regulars,' Annie said, but her eyes reflected her worry. They were living hand to mouth without the extra competition. 'At least the sun's coming up. That means we'll be busy because folks will come out.'

'I hope ye're right. It's been a hard winter, and it's time things got better.'

The thought of asking Annie to care for her children weighed on Belle's mind. She spent the morning staring out the window and, as the sun climbed higher in the sky, she knew she couldn't put off the inevitable any longer. When the eleventh stroke of the steeple clock struck, she turned to face Sarah.

'It's time,' she said. 'I need to go to the fish market to see your grandma.'

Sarah nodded and turned away from her.

Belle hesitated. Was this her daughter's way of saying she didn't care, or was it to hide tears? But she'd never known Sarah to cry, so she shrugged that thought away. Sarah would be all right. It was the boys she wasn't sure about. Would they miss her as much as she'd miss them?

'Mind the boys until I get back,' she said, picking up her shawl and wrapping it around her shoulders.

'Do we have to go to Grandma?' Jamie plucked at her skirt.

Belle hugged him. 'It's for the best,' she said, trying to keep the quaver out of her voice. He mustn't know her heart was breaking. 'You'll be able to play in the woods and skim stones into the river again. I know you've missed that.'

'You want rid of us.' Davy's voice was truculent, and he glared at her. 'But we don't care.'

'That's not true,' Belle said. 'I'll miss you, but the only way I can keep you safe is to send you back to Craigden, where you were happy.'

Sarah pulled both boys away from Belle and held them tight.

'You'd best go, or you'll miss Grandma.' Her voice held no emotion. 'Don't worry about Davy and Jamie. I'll see they're all right.'

Tears trickled down Belle's cheeks as she descended the stairs, but she brushed them away before she left the tenement to mingle with the people on the street.

A light spray misted the air, and her feet slipped on the damp cobbles. The river was high, making the ships in the harbour sway and bump against the quayside, reminding her of the awful events of two nights before. Had the sailor been missed? Were they looking for him? She shuddered and turned her head away from the river and the ships. Keeping her eyes fixed on the road, she hurried along until she reached the turning to the narrow closes, lanes, and wynds leading to the town centre.

Tenements huddled together in these narrow lanes where the sun never penetrated. The gloom and desolation pervading these crowded alleys made Belle pull her shawl closer. She hurried on with her head down. This was the part of the town where the poorest inhabitants lived. She had a foreboding this was where she and her children would end up if she didn't follow through with her plan.

Her feet didn't slow down until she reached the wider streets leading to the town centre.

Doubts filled her mind when she reached Upper George Street and heard the sing-song voices of the fishwives emanating from the fish market along with the clatter of cart wheels and horses' hooves. Annie would be there and if she wanted to turn back, now was the time.

She stiffened her shoulders, took a deep breath, and forced herself to walk towards the fish market. This was no time to think of herself. She had to protect her children. To do that meant she had to convince Annie to take them.

Crowds thronged the fish market. Portly matrons, servant girls, and country squires rubbed elbows with each other while ragamuffins ran between them, creating havoc among the crowds. Voices echoed around the fish hall as housewives with baskets slung over their arms bartered with the fishwives. She cursed herself for not coming earlier, before the market was at its height.

Belle stopped inside the door, overwhelmed by the pandemonium inside. A multitude of voices inundated her ears.

She didn't recognise any of the nearby fishwives tending the stone tables, nor the ones walking up and down the hall accosting people with their wares. Where were the Craigden fishwives?

Venturing further inside the market, she wove her way through the crowds. Her feet slipped on the wet cobbles, and she wished she'd worn less dainty shoes.

The smell of fish intensified the further in she went, reminding Belle of her life in Craigden. At the time she'd resented having to visit the big houses with creels strapped to her hips, but now, she realised, she missed that life.

Her eyes darted from fishwife to fishwife searching for Annie and, at last, she found her, halfway down the market hall. She stood in front of one of the stone tables.

54

Annie arranged the last of her fish on the stone slab. It had been a good morning, and her money pouch was heavy. With a bit of luck, she'd have no fish left when the market closed at midday.

The pouch swung as she moved. Inside was enough coin to pay Wattie what she owed him, for the provisions he'd supplied to her on tick. He was a good man, and it would be no bad thing if Jeannie were to wed him, even though he wasn't a fisher.

Lizzie's voice, harsher than usual, penetrated her thoughts.

'It's no fish, ye ken. It's men's lives.'

'Maybe so,' the woman she'd addressed scowled at her, 'but money disnae grow on trees.'

Lizzie finished wrapping the fish and handed it to her.

The woman rammed her fish parcel into the basket on her arm, glared at Lizzie, and moved away.

Annie waited until the woman was out of earshot before saying, 'Problems?'

'Ach, she comes to every market. She wants the biggest fish and disnae want to pay the price. She always comes back though. I just have to put up with her tongue.'

Lizzie rearranged the fish on her slab. 'My feet are sair. I'll be glad when we finish.'

Tired of Lizzie's constant complaining, Annie stopped listening and turned to watch the flow of potential customers. The wandering fishwives with their creels slung across their hips were always on the lookout to divert people from the displays on the stone tables and Annie was damned if she'd let them steal her customers.

Her eyes narrowed when she spotted Belle approaching.

Lizzie stepped forward to stand beside her. 'I never thought the brazen hussy would dare show her face in here.'

'Mind your tongue, Lizzie.'

Annie was in no mood to listen to Lizzie's spiteful remarks.

'Aye, well, I'm glad she's your guid-daughter and not mine.'

Annie glared at her. 'I'll not say it again.'

Lizzie shrugged her shoulders and moved back to her table, but her eyes never left the figure of Belle picking her way over the cobbles to Annie.

'I didn't expect to see you here,' Annie said when Belle reached her.

Belle's cheeks reddened and her hands tightened on her skirts, making them rise high enough to show her ankles.

Behind her, Annie heard Lizzie tutting and knew the woman was listening to every word.

'Keep an eye on my table while I have a word with Belle,' she said before leading Belle back to the doorway. She didn't wait to hear Lizzie's agreement. The woman knew better than to refuse because the Craigden fishwives looked out for each other.

Several women gossiping outside the door glanced at Annie with curiosity in their eyes. Her blue and grey striped skirt marked her out as a fishwife, and they never left the fish market until it closed.

Annie ignored them. 'It's quieter over there, away from listening ears.'

She strode across the street and stood in the lee of St George's Free Church.

It was a few moments before Belle joined her and Annie saw the girl's troubled eyes dart to the church doors and then away again.

Of course, Annie should have remembered. The minister of this church was Belle's uncle. The man who had brought her up. Belle never spoke of him, but Annie had guessed, long ago, their relationship had been problematic.

'What is it ye've come to see me about?'

Belle turned her eyes away from Annie's penetrating stare before she answered in a low voice.

'I've come to ask if you'll take Sarah and the twins.'

'Why would I do that? They're your bairns, not mine.'

'They're your Jimmie's bairns as well.'

The barb pierced Annie's heart.

'Besides, they're missing Craigden and they're not safe here in Invercraig.'

'What d'ye mean, not safe?'

Belle shuffled her feet and refused to look at Annie.

'There are too many rogues and sailors.' Her voice quavered. 'One of them attacked Sarah and I fear it will happen again.'

'You mean ye haven't been looking after her? It's a mother's job to protect her bairns.'

'I can't be with her all the time. I have to work. It's that or starve.'

'And the boys?'

'They'd be miserable without Sarah and soon get themselves into trouble. Invercraig isn't like Craigden, where they can run in the woods and paddle in the river. It's too deep on this side.'

'Ye're asking a lot.'

'I'm desperate. I need them to be safe.' Her eyes filled with tears. 'Please Annie, I'm begging you. If not for my sake, do it for Jimmie's sake. He'd want his bairns to be safe.'

Annie's heart softened as she saw the misery on Belle's face. She'd never approved of the lass and thought Jimmie had made a mistake when he married her. But she couldn't turn her back on Jimmie's bairns. They were his flesh and blood, as well as hers.

'I'll send Jeannie to collect them before the day is out,' she said. Turning her back on Belle, she strode across the street to the fish market, leaving Belle standing outside the church.

Belle's feet dragged, and she was unaware of her surroundings as she walked home. She should have been happy when Annie agreed to take her children. Instead, a sense of loss swept through her. The tears would come later after the numbness wore off.

Sarah met her at the door with a question in her eyes.

'It's arranged,' Belle said. 'Jeannie is to take you to Craigden. Use that,' she pointed to a shawl draped over the back of a chair, 'to make a bundle for your clothes.'

She turned away to avoid seeing the hurt on Sarah's face.

'I'm not going. You can't make me.' Davy pummelled her hip.

She blinked the tears from her eyes before she stooped to hug him. 'But Jamie and Sarah will need you,' she said.

'I don't care.' His voice was defiant.

'It's just for a little while. Once I sort things out, I'll come for you.' She hesitated, willing him to believe her.

'You promise.'

'Yes.' Belle's voice broke. It was a lie, and she knew it. But what else could she say? 'Now, it's time for you to be a man and look after Jamie and Sarah for me. Will you do that?'

He nodded his assent. But the look of misery on his face broke Belle's heart. She blinked back her tears and forced a smile.

'It won't be so bad when you're with your gran. Think of the fun you'll be able to have playing in the woods, paddling in the river and helping Granda with his boat. You could learn to be a fisherman like your da.'

The thought of Jimmie intensified the pain in her heart. She'd been so careless of his love. It had taken his loss to make her realise what he meant to her. And now, she was going to lose his bairns. She ached to keep them. Keep them close to her so she wouldn't be alone. But that was impossible while she had to live in Invercraig. They weren't town bairns, and they weren't safe here. Besides, they belonged in the fishing community. It would have been what Jimmie wanted for them.

It was an interminable two hours before Jeannie arrived.

'I've come for the bairns,' she said.

Belle nodded.

Jamie ran to her and buried his face in her skirt. She stroked his head. 'You need to go with Jeannie now.'

Sarah hefted the bundle onto her shoulder and pushed Davie towards Jeannie before turning and grabbing Jamie's hand.

'It's time to go,' she said. 'Jeannie's waiting for us.'

Belle closed her eyes, fighting the urge to throw her arms around her boys and grasp them to her chest. She didn't relax until after the door closed and their steps down the stairs faded into the distance.

Belle stared out of the window, seeing nothing. She'd become so accustomed to putting her own needs first, sending the children away was the hardest thing she'd ever had to do.

The door opening brought her out of her trance. For the briefest moment, she thought Jeannie had returned with her bairns, but it was Madge who stood in the doorway.

'I'll help you pack.' She entered the room and placed a carpet bag in front of Belle. 'Gregor thought you might need this.'

'Pack?' Belle struggled to pull her thoughts together. 'Gregor?'

'Aye, he's downstairs settling your bill with Granny Mutch.'

The memory of last night rushed back. Gregor telling her to move to the inn and stating his intention to marry her.

She shuddered.

'How did he know the bairns were gone?'

'He was keeping watch.' Madge opened the bag. 'I'll pack your clothes while you splash your face with water.'

Belle grabbed her arm. 'What if I refuse Gregor's offer?' Even as she said it, she knew she had no option. The secret they shared tied her and Gregor together.

'Don't be daft,' Madge said. 'You won't get a better offer. He has money salted away and there's the inn. the security that gives you will make up for spending the rest of your life with him.'

Belle closed her eyes. The rest of her life. It seemed a very long time. But Madge was right. It was security, a new start, and putting up with Gregor's attentions was a small price to pay.

55

Lachlan stood beside the four-poster bed, contemplating his father's body while he waited for his mother to join him. Every morning, for weeks now, he'd visited Sir Roderick to keep him informed, even though he wasn't sure his father understood. Sometimes he didn't respond, and at other times anger flooded his face as he struggled for breath while his frustration mounted.

Over the past two months, while his father lay in this bed, Lachlan had been responsible for all his business interests. It hadn't been easy because he'd been the laird in everything but name. Would it be any easier now he had become Lord Craigallan?

The creak of the door opening, the rustle of silk, and a faint waft of lavender announced the arrival of his mother.

'Father is gone,' he said.

He looked at the weak and aged body in the bed, a mere shadow of the powerful man he used to be. No longer the forceful and demanding laird he once was.

His mother sighed. 'It is a blessing. He is now at peace.'

Lachlan turned to her. 'Why do I feel no grief?'

She patted his hand. 'It is because your father's suffering is over. He will now pass to a better place, and I am sure he will watch over us.'

The lack of emotion in her voice struck him, and he wondered if anyone in the household would mourn his father.

'What happens now?'

'Funeral arrangements require to be made. You must liaise with Murdo about that. He will know the procedure. The family needs to be informed as well as the staff. I will see to that. Bates can take care of the servants. They will need to ensure all necessary preparations are made for the mourning period.'

With a swish of her skirts, she left the room. After a last look at his father, Lachlan followed her. The jumble of conflicting thoughts in his mind did not include grief.

The house brooded in silence the next morning, but Lachlan followed his daily procedure except for a visit to his father. Now he was dead, there was no point, and Lachlan had no stomach to show a respect he didn't have.

Flickering candles in an ornate candelabra cast shadows over the breakfast table.

Bates pulled out the chair at the head of the table and waited for Lachlan to sit.

'We have eggs, ham, and kidneys for breakfast this morning, m'lord.'

'No fish?'

'No, m'lord. The fishwife has not yet called with Monday's catch. If you recall, the fishers do not take their boats out on a Sunday.'

'In that case, I'll partake of the kidneys and the ham.'

'Yes, m'lord.' Bates busied himself with selecting the best kidneys and slices of ham.

'I'm afraid we are somewhat lacking choice this morning due to the circumstances.' Bates laid the plate in front of Lachlan.

'That will be all for the moment.'

'Yes, m'lord.'

Bates backed away and left the room, although Lachlan was sure he would be hovering and he only needed to click his fingers for the man to return.

Eating in silence he pondered the strangeness of the situation. He was sitting in his father's chair, and Bates addressed him as m'lord. It was something he'd better get used to, for this was his life from now on.

Three weeks had passed since Sir Roderick's demise and in a few days it would be May, when spring eased towards summer. During that time Lachlan's status changed, bringing with it the respect he had craved for so long. The farmworkers tipped their bonnets to him and the fishers showed him the same grudging respect they'd shown his father. But more important, Wullie McPhee, the factor in charge of his business interests in Invercraig, no longer treated him like a buffoon.

This morning, McPhee had acknowledged him without the usual reluctance he'd been prone to display in the past. He flicked through a ledger.

'The *Vigilant* docked this morning.' He glanced out the window. 'As you can see, the cargo is being unloaded, and I have ensured the excisemen will prioritise their customs inspection. Everything will be in the warehouses by evening.'

Lachlan didn't enquire the reason for the priority, but assumed it entailed the greasing of palms. He had no objection to that if it meant a smooth passage for his cargo.

'The other ships?'

McPhee turned a page in his ledger. 'The *Resolute* is on her way back from France with a similar cargo to that of the *Vigilant*. It carries brandy, cognac, fine lace, perfumes and a variety of luxury goods. The *Scotia* left yesterday for Russia with barrels of cured herring from the *White Herring Fishing Company*. They have a taste for pickled fish over there, although our fisher folk turn their noses up at it.'

'I must try herring sometime.'

McPhee shot him a sceptical stare before turning back to the ledger. 'I prefer the haddock and the sole myself. But everyone to their taste. As long as it sells abroad, I'll not complain.'

'What about the *Perseverance*? I don't see it in the harbour.'

'It left on Monday for the whaling grounds.' McPhee leafed back several pages. 'Last year's return from the whaling was disappointing,' he said. 'And the year before, it wasn't much better. You might want to consider whether it's worthwhile to continue with whalers.'

Lachlan bridled. 'I'll wait to see what this year's catch is before I decide.' He changed the subject. 'The Craigden Inn. How near to completion is it?'

'The masons have completed most of the building work, and as soon as we receive our order of slates the roof will be tiled. I reckon it'll be complete by the end of the summer.'

'I had expected the work to be completed much earlier.'

'There have been some unanticipated delays.'

'How so?'

'Our first order of Norwegian timber was lost in a shipwreck, and we had to reorder. Plus, there has been a delay in acquiring the roofing slates.'

'That may be so, but perhaps closer supervision of the workers is required.'

McPhee stiffened. 'I keep a close check on the work, and I see no signs of slacking.'

Lachlan smiled, pleased he had rattled the man. He rose from his chair. Pausing in the doorway, he said, 'Once the unloading is complete, send half a dozen bottles of cognac to the house. I fancy a taste of it with my dinner tonight.'

The fresh spring air and warmth of the sun refreshed him after the confines of the factor's office. Lachlan strode to the quayside and watched the dockworkers scurrying up and down the gangplank, ferrying the cargo to the dockside. He was getting a grip on the business interests, and it pleased him to observe the activity which would line his pockets.

His mind turned to the incomplete Craigden Inn. The previous inn had been a thriving business before it burned down. He'd spent many pleasant times there, and he was sure Madge had made a decent profit. Perhaps he should employ someone to run the new inn rather than rent it out. And with that thought, he turned away from the ship and strode toward the tenement house where Belle lived.

She had rejected him when last he saw her, but he was certain she would jump at the chance to run the Craigden Inn. And once she was back in the village, she might soften towards him.

The steady thump of Gregor unloading ale barrels in the yard resonated through the empty taproom. Belle pushed a strand of hair away from her face before placing the wet cloth on the tabletop. The inn was a lot cleaner since she'd taken up residence, although the smell of stale liquor and tobacco smoke lingered.

Madge had remained upstairs this morning. Since Belle's arrival, she'd left her with more and more to do. Belle didn't mind. It kept her mind off the promise she'd made to Gregor.

She looked up when the door opened, and air wafted through the room. Her eyes widened when she saw Lachlan framed in the doorway. It had been two months since she'd last seen him and refused his offer to protect her. What was he doing here now? She quelled the slight flutter of her heart. This man had made a fool of her once, she had no intention of allowing him to do it again.

'I was told you were here.' He grasped her arm.

She shook his hand off and rubbed at the table with a vicious swipe of the cloth.

'Why have you come? You must know you are unwelcome here.'

Slapping the cloth into the pail of water at her feet, she turned to glare at him.

'I have come to make you an offer.'

Belle laughed. 'I refused your offer the last time and I haven't changed my mind. I will not be your whore, sir. You should accept that and return to your wife. There is nothing for you here.'

'I am sad you feel that way, but that is not the offer I had in mind.'

She laughed again. 'There is nothing you can offer me I would find acceptable.'

'It is a business offer, Belle. If you accept, the independence you want is yours. You could be your own woman.'

Despite her anger with him, Belle found herself intrigued. A business offer? What on earth did he mean?

When she didn't answer, he continued, 'The new inn at Craigden will require someone to manage it, and who better than you, Belle? With the experience you have, it can't fail.'

Her eyes narrowed with suspicion. 'And what would you expect of me if I accepted your offer?'

'There are no strings attached. You would be your own woman in charge of the new inn.'

His offer tempted her. If she returned to Craigden, she could have her children with her. She'd have her independence, and she didn't doubt her ability to keep Lachlan at arm's length. But it could never work. Without a man at her side, the women would never accept her.

'You're very sure of yourself,' she said.

'It could work, Belle. All you have to do is agree.'

'Then I am sorry to disappoint you, for I cannot agree. Your offer has come too late because I am to be wed before the year is out. I will be the wife of the owner of this establishment, which is a more lucrative prospect than the Craigden Inn.'

'There is no more to be said then.' His eyes reflected his pain.

After he left, she went to the door and watched him walk along the road. She sensed his despair and bit her lip to quell the sadness rushing through her, for she took no pleasure in hurting him. As if aware of her eyes watching him, he turned to look back. He stood for a moment, staring at her before straightening, squaring his shoulders and striding off. His confident swagger sent a message back to her that, as far as he was concerned, she no longer mattered.

Belle slammed the door. She had done the right thing by rejecting Lachlan. Her future lay with Gregor.

Belle's words rang in Lachlan's ears. He would not approach her again, even though his mind and body longed for her.

Pulling on the reins he brought Raven to a halt when they were in sight of Craigallan Castle. He had always thought it a grandiose name for a mansion house for, although it was large and impressive, it did not have the ramparts he associated with castles. Today it brooded in the sunshine, mourning its former master.

Raven pawed the ground and whinnied while Lachlan contemplated what to do. Now he was the laird, he felt he should assert his authority. Until he did that, his father's ghost would linger on.

His mind made up, he urged Raven towards the house. He would issue the order for the closed curtains to be opened and for the mourning period to end. His mother would disapprove, but she wouldn't interfere.

Despite all his efforts, his father's voice invaded his mind. 'It is time you had an heir. With no heir, the bloodline will end.'

'Yes,' he thought. 'It is imperative the bloodline continues.'

By the time Lachlan dismounted at the stables, he knew what he had to do.

A stray tear slithered down Belle's cheek as she stood with her back to the door. She wiped it away with an angry finger and strode over to the table she'd been cleaning when Lachlan arrived. She grabbed the cloth from the pail, wrung out the excess water and scrubbed at the tabletop. This was her life from now on, and Lachlan had no part in it. So why were her thoughts in turmoil? Where was her anger directed? Herself, Lachlan, or Gregor?

Her hand stilled and she stared towards the window. Had she made a mistake sending Lachlan away?

No, she shook her head while she swiped angrily at the tabletop. She'd made her decision, and she would abide by it no matter how much it cost her.

Dropping the cloth into the bucket she strode to the window to stare across the river to the huddle of cottages at Craigden. Jimmie had taken her there as his new wife and she'd hated the place. But as time passed, she'd grown to think of Craigden as home and become content with her lot. But that was in the past. This was now her home and there was no going back.

'What are you thinking about?'

Belle hadn't heard Madge approach.

Without turning, she said, 'I was thinking about the bairns and wondering how they were settling with their gran.' That wasn't strictly true but wasn't far off.

'The bairns will be fine. You did the right thing sending them back to Craigden.'

'Did I?' Belle wasn't so sure, and her heart ached for them.

'Yes, you did. If you'd kept the bairns, it would have meant a life of poverty never knowing where your next meal was coming from. By sending them away, it allows you to build a new life for yourself. A prosperous life.'

'Yes, you're right.'

Belle turned, picked up the pail of water, and headed for the back door. As she poured the water down the drain, she couldn't help thinking she was pouring her life away as well.

56

The tempting aroma of roast venison and freshly baked bread permeated the corridor which led into the house from the courtyard. Lachlan closed his eyes and savoured the smell. At moments like this, he regretted the loss of his carefree life before his father's illness and death.

In previous times he'd felt welcome in the kitchen, where cook spoiled him with titbits. But the atmosphere had changed over the past few weeks and now they bobbed curtseys and called him m'lord.

He squared his shoulders. This was no time for regrets. He was no longer young Master Lachlan; he was the laird and had a position to maintain.

Bates materialised at his side when he entered the main hall. The man had an uncanny knack of appearing out of nowhere.

'M'lord?'

It was the butler's customary greeting, his way of inquiring if Lachlan had any orders for him.

'Open the shutters and curtains. We cannot remain in mourning forever. This house has been gloomy far too long.'

'Yes, m'lord. Will there be anything else?'

'My mother?'

'She is in her sitting room, m'lord.'

'And Clarinda?'

'My lady is in her rooms.' He did not have to say, 'as usual', but it was implied.

Lachlan was halfway up the stairs when he turned around to look down at Bates.

'There is one other thing. I want the locks on Lady Clarinda's doors removed. Make sure it is done.' He bounded upwards without waiting for the butler's response.

Clarinda's suite of rooms spread over a large part of the third floor. It contained two sitting rooms, two bedrooms, and the nursery. This was where she and Aunt Beattie spent most of their time.

Aunt Beattie concealed her surprise when she opened the door to his knock, making Lachlan realise it had been a long time since he'd attempted to see his wife.

He wanted to impose his authority and demand entrance, but he liked Aunt Beattie. She wasn't responsible for her niece's refusal to welcome Lachlan into her presence. So, he turned his demand into a request to see Clarinda.

Aunt Beattie looked apologetic as she said, 'I'm afraid my lady is indisposed.'

Lachlan smiled at her. 'I'm sorry. I must insist.'

Unable to refuse now he had become the laird; she nodded her assent and ushered him inside.

'I will inform my lady you are here,' she said.

He followed close behind her, making sure she could not stop him from entering Clarinda's sitting room.

'You may go now,' he said. 'I wish to speak to my wife in private.'

He waited until she closed the door, not caring whether she listened outside. They both had to know he would no longer accept Clarinda's rejection of him.

Clarinda lay on a chaise longue with a cushion at her back. She looked up at him with languid eyes and raised a handkerchief to her brow.

'As you can see, I am unwell,' she said.

Lachlan narrowed his eyes. He had not forgotten her ability to present herself as delicate, using her blonde beauty to disguise her steely will. It had worked in the past, but he was stronger now.

'I fear your indisposition,' he stressed the last word, 'is no excuse for refusing to fulfil your role as Lady Clarinda. You will take on the duties formerly performed by my mother.'

He saw her stiffen and waited for her response.

'I cannot presume to replace your mother as lady of the house.' The softness of her voice masked an undercurrent of anger.

'Nonsense,' he said. 'As the laird's wife, your duty is to me and that involves becoming the lady of the house. My mother will expect no less and it will give her time to retire from those duties. I am sure she will guide you in what is expected.'

He strolled to the chaise longue and waited for her to make room for him. When she didn't move, he grasped her ankles. 'I think you will be more comfortable if you sit up.'

Apart from glaring at him, she offered no resistance when he repositioned her feet on the floor.

'That's better,' he said as he sat beside her. He waited while she adjusted her skirts before continuing.

'As lady of the house, I cannot allow you to isolate yourself and I have ordered the servants to stop delivering meals to your rooms. From now on, you will attend meals in the dining room with the family.'

'If my health does not allow this, I am sure Aunt Beattie will step into the breach. She will not have me starve.'

'No, my dear, that will not do. If Aunt Beattie flaunts my orders, I will ensure her speedy return to the London house and I will arrange for you to have your needs tended to by a servant.'

'You cannot do that.'

'I'm afraid I can, and I will,' he said.

'If you send Aunt Beattie away, I shall accompany her. Scotland does not agree with me. The weather is too cold, and I am surrounded by bumpkins. London is more civilised.'

'I doubt you will enjoy living in penury. Nor will you enjoy the notoriety when I apply for divorce.'

She gasped. 'You wouldn't.'

'Oh, but I would. You are a wife who refuses to do her duty by her husband, so what other choice do I have? You, madam, would be the talk of London and reviled by society.'

He strode to the door. Turning on the threshold, he said, 'I have instructed the locks to be removed from your doors. Your duty is to provide me with an heir, so when I visit you, I will expect you to be a full wife to me. Otherwise, you know what to expect.'

The slump of Clarinda's shoulders, combined with the defeat reflected in her eyes, gave Lachlan satisfaction. She despised him, but he had proved himself to be her lord and master, and never again would she have the power to belittle him.

There was a spring in Lachlan's step as he descended the stairs.

April to July 1840 - The Arctic

Jimmie woke when Nukilik slipped out of the bed, leaving behind a hollow of warmth where his body had lain. He struggled to follow him, but Nukilik shook his head and mimed for him to sleep.

'Where are you going?' he said, although he knew Nukilik did not understand the words.

Nukilik pointed to his spear and said, 'Nanuq.'

Jimmie knew that meant he was going to hunt the bear that had been snuffling around the settlement for the past few nights.

He pointed to his chest and held out his hands in a mute plea to go with him, but Nukilik shook his head and again mimed sleep.

Jimmie closed his eyes after Nukilik left, but sleep didn't come. The warm bodies of Kanguq and Quamnanic snuggled beside him reminded him of Belle, and his mind drifted back to his life in Craigden.

Bittersweet memories flooded through him, and he shook his head in despair. What was the use of thinking back to a time and a place he could never go back to? He had to reject his yearnings, accept his fate and make his life here.

Nukilik would like him to mate with Quamnanic, and he didn't know how much longer he could resist because of the proximity of her during the night. But she was little more than a child. It wouldn't be right.

He struggled into his fur clothing before venturing outside. The intense cold nipped his exposed skin and his breath hung in the frigid air, so he pulled the furs over his face until only his eyes were visible.

It was early, and nothing stirred. He walked past the dome-shaped dwellings and, squinting his eyes, he scanned the horizon for signs of the hunting party. But all he saw was snow and ice, an endless expanse of white with jagged ice formations here and there.

The rising sun cast long shadows as it crept up over the horizon to lighten the sky. Not so long ago, there had been no sun. It had been a world of eternal night which Jimmie thought would never end. But as the season advanced, daylight returned, and the sun slid from left to right along the horizon.

Keeping track of time in this land of ice and snow was impossible. How long had he been here? It might have been weeks or months. He had no way of knowing except for the passing seasons. He knew it had been September when the ice crushed and swallowed his ship. There had been daylight then but, as time passed, it diminished until only night and darkness remained. He thought the dark time must have been winter. But with the return of daylight, the intense cold lessened, and he thought he detected a faint warmth when the sun was at the midpoint on the horizon. He guessed this must be spring.

A thunderous crash in the distance made him start. Since the coming of the sun, they were becoming more frequent. He preferred these sounds to the eerie silences that came after the dark time's frequent storms when the wind howled, and blizzards raged. The crashes sounded more like explosions or falling rocks rather than thunder. He gazed over the ice field, peering into the distance, to locate the source of the noise, wondering if the crashes were chunks of ice falling into the sea.

He ventured further onto the ice until he saw the glimmer of water in the distance where none had been before. A surge of hope flickered through him, and he clasped his arms around his body. If that was the sea in the distance, perhaps it would bring ships.

As time passed, the days grew longer and the cold less intense. The ice sheet shrank, and the icehouses cracked and dripped water. That was the signal for the men in the community to erect their tupiks; tents protected from the elements by their covering of animal skins.

As usual, Jimmie felt helpless. He wanted to help, but didn't know how. Everything here was so different. The weather, the strange seasons, the icehouse dwellings and now, tupiks. All he could do was observe and marvel at how these people coped with their environment.

He stamped his feet and beat his hands on his sides while he watched the men build the tented village. Whalebone and antlers shaped into dome or pyramid-like structures formed the frames for tupiks. Earlier, Jimmie had watched the women sewing skins and pelts together which had puzzled him. But now he understood as he watched the men take the seal skins and caribou hides and stretch them over the frames.

Life continued, and the weeks passed. The iglus were no more and life in the tupik was less claustrophobic. Jimmie had done his best to adapt but wondered whether he would ever become a part of this community for the people here treated him more like a guest than one of their own.

With the coming of summer, the sun circled the land, never rising or setting.

Jimmie couldn't tell how long ago it had been since he first saw clear water in the distance. But as each day passed, and the ice shrank more, his compulsion to watch the horizon grew. It was now clear to him what he'd thought was land and ice stretching as far as the eye could see was a bay into which seawater now rushed. If a ship were to come, then all was not lost.

In the distance, he spotted slabs of ice floating in the water, and even though the encroachment of the sea meant the ice he was standing on was thinner, he didn't move. He became like a statue, rooted to the spot, ignoring everything else around him. Hope was the only thing keeping his spirits up.

Apart from Nukilik, who regarded Jimmie with troubled eyes, the men paid him no heed. With the passing of the dark time, they had too much to do. At this time of the year, when caribou, bears, foxes, hares, lemmings and wolves abounded, they concentrated on hunting. And with the lessening of the ice fields, seals and whales were not safe from their spears. On their return, once the butchering was complete, the women busied themselves cleaning the skins, selecting some to make into clothing and laying others aside to trade for things they couldn't make themselves.

If Jimmie had paid more attention to what was going on around him, he might have questioned why so many skins and pelts were being stored inside, forming a mountain of fur on one side of the tupik. But all he could think about was the sea and how much closer it was getting to where he stood on the edge of the ice field.

Today, it was the nearest it had ever been, and he watched with envy the small boats bobbing up and down in the water. He yearned to join them but didn't have his own kayak. Yesterday's hunt had been for caribou, today they searched for signs of seals or whales. If successful, they would return to launch the umiak with its larger capacity, and maybe he could join the hunt.

A tug on his arm made him turn. Kanguq stood beside him. She mimed a sad face and pointed to him.

He nodded.

'Imaq?' She gestured to the water and made another sad face.

'My home is over the sea,' he said with a break in his voice. 'Too far away to travel in one of those boats.'

She looked puzzled.

'Illuk! Home!' He pointed to the tupik. 'My home.' He patted his chest then swept his arm around, encompassing the expanse of sea in front of him, 'Is far away.'

58

August 1840 - Homeward bound

Belle reached up and placed the scrubbing brush on a nearby bench before mopping up the soap suds and wringing the washcloth out. A lock of hair fell over her face, and she pushed it back with a wet hand. Sitting back on her haunches, she inspected the floor. Satisfied it was clean, she placed the cloth beside the scrubbing brush.

She glanced over to where Madge was cleaning behind the bar and said, 'I'm away out to empty the bucket.'

'I'll give Gregor a shout. He'll do it for you.'

Belle shook her head. 'He's busy. The brewer's dray cart was here earlier and by the sound of it, he's hefting ale barrels.'

She lifted the bucket and headed for the door. The oppressive heat following the thunderstorms of the day before, struck her as soon as she stepped outside. But she welcomed it after the claustro-phobic atmosphere inside the inn where she seemed to spend most of her daytime hours cleaning. She turned her face towards the sun, basking in its warmth before crossing the road to the river's edge.

She balanced the pail on the low wall and tipped the water into the river. A shiver rippled through her. Four months ago, it had been a body she and Gregor tipped over this wall, hoping and praying it would be swept out to sea. That had been the grimmest day of her life and the act that made her beholden to Gregor and led to her agreement to wed him.

At the time she had despaired and thought her life was over, but from that day Gregor changed from the surly ruffian he had been, into the man he was today.

Keen to please her he'd made more of an effort to be sociable, he smiled more and argued less. He'd even allowed his sister to cut his hair and trim his beard.

Surprised to discover a presentable man underneath his unkempt exterior, Belle found his presence more bearable. Swarthier and less tall than either Jimmie or Lachlan, he was someone she would not be ashamed to be seen with in public.

Despite this, she kept putting him off when he pressed her for a wedding date.

'It's too soon,' she told him. But, after four months, he was becoming more insistent.

'It's not even a year since I lost Jimmie,' she'd argued.

'When the year is up,' he'd said.

And she had agreed.

'We'll set the date when the laird's whaler docks. That will make it a year since you lost your husband at sea.'

She'd nodded, although her heart was heavy.

'I'll be good to ye, Belle. Ye won't regret it.'

She looked out over the river to Craigden. Her eyes misted as she looked at the cottages squatting at the shoreline. That was where Jimmie had taken her when they were first wed, where Sarah was born and where her bairns now lived with their gran. She hadn't seen them for four months, and she missed them.

Dashing tears from her eyes, she turned back to the inn. There was no use crying for a lost life. This was her life now, and the sooner she accepted it, the better.

59

It was the day after the whale hunt when Jimmie spotted a ship.

His heart lurched as it usually did when he saw ships far out at sea. This was the seventh one he'd seen over the past few months. But each time they had sailed on until they vanished over the horizon. Despite this, a niggle of hope burned in him, and he jumped and waved and shouted, although he knew this was useless and they would neither see nor hear him from that distance.

He closed his eyes to prevent tears from spilling out of them to freeze on his cheeks. When he opened them again, the ship seemed nearer.

He watched its sails billowing in the wind as it negotiated the entrance to the bay, convincing him it was heading shoreward. When it dropped anchor, Jimmie, unable to believe his eyes, pinched himself to make sure he wasn't dreaming. Ignoring the creaking ice beneath his feet, he edged forward until he stood on the spot where the ice met the sea.

However, he hadn't been the only one to spot the ship's arrival, and it was only when Nukilik drew him back to safer ground he became aware of the villagers clustering nearby.

'It's a ship,' Jimmie gasped. 'A ship has come, and I am saved.'

Tears froze on his eyelashes, his heart thumped and, staring into Nukilik's face, he pointed to himself and then to the ship.

'Quajaq,' he said. He knew this was the word for the kayaks they used when they fished in the bay.

Nukilik shook his head and pointed to where men were pulling several larger boats to the edge of the ice.

'Umiak,' he said, pointing Jimmie in that direction.

Fearing the ship would sail before he reached it, Jimmie raced over the ice to help launch the boats. The men made way for him, and he grabbed the side of one and pulled. The ease with which it slid over the ice amazed him. He had expected it to be heavy like the wooden boats back home. But the boat was light and made of skins, making it feel flimsy.

Despite his reservations, he hopped aboard when it reached the water. It must be seaworthy, he told himself. He'd seen the men out in them several times with no ill effects.

The whalebone paddles rose and fell as the men sped the boat to the ship and soon, they were circling it.

Rope ladders slung from the deck walloped off the side of the ship before steadying and dangling within hand's reach of the umi-aqs. The boat rocked as Jimmie struggled to his feet and reached out. Nukilik pulled him back. He tried to shake off the restraining hand, but Nukilik pointed to the shaman seated in the prow.

Shame washed over him, and he relaxed back. Of course, he should have remembered. The native people respected their elders and shamans. It was the custom to show deference in their presence. To board the ship before the shaman did would be a gross act of disrespect.

Jimmie followed the shaman aboard, staying as close behind him as it was respectful to do. A man whom he guessed must be the captain approached them.

'Ai,' the shaman said.

He extended both hands and offered the captain a bone carving of a fish.

The captain accepted the offering and said, 'Ai,' in return. He gestured for the shaman to follow him to a rowboat on the starboard of the ship.

Jimmie fidgeted. His anxiety mounted as the shaman and the captain communicated with each other with a series of gestures and the odd word. He couldn't let this chance of escape slip through his fingers. But Nukilik's hand on his arm continued to restrain him.

After what seemed like an eternity, the shaman left the captain's side to walk back along the deck. Jimmie took his chance and scurried to the captain's side.

'Captain,' Jimmie said, his voice faltered. After all this time, he couldn't find the words he wanted to say.

'What have we here?' The captain turned to inspect Jimmie. 'Where did you come from?'

'I'm a whaler, captain. After my ship went down, Nukilik rescued me. He has been my saviour.'

'Ah, yes. Nukilik is indeed a good man.' The captain looked him up and down. 'Shipwrecked, you say. How long have you been here?'

'I don't know. Months, maybe years.'

'Well, you certainly weren't here when I called in on my way home last August.'

'You've been here before?'

'I call in every year on my way home.'

The captain turned away from Jimmie to issue an order to the seamen preparing to lower the rowboat.

Jimmie grasped his arm. 'Take me with you when you sail,' he entreated. 'I'll work my passage.'

'I have no need of an extra crew member, and it would unsettle the men.'

'Please,' Jimmie said.

'We'll talk later, and I suggest you hurry to your boat lest you have to swim ashore.' He nodded to the rope ladder further along the deck where Nukilik stood waiting to descend to the boat below.

Obedience was something sailors learned as soon as they set foot on a ship, so Jimmie obeyed the captain's instruction. But with every stroke of the paddles on their way back to shore, his heart became heavier and the likelihood he would never leave this place took root.

The umiak, a much lighter craft than the rowboat being lowered from the ship, nuzzled its way to the shore. Jimmie was the last person to disembark. Skimming over the water, feeling the splash of the waves, and hearing the paddles rise and dip in the water had felt good. The sea was where he felt most at ease, and he wanted to remain in the umiak. Sail with it across the seas until he reached home. But it was a vain hope. The boat was too small and frail for such a journey. What he needed was a ship like the one anchored in the bay.

Thoughts whirled through his mind. He had to convince the captain to take him home. But what if the captain refused? He had said he had no need of another sailor. Perhaps if he smuggled himself on board, he could hide. Be a stowaway. But he knew ship captains often marooned stowaways ashore after finding them. And, if that happened, there was no guarantee it would be a hospitable place.

There was no other way. Jimmie would have to throw himself on the captain's mercy. But remembering the man's stern face, he knew it would be no easy task.

While he waited on the shore, Jimmie cast his eyes towards the approaching boat. It was so close he saw sailors straining at the oars and the captain standing in the prow issuing orders. He looked formidable, and Jimmie quailed, wondering what he could say to convince the man to allow him to accompany them when they sailed.

Nukilik prodded him and pointed towards his tupik. Jimmie pulled away from him, but Nukilik was insistent, and Jimmie had no other option but to follow him. After all, he relied on this man.

Gathering up several caribou pelts, Nukilik thrust them into Jimmie's arms. He gathered up more furs and pelts and led the way outside to add them to a growing pile, for this was a community where they shared everything.

By this time, the sailors had shipped their oars and pulled their boat onto the shore. The captain gestured to the men to unload the boat before striding forward to meet the group clustered around their pelts.

'Ai,' he said, pointing to the furs and gesturing towards his men who were unloading pots, pans, kettles, knives, and spoons.

Understanding flooded through Jimmie. Until that moment, he had never questioned the use of anything metal within the community. Now he knew where Kanguk had come by her metal pot and the spoon she gave him to eat the watery soup she made.

Jimmie laid his bundle of skins beside Nukilik's and turned to the captain. 'May I speak with you, sir?'

The captain frowned. 'Not now, I have business to conduct.' He waved Jimmie away and joined the group clustered beside the animal skins.

A familiar feeling of despair washed through Jimmie. Several times, he'd approached the captain, only to be dismissed each time. How was he to get home if he couldn't get the man to listen to his pleas?

He hovered on the edge of the group while they bartered for the goods. As soon as the deals were done, the captain ordered the sailors to load his accumulation of furs and pelts into the rowboat.

Afraid the boat would leave without him, Jimmie once again approached the captain.

'Sir,' he said, his voice cracking with desperation. 'Please do not leave without me. Please do not leave me here. I am desperate to return to my family.'

'I had not forgotten you,' the man said. 'But I have no need of another crew member, and it would create unrest among the men. If you were to buy passage on the ship, then I could ensure your return home.'

Jimmie's shoulders slumped, and his despair increased. 'But I have nothing, sir. I lost everything in the shipwreck.'

'Then, I am afraid here you must stay unless you find some way to provide the means for your passage.'

'You are a hard man, sir.'

'Ah, but this is a hard world and nothing in it is free.' The captain considered him. 'Perhaps your friend Nukilik will provide a solution?'

He turned to Nukilik, who stood nearby. Pointing to Jimmie and then to the ship, he held up six fingers and gestured towards the remaining pelts.

Nukilik nodded and Jimmie's spirits soared until he remembered that in this community a nod of the head meant no, while a shake of the head meant yes. Nukilik was saying no.

The captain frowned and held up five fingers. Nukilik held up two.

They continued to barter until they settled on three caribou pelts and a small fox fur.

'The deal is done,' the captain said. 'Nukilik has paid for your passage home.' He stroked the fox fur. 'This will make a fine present for my wife. She has wanted one of these to wear around her neck.' With that, he strode towards the boat. 'Come on then. We don't want to miss the tide.'

60

The voyage home seemed interminable to Jimmie even though the ship made good time. He would have liked to work his passage alongside the men, but following Nukilik's payment, the captain insisted on treating him as a passenger. So, he spent a lot of time leaning on the ship's rails watching the sea. Once they left the Baffin Straits, they followed the coast of Greenland, where he spotted seals, walruses, and the occasional whale. But the captain was eager to return home in time for his daughter's wedding, so they didn't tarry.

The captain often joined him, and they talked about the sea, life back home in Scotland, and Jimmie's time living with the Inuit people. When the weather turned foul, they went below decks to the captain's cabin, where they shared a glass of rum and continued their conversations.

Jimmie wondered if the man was lonely. He'd never given this any thought before, but how did a captain become friends with anyone under his command?

They were several days out when the captain confessed. 'I'm a bit of a scriever.' He gestured towards a pile of papers and the ink well on his desk. 'I've been documenting my whaling trips and I've been studying the Inuit people for over twenty years.' He paused for a moment of reflection and to refill his pipe with tobacco.

'I feel the time is fast approaching when there will be no more whales and my time as a whaling man will end. When that happens, I intend to concentrate on writing a history of the whaling and the people who frequent these Arctic shores. I was thinking,' the captain continued, 'that if I included a document written by yourself, it would have an impact. If you are agreeable?'

Jimmie swallowed a mouthful of rum while he wondered what to say.

'You are strangely silent, my friend,' the captain said. 'Does the idea not appeal to you?' He studied Jimmie with narrowed eyes. 'Or is it something else?'

Unwilling to admit he could neither read nor write, Jimmie considered his response. At last, he said, 'I'm afraid my education is somewhat lacking. Writing about my experiences is beyond me.' He focused his eyes on the pile of papers with their meaningless squiggles.

'Ah, I see.' The captain removed the pipe from his mouth and leaned towards Jimmie. 'You have not the ability to read or write.'

Jimmie nodded and turned his eyes away from the captain's face to avoid seeing the man's disapproval.

'I am sorry if I have embarrassed you,' the captain said. 'You have nothing to be ashamed of. You are no different from most of the men aboard this ship. However, it is not difficult to learn these skills and, providing I have your consent, I would be happy to teach you.'

'You would do that for me?'

'Of course, provided you apply yourself and, in return, you must provide me with a written account of your experiences in Baffin Land.' He refilled Jimmie's glass. 'Have we a deal?'

Jimmie nodded his agreement, although, when he looked at the cabin's bookshelves, the task seemed immense.

The captain grasped Jimmie's hand and shook it vigorously. 'In that case, we start right away. We have much work to do.'

He was as good as his word and by the time the ship reached Scotland six weeks later, not only could Jimmie read and write, but he had provided the captain with the story of his life in the Arctic.

Jimmie's eyes misted with tears and his heart thumped when the ship left the stormy North Sea and sailed into Peterhead Bay. This was his first glimpse of Scotland since he'd left its shores over a year ago and he couldn't remember a time when he'd been so happy.

'Glad to be back?'

Jimmie hadn't heard the captain join him at the ship's rail.

Overcome with emotion, he nodded. When he found his voice, he said, 'I've never been to Peterhead before. I'll need some advice on how to get to Craigden from here.'

'Ach, there's no need to worry about that. My brother's the skipper of a herring boat. He can drop you off on his next fishing trip. I'll speak to him and provide you with a bed until then.'

61

September 1840

The wind almost tore the shirt from Annie's hands as she pegged it on the washing line stretched between two poles on the pebbled edge of the river which flowed past the gable end of the cottage.

'I'll need some more clothes pegs,' Annie said. 'Don't want the washing to end up in Norway.'

Silently, Sarah handed her the pegs she'd asked for.

Annie sighed as she lifted a gansey out of the basket at her feet. Sarah was too quiet for a bairn, and she often wished the lass was as boisterous as her brothers. The two boys had settled after their return to Craigden, but Sarah always held back. Annie couldn't shake the feeling something troubled the girl, but until she opened up to her, there was nothing she could do.

After she finished pegging the oiled wool jersey to the line, she bent to pick up the basket. As she straightened, she looked seawards. It was a habit common to fisherfolk, for the sea was a part of their lives.

A sailboat entering the river's mouth caught her eye. It wasn't a Craigden boat; they were pulled up on the foreshore and there they would stay until Monday, for tomorrow was the Sabbath. Yesterday's catch had been larger than usual, so there had been no need for the boats to go out again today.

As she watched the boat's sails billowing in the wind, she admired its lines. What James wouldn't give to own a boat like that? But, although the fishing had been better this year, it wasn't enough to provide the finance for such a boat.

Ah well, there was no sense in wishing for something they couldn't have, so she tucked the basket under her arm and turned towards the cottage. She paused on the threshold and glanced back upriver. The boat wasn't heading for Invercraig as she'd thought; it was on its way to Craigden.

'James,' she shouted as she rushed inside. 'There's a boat heading here, and it's not one of ours.' She plonked the basket in a corner of the room before rushing outside again.

When she reached the foreshore, a few of the other women and some of the men had gathered to watch as the boat manoeuvred closer before dropping anchor.

Annie elbowed her way to the front of the group in time to see a sailor drop from the boat into the water. There was something familiar about him as he waded ashore.

Her heart lurched. It couldn't be, but it was. Tears sprang to her eyes, and she ran to the water's edge to meet him.

'Jimmie,' she said in a voice choked with emotion. 'You're alive.'

'Yes, Ma. Alive and well.' He grabbed her in his arms and hugged her so hard she thought her ribs would break.

The relief at being on his home soil made tears spring to Jimmie's eyes. His arms tightened around his ma, and he hugged her until she squealed.

'Take care, laddie,' she gasped. 'Or ye'll break me in two.'

He loosened his grasp. 'Have I hurt ye?' he said as he watched her eyes fill with tears. He'd never seen his ma cry before.

'No, son, it's because we thought you were lost to us.'

'I wanted to come back, but I was stuck in the Arctic with no way to get home. If the Peterhead whaler hadn't come, I'd still be there. I thought I'd never see home again.' His voice broke and overcome with emotion, he caught his breath.

He slung his arm around her shoulders, hugging her to him as they walked back to the house. They'd never been a demonstrative family, but it felt good, and Annie didn't object.

James was standing on the riverbank at the side of the house, watching the Peterhead boat sailing down the river to the sea.

'That's a braw boat,' he said, before turning to look at them.

His eyes widened.

'It cannae be,' he said. 'Is that you, Jimmie?'

'Aye. It's me.' Jimmie rushed to his father and grabbed his hand. He wanted to throw his arms around him but held back. He didn't think his da would appreciate a hug.

A movement behind him made him turn.

Sarah stood at the corner of the house staring at him, eyes wide, as if she couldn't believe what she was seeing.

He held his arms open, and she launched herself into them, burying her head in his chest. Her body heaved, and he thought she was crying.

'There, there,' he soothed, 'I'm back and I'll never leave you again.'

She lifted her head and looked at him.

'You promise,' she said.

'Aye, I promise.'

He wiped the tears from her cheeks.

'Now, off you go. Get your ma and the twins so we can all be together again.'

Sarah bit her lip as she looked up at him with troubled eyes. 'Ma's not here, but Davy and Jamie are down by the river throwing stones. I'll fetch them.'

Annie grabbed Sarah's arm. 'Run along to Uncle Ian's house first and ask him to come.'

'What did she mean?' Jimmie turned to his ma after Sarah left. 'Where is Belle?'

Annie stared out over the river. 'A lot has happened while ye've been gone. It started when the inn burned down.'

Jimmie's eyes turned towards the village square. It looked different.

He stepped onto the road to get a better view. The wooden inn where he'd lived with Belle was gone. In its place stood a stone building which lacked doors and windows.

He stared in disbelief, with the words of his mother, 'The inn burned down,' racing through his mind.

'What happened?'

'It was the women.'

Annie's voice was so low Jimmie had to strain to hear her.

'They didnae want their men drinking at the inn and they set fire to it.' She paused. 'It was bad. The fire took hold so fast it was impossible to put out.'

Dread swept through Jimmie, and he struggled to speak.

'Was Belle hurt? Is she,' he hesitated, afraid to say, 'dead?'

'No, she left to seek shelter in Invercraig.' She hesitated. 'It's best to wait for Ian. He knows more than I do.'

Jimmie paced up and down in front of the house while he waited for Sarah to return with Ian. His mind was so full of questions about Belle he paid no heed to the cluster of villagers congregating on the road. It was only when his ma suggested they'd best wait for Ian inside the house he became aware of them gathering with their whispers and nods.

Once inside, his mother coaxed him to sit in the chair beside the unlit fire. 'Don't fret,' she said. 'Ian will soon explain everything. But while ye're waiting, mayhap ye can tell us what happened to ye.'

'Later. I need to find Belle first.' He stared at her, unable to stop his mind whirling. Why wouldn't she tell him what happened to Belle? Why did she need to leave it to Ian to tell him? At least she'd said Belle wasn't dead, but that didn't mean she hadn't been injured, or worse. And why had she felt it necessary to go to Invercraig when she could have stayed here?

Unable to rid himself of the sick feeling in his gut and his dread about Belle's fate, he got up from the chair to stare along the road. Why was Ian taking so long?

Jeannie finished wiping down the counter. Some oatmeal had spilled when she served the last customer. She'd been working in the general store for several months now and she was getting the hang of it. Feeling Wattie's eyes on her, she laid the cloth aside and turned to face him.

'Have you decided yet?'

'I'll need to speak to my ma first.'

A worried expression crossed Wattie's face. 'I'm not a fisher,' he said. Jeannie knew what he meant. He was afraid Annie would refuse her consent. Her da wasn't a problem. He always agreed with her ma.

'She knows you're a good man,' Jeannie said. 'I wouldn't worry about it.'

Jeannie turned away from him. He was a kind man, and she was fond of him. She could do a lot worse. Besides, the fisher lads weren't interested in her. She was too wee to carry them to the boat. So, her decision was a simple one. Stay an old maid or take Wattie. It wasn't much of a decision.

The jangle of the shop bell interrupted her thoughts.

Lizzie McNab shuffled inside and leaned her arms on the counter.

Jeannie sighed. Lizzie wasn't the cleanest person, and she'd have to wipe the counter again after she left.

'Ye hivnae heard the news then,' Lizzie said. Her eyes roamed around the shop, stopping when they rested on the ham displayed on the shelf behind Jeannie.

'I'll have a slice of that,' she said. 'Mind and don't charge too much for it.'

'What news?' Jeannie lifted a knife to slice the ham.

'Your brother. Jimmie, is it? The one lost at sea.'

Jeannie sighed. Lizzie knew it was Jimmie who was lost at sea.

'Aye. What about him?'

'He's come back.'

'What do you mean, come back?' Jeannie felt like shaking her.

'He's home. Sailed in on a Peterhead boat. It's him all right. Seen him with my own eyes.'

Jeannie gasped and handed the knife to Wattie. 'You tend to Lizzie. I need to go home.'

Her feet sped down the road to the house and she burst inside, determined to see if what Lizzie said was true. And there he was. His beard was longer, and he looked a bit more grizzled, but she would have known him anywhere.

'Jimmie,' she said as she flung herself into his arms.

'Jeannie.' He hugged her tight and whispered her name over and over again.

And so they stood. Sobbing and hugging each other, reluctant to let go.

62

Ian scrubbed the fish scales from inside the boat. It would have been done earlier if he hadn't been so exhausted after yesterday's fishing. Hector wasn't much help. He'd become despondent after they committed Ellen to the asylum and seemed perpetually tired. Ian suspected it wouldn't be long before Hector lapsed into the house and left all the work for him. Not that it would make much difference, as he was doing most of the work now. Ian scowled and scrubbed harder at a stubborn patch.

'Uncle Ian. Uncle Ian.'

Sarah's voice cut across his thoughts.

He sat back on his heels. 'What's up, lass? Ye look flustered.'

'Granma says you need to come.' She stopped for breath. 'My da's come home.'

'Your da? Jimmie? He's back?' His eyes widened with astonishment, not taking in what she was saying.

'Yes. You've got to come. Granma says.' Her words came in short gasps.

He threw the scrubbing brush into the boat and bounded over to her.

She grabbed his sleeve and pulled.

'I'm coming,' he said, catching her hand.

They ran along the road, ignoring the clusters of women whispering between themselves. Ian had little time for them after what they'd done to Belle and their malicious gossip about Ellen.

He slowed to catch his breath when they approached the cottage, but Sarah's hand pulled him on until they stood on the doorstep.

281

A moment of doubt crossed his mind. How could Jimmie be back after such a long time? He'd been gone more than a year.

'You're sure your da's home? You're not imagining it?'

'I'm sure.' Sarah tugged his hand.

Taking a deep breath, Ian turned the door handle and stepped inside. It was only then he was convinced. For there stood Jimmie with his arms wrapped around Jeannie while she sobbed into his chest.

Jimmie pried Jeannie's arms loose and turned to face his brother.

'Ian, it's yourself.' His voice cracked as he struggled to suppress the tears welling in his eyes.

Ian took a step towards him and grasped his brother's shoulders. 'Jimmie! I thought you were dead. I cannae believe my eyes.' He paused for breath. 'I couldn't believe it when Sarah told me ye were home. But here ye are.' His voice faltered.

'Aye, it's me. Back from the dead.'

Jimmie flung his arms around Ian, and the two men hugged for the first time in their lives. 'All these months while I've been away, I've yearned for this moment. Now it's here, I'm lost for words.'

Embarrassed, Ian let go and stood back to stare at his brother.

'You're not getting any bonnier, that's for sure,' he said.

'Aye.' Jimmie fondled his beard. 'It's a wonder anyone recognised me.'

Annie looked up from her stool at the fireside. 'A mother knows her bairns, no matter how changed they are. And right glad we are to have Jimmie back home, safe and sound.'

Jimmie crossed the room and laid a hand on her shoulder.

After a moment, he turned back to face Ian.

'Ma wouldn't tell me what happened to Belle.' Desperation shone out of his eyes. 'I need to know. Was she hurt? Why isn't she here? And what on earth happened?'

'It's a long story,' Ian said, wondering where to begin.

Annie stirred on her stool. 'Best you take Ian outside to tell him.'

'No, Ma. I think we all need to know the full story of what happened after the fire.' He paused to look over at his mother, wondering how she would react to what he needed to say.

'We didn't treat Belle right after the fire. She was family and we should have done more. Instead of helping her, we left her to her fate.'

Annie looked away from him to stare into the dead ashes in the fireplace. Her shoulders slumped, and she reached for the comfort of her clay pipe. It seemed to Ian she had aged before his eyes.

Silence descended on the room as he told the story of Belle's escape. How she had sought refuge with Madge's brother and her life in Invercraig. He even told them about her persecution and near-death experience at the hands of Ellen, although it pained him to do so.

Jimmie shifted uncomfortably in his seat at the table as Ian talked about Belle's burgeoning relationship with Gregor and their impending marriage.

'It didn't take her long to find someone else.' Jimmie's voice echoed through the room.

'That may be true, but I'm not sure she had much choice.'

Jimmie glared at him. 'This Gregor. Does she have feelings for him?'

'If she does, they aren't the kind of feelings she has for you. I think she feels indebted to him.'

Jimmie snorted. 'You don't choose to wed someone because you owe them.'

Ian understood Jimmie's anger, but his patience was becoming thin. 'Unless the only other choices you have are to be thrown onto the street to earn your living or enter the poorhouse.'

A mixture of pain and anger crossed Jimmie's face, and he buried his head in his hands.

Ian continued to speak. By the time he related everything that had happened since the fire, silence cloaked the room.

'Ye're right, lad.' Annie's voice broke the silence but was so low he had to strain to hear it. 'We should have looked after Belle better than we did.'

Ian swallowed to rid himself of the lump in his throat. He hadn't wanted to hurt his ma, but she had to understand the part the family had played in what happened to Belle after she left Craigden.

'It's no good crying over spilt milk. What's done is done. Now we need to think about how we can sort it.'

'But it's too late for that.' Jimmie's voice was bitter. 'Once she weds Gregor, she's lost to me.'

Ian laid his hand on Jimmie's shoulder. 'The wedding won't hold. She's married to you.'

'You don't understand. My wedding to Belle was never blessed by the church. We jumped over the broomstick.'

Annie looked up, aghast. 'You mean you're not legally wed?'

Ian jumped to his feet. 'There's no time to lose. We need to get there before the wedding takes place.'

63

The stern of the boat dug into Jimmie's back when he exerted his weight to wrest it off the shingle.

The boat slid a few inches before a small rock halted its progress.

'Stop pushing, Jimmie, while we reposition the boat. We don't want to tear a hole in the bottom.'

Despair flooded through Jimmie. If they couldn't get the boat off the shingle, he'd never get to Invercraig in time.

'You push to the starboard and I'll pull,' Ian shouted to his father from his side of the boat.

'That's it,' Ian said after they manoeuvred the boat into a better position.

Jimmie put his back to the stern, held his breath and heaved.

His muscles ached with the effort of moving the boat from its berth, but he refused to allow himself a breather.

At last, the boat slid into the water and the weight lifted from Jimmie's shoulders and back. His feet slithered on the shingle, and he staggered before joining James and Ian onboard

He grabbed an oar. 'We'll row while you steer,' he said to his father. 'You ready, Ian?'

The tide was in their favour, sweeping them towards the middle of the river. But Jimmie braced himself, knowing he needed all his strength to avoid the treacherous whirlpools and the angry currents, swirling around the island dividing the north and south shores of the river.

Ignoring the excruciating pain in his shoulders, he bent forward and back, keeping time with the rhythm of the oars slicing through the water. A quick glance at Ian reflected his pain, but Ian was as determined as he was to reach the other shore.

Choppy waves splashed over the bow as they rounded the point of the island and, for a moment, Jimmie feared the boat would capsize, but they bent over their oars and pulled hard until they were clear of the current.

Ignoring the three-masted ship berthed at the dock, they searched for a place to moor their boat among the smaller boats tied to the harbour wall.

By this time Jimmie's impatience was out of control and, as soon as they were level with one of the boats, he stood ready to leap into the nearest one.

James, as if sensing what Jimmie intended to do, guided the boat closer to the moored boats.

'May God go with you,' his father said as Jimmie leapt onto the deck of the nearest one.

The boat rocked when Jimmie's feet landed on its deck, but he paid no heed and leapt onto the next one and then the next until he reached the harbour wall. He clambered up, ignoring the scrape of stone against his skin, and didn't draw breath until he stood on the ground at the top.

He was here, and Belle was within his reach. But was he too late?

He suppressed his panic and strode towards the Ship Inn.

Sunlight filtered through the bedroom window, making Belle's image in the mirror shimmer. The yellow silk of the dress was the perfect foil for her dark curls. Gregor had chosen well. It was his gift to her for their wedding day.

Madge elbowed herself up in the bed. 'You look beautiful,' she said. 'Are you happy?'

Sadness welled up in Belle. Happy? She hadn't been happy for a long time.

She forced a smile. 'A bride is always happy on her wedding day.' Her voice broke on the last words.

'But, somehow or other, I sense you are not.'

Belle ignored the suggestion. 'Gregor is good to me, and I owe him a lot. Besides, by tonight I'll be mistress of this establishment.'

She walked to the window and stared out.

On the other side of the road with his back to the river, a man stood watching.

The sun was behind him and his face was in the shade. His clothes were shabby, and his long beard made him look old. But he had the stance of a younger man and as the sun glinted off his hair, she realised it was a light shade of brown and not grey as she had first thought. He was too far away for Belle to see his face clearly enough, but there was something familiar in the way he stood. Who was he?

'What are you looking at?' Madge heaved herself out of the bed and joined Belle at the window.

'It's that man over there.' She pointed towards him.

As she watched, he turned his head and looked up at the window. He raised his hand in a wave, and after a moment, walked across the road.

Belle knew if this man claimed to know her, Gregor would give him short shrift and she would never find out his identity.

'I'm going downstairs. I need to know who he is?'

The taproom was gloomy, and both Gregor and the man stood in the shadows of the doorway.

'There's no one of that name here,' she heard Gregor say. 'Now be off with you. We want no tramps here.'

Gregor advanced towards him, and the man took a step back out of the gloom of the doorway. Sunlight slanted over his face.

Belle drew nearer to the two men, her curiosity aroused.

The man's head turned in her direction. 'Belle!'

His voice was hoarse, but strangely familiar.

'Go back upstairs,' Gregor snapped, without looking at her.

Belle ignored him.

There was something familiar about this stranger, but his long beard masked his face. It was the way he stood. The way he held his head. But it was only when she was near enough to see his eyes that she knew.

She could never forget those piercing blue eyes; bluer than any other eyes she had ever known.

'Jimmie,' she gasped. 'I thought you were dead.'

'Not dead, Belle. But very much alive.'

She ran to him then, pushing Gregor aside when he tried to block her, and threw herself into Jimmie's arms.

Jimmie, the only man she had ever truly loved, had returned to her.

She sobbed and clutched at him while he held her close.

Madge, who had followed Belle to the door, stared in disbelief. Gregor, scowling with puzzlement, stood at her side.

'We need to go home, Belle,' Jimmie said. 'Back to Craigden. Ma and the bairns are waiting for you.'

Belle drew back from him. Sadness filled her. She desperately wanted to go home with Jimmie, but so much had happened since Jimmie left. It was impossible.

She suppressed the tears welling up inside her before she answered him.

'I can't.' Her voice shook. 'The village women don't want me there. That's why I had to seek refuge here.'

'What the village women want or don't want doesn't matter. I'm here and I'll protect you. I'll make sure they don't harm you.'

'What's to stop them when you return to the sea?' Her voice quavered. She wanted so much to return to Craigden but feared the women and their jealousy.

'I'm done with the sea, Belle. I'll always be there for you.'

He wrapped his arms around her, and she laid her head on his chest to calm the thoughts circling in her mind. Craigden was home. She'd be with her bairns again. Jimmie had sworn to protect her. She'd talk to Lachlan and accept his offer of the tenancy of the new Craigden Inn. She would have everything she'd ever wanted.

'Belle!'

Gregor's voice, husky with emotion, sent a shiver through her. In the excitement of the moment, she'd forgotten he was there.

Forgotten her promise to him.

Forgotten, this was the day they were meant to wed.

'Give me a minute to speak with Gregor,' she said, wriggling free from Jimmie's arms.

Jimmie nodded, although his eyes watched her as she walked over and grasped Gregor's hands.

'You do see I can't marry you now, Gregor,' she said. His hands trembled within hers. 'It's impossible when my husband is still alive. But I'll never forget you, nor what you did for me.'

She planted a kiss on his cheek before turning back to Jimmie.

'Let's go home,' she said.

<<<<<>>>>>

Also by Chris Longmuir

Dundee Crime Series
Night Watcher
Dead Wood
Missing Believed Dead
Web of Deceit
The Kirsty Campbell Mysteries
The Death Game
Devil's Porridge
Death of a Doxy
The Suffragette Mysteries
Dangerous Desire
Historical sagas
A Salt Splashed Cradle
Song of the Sea
Nonfiction
Nuts & Bolts of Self-Publishing
Crime Fiction and the Indie Contribution

About the Author

Chris Longmuir was born in Wiltshire but now lives in Angus. Her family moved to Scotland when she was two. Chris has a wealth of life experience and has worked in shops, offices, mills and factories, as well as being a bus conductor for a spell. As if this work experience wasn't sufficient, she also worked as a social worker for Angus Council (latterly serving as Assistant Principal Officer for Adoption and Fostering). Her experiences as a social worker gave her an insight into the dark underbelly of Dundee, Scotland, where she sets most of her novels.

Chris is a member of the Society of Authors, The Crime Writers Association and the Scottish Association of Writers. She is a multi-award-winning author who writes short stories, articles, historical novels, and crime thrillers. Her first book, published by Polygon, won the prestigious Dundee International Book Prize. She confesses to being a bit of a techno-geek who builds computers in her spare time.

https://www.chrislongmuir.co.uk

www.ingramcontent.com/pod-product-compliance
Lightning Source LLC
Chambersburg PA
CBHW031253120726

47906CB00003B/724